4-2-24

A Mah Jongg Mystery

Dangerous Pastimes Series, Book 1

By Violetta Armour

Published by Take Me Away Books, an imprint of Winged Publications

Copyright © 2018 by Violetta Armour

All rights reserved. No part of this publication may be resold, reproduced, stored in a retrieval system, or transmitted in any form or by any means, electronic, mechanical, recording, or otherwise, without the prior written permission of the author. Piracy is illegal. Thank you for respecting the hard work of this author.

This is a work of fiction. All characters, names, dialogue, incidents, and places either are the product of the author's imagination or are used fictitiously. Any resemblance to actual events, locales, or people, living or dead, is entirely coincidental.

All rights reserved.

ISBN-13: 978-1-946939-77-7
ISBN-10: 1-946939-77-3

DEDICATION

Dedicated to all the ladies who play Mah Jongg in AFFAN, Phoenix, Tempe and Munds Park Arizona. The game brought us together. The friendships formed keep us together.

-Wishing you many life-long friendships!

Violetta Armour

- 2018

In China there is a belief that an invisible red thread connects people who are destined to be together in life. –Ann Hood

Chapter One

Present Day 2010

When Angelina hears that they found Myra's dead body naked in the shower with the water still running, she immediately suspects foul play. Knowing Myra was frugal—one might even say a penny pincher—Angelina believes Myra would have turned off the water even if it was the last thing she did.

Now as she stands beside Myra's graveside, her thoughts drift as the minister drones on. This isn't her first funeral and won't be her last as her friends are aging, yet each death causes her to evaluate and judge her entire existence.

Will I have regrets on my deathbed for things not done? What about my bucket list? Will I have time to make amends with those I've offended? Yes, death definitely makes one examine one's life.

A cactus wren chirps cheerily, oblivious to sadness as it flits from tree to tree. Orange blossoms emit wafts of sweet citrus fragrance. Springtime is in bloom in the Phoenix desert with the ocotillos' fiery russet buds and the Saguaro cactus sprouting pink floral trumpets. So many reminders of new life, but while the crocus is pushing up, Myra is pushing down. Six feet down.

Myra's three daughters stand together in somber dresses, holding hands. Angelina thinks of her daughter, April, and feels the familiar pang of regret for how her relationship with her has crumbled. Myra's sudden death reminds her that life is precarious.

Behind Myra's daughters stand the grandchildren with their dads. One of the sons-in-law keeps looking at his watch. It's Debbie's husband, the dentist. *Does he have an urgent root canal waiting or what?*

Beside Angelina, June sniffs in her handkerchief, while Clara stands stoic with head lowered. Even their shoes reflect their personalities. Clara is wearing sensible Oxfords. June has cutesy, open-toed heels that will, in spite of her petite stature, sink into the moist sod with each step she takes. Eccentricities and all, Angelina is glad to have them beside her now and grateful for their friendship. She is also reminded that with Myra gone, their Mah Jongg foursome is reduced to three.

Like the cactus wren's flight, her thoughts flit from one thing to another. What really caused Myra's death? Angelina has read enough whodunits to know that the unattended death of a healthy woman is labeled suspicious and requires a police investigation, but maybe she should also do a little sleuthing herself. This is after all just like page one of the mysteries she devours—a sudden death, a funeral scene, a curious friend with a vivid imagination.

A wayward thought strikes her. Another irony. Today is Monday. Myra said it was her favorite day for the 3 M's. Mah Jongg Mavens at Myra's."

Is it possible there is a fourth M in Myra's life? M as in murder?

Detective Guy Lucchino tries to be inconspicuous as he stands a distance away from the gravesite, half hidden by a flowering oleander bush. He stands poised, almost holding his breath, so as not to crunch the gravel or step on a branch. Watching and waiting. He never knows exactly what he's looking for when he attends funerals of suspected victims, but he always scans the guests' faces and studies their body language. Possibly a weird gesture. Always the chance that he'll detect the unusual—the person there for the wrong reason. In his many years as a detective, he has seen all kinds of killers, but one thread runs constant through them all. Like salmon to spawn, they return to the scene of the crime one way or another, often to see what havoc their violent act has caused. Sometimes to see what progress is being made in the search for them. Sometimes perverted pleasure.

Guy also knows that many murders, particularly crimes of passion, are committed by a family member or someone who knows the victim well. As Guy tells his partner, Bill, "What better place than a funeral to observe all the potential suspects. A group lineup, so to speak."

From his makeshift command post, the oleander bush, he watches mourners as they leave the site and walk to their cars, murmuring in hushed tones. He strains to eavesdrop, to hear snatches of their conversations.

Almost everyone has left the gravesite and the last ones who file past him are three women about the age of the deceased. They help each other over the uneven terrain of a bulging tree root. Unlike the other mourners speaking in hushed tones, they speak in a normal volume. In fact, they all talk at once. Guy has interviewed Myra's family so these must be friends. If his instincts are right, as they often are, this little trio is probably a goldmine, a triple nugget, of information.

He returns to his car, the only one left there, and jots a note. Three ladies at gravesite. Find. Talk.

He drives slowly toward the exit gates of the cemetery when he reaches for his cell phone on the passenger seat. It's not there.

Stopping the car, he searches the floorboards of both seats. Nothing. Climbing out he checks to see if he sat on it as he's done often, resulting in embarrassing butt calls. No. A brief second of frustration. He hates losing things and lately seems to be misplacing items often. *Maybe I am getting too old for this.*

He makes a U-turn in the entryway and returns to the gravesite.

When he parks his unmarked car on the shoulder, a car pulls away from the site and drives toward the other exit. He recognizes it from the taillights. A 1976 Dodge Dart. An unmistakable model to him because he proudly purchased it the last year they made the Dart. Was this a late visitor to Myra's gravesite or someone passing through? He wishes he had hung around a few minutes longer. His chief always said patience was the key to a good investigation, and what was his hurry? *Not like I have anyone waiting at home.*

Now he's doubly frustrated. His phone is missing and he's possibly missed a clue. He walks to the pink oleander bush, checking the ground between the car and the bush. Nothing. He hears a truck and turns to see the cemetery workers approaching. Although he didn't stand close to the burial site, he now approaches the casket. There is a headstone already in place with Myra's husband's date of passing. At the raised base of the stone, a thin red ribbon stretches from one end to the other.

Strange. Has it fallen off one of the wreaths? No, it's placed too perfectly. It seems deliberate, as much as a piece of ribbon can be. Possibly a religious symbol or sentimental family gesture?

After retracing his steps to the car, a shiny reflection peeks out from under the bush and catches his attention. His phone. He exhales a sigh of relief and grabs it with the urgency of a passenger reaching for a life jacket on the Titanic.

Mah Jongg is a game of skill coupled with wit and fortune. It originated in China and dates far back into ancient times of 2000 years ago.

Chapter Two

Present

After the funeral luncheon, Angelina drives home remembering the promise she made to herself at the gravesite. Call April. How will she begin the conversation? With polite and phony small talk or will she have the courage to get to the heart of the matter?

Once home, she procrastinates with mundane tasks. Changes her clothes, pours an iced tea she doesn't want, shuffles through the junk mail, mostly ads and coupons which she discards. She has no need for garage door openers or new storm doors. The TV evening news repeats a familiar and repetitive chord. Thirty depressing minutes about the economic crisis facing the housing and job market. She hits the off button on the remote.

Instead she goes to her desk and finds one of her black-and-white speckled notebooks, the kind that says Composition on the cover. The kind that always takes her back to her elementary school days with feel-good memories.

Several of them are stashed away because even now at age sixty-eight, she can't resist shopping for school supplies each September. A foolish notion, but she sees it as a harmless indulgence as she strolls leisurely through Staples, filling her cart with notebooks, highlighters, colored index cards and pencils she can't wait to sharpen. Angelina loves a sharp pencil.

As awful as the thought of someone killing Myra is, she also feels a sense of curiosity. She fashions herself quite the amateur sleuth.

Angelina, who at age ten had to wear glasses with lenses as thick as the Coca Cola bottles of her 1950s childhood, is convinced her near-sightedness was the result of her voracious reading of every Nancy Drew book, many nights by the flashlight she kept under her pillow. Then she discovered Miss Marple and Hercule Poirot, often finding the elusive clue before Agatha Christie revealed it.

After Peter passed, she found some comfort immersing herself in a mystery to relieve her loneliness for a few hours. She never missed an episode of *Murder She Wrote*, and Peter often called her Jessica, as in Fletcher, when she became too snoopy.

In her clean notebook, she wants to record everything she can remember about Myra. One never knows what fact will lead to the discovery of what she suspects could be foul play. At the top of the first page she writes the year she met Myra. 2002. Beneath that she writes Mah Jongg.

Thinking of her remaining two Mah Jongg friends, she calls Clara and June.

"We need to talk about Myra's death. Come for lunch tomorrow. Something is fishy."

They each respond as she expects. Clara sardonically. June kindly.

"We're not having fish, are we?" Clara asks. "You know I don't do fish."

"Trust me. I'll have something to your liking," Angelina says.

June replies, "That's a wonderful idea. We need to be together now. We shouldn't grieve alone."

As Angelina ends the call, she shakes her head. It could be a huge mistake involving them in her sleuthing, but perhaps they know something about Myra that she doesn't. *We shouldn't leave any stone unturned.* Or as June, who jumbles all the proverbs, might say, "A stone unturned gathers no moss."

Chapter Three

Present

Guy pours his nightly two fingers of Johnnie Walker Red and sits at the kitchen table with the Steno book. He transfers the day's notes from the small tattered notebook he carries. He takes a sip and waits for the warm, smooth sensation to trickle down.

Even after three years, the dinner hour is the hardest—remembering when he and Monica would enjoy a patio cocktail on warm fragrant evenings. Or he would sit at the kitchen counter watching her chop veggies. Some nights he chopped. Both recapped their work day, her patients and his cases, especially the difficult ones. Often in the retelling, he stumbled onto a clue he had missed earlier.

He takes another silky sip as he glances at the needlepoint above the kitchen alcove desk. Monica gave it to him when he first made detective. Although now bittersweet, it makes him smile. It shows a magnifying glass, a Sherlock Holmes cap, and the words, "Detect. Verb. 1. discover, find out, dig up, unearth. 2. get to the bottom of, uncover, bring to light. 3. observe, spy, apprehend."

He reviews the notes in the Steno. Although he doubts foul play, he is required to rule that out through a thorough investigation. There are, however, a few unusual triggers. Would a lady leave her front door unlocked while taking a shower? And what about the lack of any fingerprints on the wine bottle on the counter next to the half-full glass. As if someone wiped the bottle clean and in doing so removed Myra's also. Who poured that glass of wine?

He makes more notes. Would anyone besides her family benefit from her death? Did the retirement center stand to gain anything by her death? Does her unit revert to the center for resale or to the family? Check Myra's financials. And what's the red ribbon about?

Guy likes the words of the needlepoint: To discover, to uncover, to bring to light. Although he could have retired last year as he and Monica planned, he doesn't know how he'd fill his days now, so he continues to work. He's no longer given the high-profile cases and that's fine with him. It's good to have a place to go each day. A reason to get up, shower and shave. He closes his Steno book and walks out to the patio with Johnnie in hand.

It's a warm spring evening and the citrus scent of the orange tree fills the air. Monica's hibiscus bush is in bloom and a hummingbird is also having his evening cocktail as his beak enters the yellow center of the red petals. Just a sip, then he hovers like a helicopter and flits away.

After a few minutes, Guy decides to make the evening hours pass by indulging in a favorite pastime—watching a Kevin Bacon movie. His collection contains most of them.

Tonight, he picks a comedy, wanting something light after the somber funeral. He debates over *Animal House* and *Planes, Trains and Automobiles*, two of Kevin's early films with minor parts, but each one causes him to laugh no matter how many times he's seen it. He slides the disc in the DVD player and while the opening credits run, he goes to the freezer for a frozen dinner. He loves to cook but rarely has the desire to cook for only himself. He agrees with Three Dog Night. One is the loneliest number.

Chapter Four

Present

April answers on the third ring in what seems a hurried and breathless, “Hello.”

“April, is this a bad time?” Angelina asks, thinking any time a call from her mother might be a bad time.

“No, I was on the patio and ran in before it went to voice mail.”

“Good. How are you?” Angelina tries to sound calm despite an uneasiness in her chest.

“I’m fine. And you?” April asks politely, but Angelina senses a coolness, as has been the case in their conversations since . . . since when? Since she blatantly criticized her lifestyle and choice of men. And so rudely interfered.

Angelina starts to say, “I’m fine too,” but realizes this charade defeats the purpose of her call. “Actually, April, I’m not fine and that’s why I called.”

“Are you sick? Is something wrong?” April sounds genuinely concerned, which encourages Angelina to continue with honesty.

“No, dear, it’s not that. I just came from Myra’s funeral…”

“Myra? Your Mah Jongg friend? Was she ill?”

“No, no, it was very sudden. And sad. But that’s not why I called you.” Angelina takes a deep breath and continues.

“As I stood there at the graveside and saw her daughters looking so grief-stricken, I thought of you . . . of us . . . and realized how much I miss you. How much I miss us . . . the way we used to be.”

There is a pause and then April says, “You mean before you felt the need to interfere, under the guise of ‘I just want what’s best for you’?”

"Yes, I . . ."

"I appreciate your call, Mom, but as long as you feel the way you do about Gary, and I don't see that changing after all the things you said to him, I don't think we're going to have that close relationship you are missing."

"But can we try? I'd like to try. I'd like to get to know Gary better if he's your choice."

"He is my choice. And my other choice is not to discuss this now. I'm sorry about you losing your friend. I really am. But . . . but I need to go. I have something in the oven that needs my attention before it burns. Goodbye."

When Angelina hears the click ending the call, she feels the sobs starting and then the tears come. Tears she hadn't shed at the funeral but are flowing freely now for . . . for the entire day. Myra's death, her longing for April and the realization that she has hurt someone she loves very much.

April's dinner needs attention and Angelina knows in her heart their relationship needs attention also. She is determined to give it all it needs and hopes it isn't burned beyond repair.

A Mah Jongg set has 152 tiles, consisting of Bamboos, Cracks, Dots, Winds, Dragons, Flowers and Jokers. The goal is to display a hand consisting of different combinations of the tiles as designated on the Mah Jongg card.

Chapter Five

Present

Clara and June enter Angelina's home to Italian aromas. Pavarotti is bellowing in the background and three wine glasses are at the place settings.

"So what army are you cooking for today?" Clara asks as she walks into the kitchen and sees all four burners going. "What are you going to do with all this food?"

"I have no idea," Angelina replies as she chops an onion with the vengeance of a jilted lover. "Actually, I do know. I'm preparing a dish for each of Myra's daughters and one for our lunch. You know I do my best thinking while cooking. A little music, a glass of wine …and the grey cells work even better."

"I thought you cooked to avoid thinking," says Clara who lifts one of the lids. "Ah, this sauce smells delicious. I can't believe I'm hungry when I am so grief-stricken. But it makes sense. When our dog died, I ate a whole tub of ice cream that very night. None of that low-fat stuff. It was Haagen-Dazs. It's not like that would bring him back, but still . . ."

June interrupts, "That's what Jennifer Aniston did when Brad Pitt left. But I think she did it for a week straight. That's what *People magazine* said. Didn't bring him back either. But people do love to eat at funerals. They eat like men on death row—you know, their last meal and all."

“Now how would you know how men on death row eat, June?” Clara asks.

“Well, I’ve seen movies, Clara,” June says. “As for funerals, what about all those casseroles widows take to the widower before the wife’s body is even cold? Shameless hussies, that’s what they are.” June finds a dish towel to help dry utensils that Angelina is rinsing.

Angelina smiles, recalling. “Yes, Myra called them funeral sluts.”

“She did? I never heard her say that,” June says.

“Well, she probably didn’t want to offend you, June.” Clara says, searching for a spoon to taste the pasta sauce.

“It’s not like I never heard the word before. I’ve been around the block a few times too, you know,” June says and briskly folds the towel. She folds it twice again as if to emphasize her words, but her expression indicates her hurt feelings.

“Oh, Junie, don’t be upset,” Clara says. “I think it’s a compliment that Myra was protective of you. She thought you were sweet. For a Jewish girl, you are definitely missing some Chutzpah.” Clara walks closer to the stovetop. “So, what’s in the other pots?”

Angelina has prepared pasta for them with a lemon Alfredo sauce and a Bulgarian stew for Myra’s two daughters who live in town. The stew is called *chomlek*, which translates as Pope’s Stew, normally made on Sundays in her parents’ homeland Balkan village. Beef and onions are layered in an earthenware pot to simmer for hours during the lengthy Orthodox service.

Angelina serves the pasta and lets them enjoy it for a few minutes before she shares her thoughts. “I called this meeting not just to give us a chance to commiserate. I suspect foul play with Myra.”

“Like in murder?” June’s big blue eyes open wide. “Oh, I can’t believe that. I won’t believe it. Who would murder Myra? Sweet, kind Myra?”

“Her son-in-law, that’s who,” Clara says.

“Now, you can’t jump to conclusions like that, Clara,” Angelina says. “We need to lay some groundwork. A list of all the family and everyone else she knew. Anyone who would benefit by her death.”

"The son-in-law," Clara says again as she butters another piece of Italian bread.

"Clara!" June exclaims. "Angelina said we have to be systematic. You can't keep accusing the son-in-law. Besides, every time I met him he was polite."

"Well, June, killers don't walk around angry and rude all day long, you know," Clara replies.

Angelina rolls her eyes, takes a sip of wine and wonders again why she thought including them might be a good idea. In eight years they've never agreed on anything. Perhaps that's why they are still together. Clichés fill her mind. Never a dull moment. Variety is the spice of life. Or as June with her mixed metaphors might say, the spice of life is never dull.

Even their appearances cry diversity. Clara is tall, stately and in excellent shape. She was one of those bone-skinny girls in high school, but now she sports a nicer figure at age sixty-nine than she did at seventeen.

June is a petite blonde who said she was named after her mother's favorite starlet of the fifties, June Allyson. Surprisingly, June favors her, although now her blond hair is wispy and faded.

Angelina is also on the short side. Her olive complexion looks young and supple, which she credits to her ancestors' Mediterranean diet. She is certain that Eastern European embryos float in sacs of olive oil. Or maybe it was the homemade yogurt, a staple at the Bulgarian table long before Americans discovered its health benefits. Angelina buys only Dannon yogurt since she heard that they bought the Bulgarian culture stock, attributing to their long life spans.

Her black curly hair still has a sheen although she has been doing grey touch-ups for years. At five-foot-two inches, she struggles constantly with an extra twelve pounds. Six pounds off in the summer, usually back on during the holidays. She admitted, in one weak moment, to her Mah Jongg friends that she has some of her favorite outfits in two sizes.

When Angelina confessed this, Clara asked if she had the little size tags on hanger dividers, so she knew which part of her closet to shop. Angelina thought it was a splendid idea and asked a friend who worked retail if she would get her a few. Size ten to fourteen would suffice.

In the past eight years, the Mah Jongg Mavens have built a trust that only comes with revealing such confidences.

"Angelina, Earth calling Angelina," Clara says. "What are you thinking about?"

"How valuable your input will be." *One can only hope.* Angelina rises and sets her empty dish in the sink. She grabs her speckled notebook and pencil and returns to the table. "I don't want to rush you. Keep eating. I want to record our thoughts before we lose them."

SUSPECTS. Angelina writes this at the top of a clean page and asks, "Clara, why do you say the son-in-law? His name is Randy, right? The dentist."

"Yes. I think it was Randy in the dentist chair with the drill." She smiles at her feeble joke.

"Clara, how can you joke about this? Myra is dead," June pouts.

"And crying isn't going to bring her back. She'd want us to have a few laughs. She had a great sense of humor," Clara responds and takes another bite of crusty bread.

"Seriously, Clara. Why do you say Randy?" Angelina is poised with pencil in hand.

Clara holds one finger in the air to indicate she needs to finish chewing. "We all know he borrowed money time and time again from Myra. And Myra told us that neither she nor Randy told Debbie. Isn't that Myra's daughter's name? Didn't want to upset her." Clara raises an eyebrow. "And I don't think he considered them loans. He had no intention of paying them back."

"Now we can't assume his intentions," Angelina says, "but I see your reasoning. With Myra's death, the loan issue is wiped out and . . ."

"And he stands to gain quite a bit more. We know Myra was financially well-off. How else could she afford that luxurious retirement center?"

"Well, if we're looking at family, for the sake of discussion, you understand," June says, "How about Myra's oldest daughter, Janet? She's running for that big political office. Maybe she wants the sympathy vote."

"That's far-fetched," Clara shoots June down.

Angelina taps her pencil on the notebook as if it were a gavel. "Ladies, in true brainstorming fashion, we pitch our ideas with no judgments from others. We'll get back to each idea and discuss its merits."

Clara and June look at each other and form a truce out of respect to their hostess. After all, they are enjoying the benefits of her cuisine.

Surprisingly, Angelina blinks back the tears she feels coming on.

June is the first to respond, "Angelina, I know how much you're going to miss Myra."

Clara leans into Angelina and pats her reassuringly on the shoulder. Angelina dabs at her eyes with her napkin.

"It's not Myra I'm crying about." she sniffles as she speaks. "I mean I am very sad about Myra. But when you mentioned Janet, it reminded me of the daughters standing at her graveside. How forlorn they looked, and I was thinking that if I passed today, would April look that sad?" Angelina shakes her head. "I don't think so."

Clara speaks, "Angelina, what on earth are you talking about? Of course, April would be sad. This is so unlike you. What is bringing on this pity party?"

June says, "Angelina, your daughter loves you. Why wouldn't she?"

Angelina takes a sip of water. "I haven't been totally honest with you about April. Myra knew but I didn't tell either of you. I think I was too embarrassed and ashamed of my behavior."

Clara and June wait for an explanation.

"You do know that April has been in a relationship with her boyfriend for the past four years. Gary. I liked him from the start. He was kind to April, seemed ambitious, always pitched in after a dinner to clear the table. Many good qualities. But April is not getting any younger and I know she wants a family and . . . and . . ." Angelina takes a deep breath. "Well, I just didn't think he was ever going to commit to her . . . to marriage and family. And then when he moved in with her, I thought, big mistake. The old 'why buy a cow when the milk is free,' of course, is what kicked in. When I brought it up with her . . . ."

"You actually said those words—the cow and the free milk?" June asks.

"Not exactly, June. But I talked about marriage. She brushed me off and I knew it was sensitive, so I stopped inquiring. But each time we were together it was like the elephant in the room. And it seemed she was calling me less and less."

Angelina peers up at the ceiling, takes a deep breath, and then says, "Then I did the stupidest thing. I called Gary and arranged a lunch with him and asked him what his intentions were. It was awful."

Clara asks point-blank, "What did he say?"

June is kinder. "Oh, I'm sure it wasn't as bad as you imagined."

Angelina looks directly at June and gives a wry smile at her friend's constant optimism. "No, it was worse. He said their relationship was between him and April and if she had concerns, it was her place to voice them. Not mine. He became defensive and I knew immediately I had overstepped. I accomplished nothing good. And I also knew right then that this mistake was going to cost me. A terrible cost—the trust of my daughter."

"Oh, Angelina . . ." June starts to say when the phone interrupts. Not one to ignore a ringing phone, Angelina jumps up and answers. After a brief conversation, she says, "Seven o'clock would work. See you then, Detective."

At the mention of Detective, Clara and June both glance up.

"Who was that?" Clara asks.

"A Detective Lucchino. Wants to talk about Myra."

"Doesn't he want to talk to all of us?" Clara asks.

"He didn't say. But maybe this list we compiled will be helpful to him tonight."

Clara mumbles to June, "I don't know why he didn't call us."

Angelina starts to clear the table. "Thank you, ladies, for listening. I shouldn't have burdened you with my concerns about April now, with Myra and all."

"But, but …" Clara says.

"We'll talk further. And I did call April after the funeral service. I'm trying to make amends and I'll let you both know how that goes."

"Yes, please, please do," June says.

When they leave, Angelina studies the list of people they have compiled who knew Myra.

It includes family members, acquaintances and staff members at Friendship Acres Retirement Center where Myra lived. Their names are listed on the left side of the page. On the right side of the page, Angelina has a column entitled "possible motive." Other than notes beside Randy's name, that side is totally blank.

Chapter Six

Present

When the doorbell rings promptly at seven, Angelina opens it to Detective Guy Lucchino, who immediately strikes her as a Columbo look-alike. He's wearing the rumpled trench coat, and a lock of dark hair is falling near one eye. Eyes she would assume to be brown with his swarthy complexion are instead an unusual and striking shade of bluish grey. Interesting. A Columbo wannabe with Paul Newman eyes.

"I'm sorry to bother you, Mrs. Popoff. I won't take much of your time," he says with a somewhat shy demeanor.

Not what she expected at all from the authoritative voice on the phone. His body language seems apologetic, as if he's sorry to be troubling her. What did she expect? Perhaps someone more serious like a Sam Spade or a Sergeant Friday from *Dragnet*. Just the facts, ma'am. Just the facts.

"Come in, Detective," she says. She's about to ask if she can take his coat but remembers that Columbo never removes it so she refrains.

"May I offer you some water, coffee, iced tea?" She leads him to the living room.

"Water would be good. I think I overdid it at the little Mexican restaurant around the corner." He taps a fist to his chest to indicate gastric distress.

"I have Ginger Ale if you like," Angelina offers.

"No, water would be fine. Actually, it was a delicious burrito. Have you been there? Chino Bandito?"

"Chino?" she asks as she walks into the kitchen. "Sounds Chinese to me."

"Actually, it's Chinese and Mexican. The wife is Chinese and the husband is Hispanic. They have both menus and, believe it or not, a combination of both. You can order a Mexican egg roll or Chinese nachos."

"Really?" she asks as she sets two waters down.

In three gulps he drains the glass.

"Please sit down." She motions to a wingback chair. "No, that one might have cat hair all over it," she says with a touch of embarrassment. "Here, sit on the sofa." Then she wonders why she bothered. What's a few cat hairs on a coat that looks slept in?

As he sits, he notices the big yellow and white Garfield cat curled up under the coffee table.

Angelina comments, "That's Henry. Strong silent type. Won't repeat a word of our conversation, I promise."

Guy smiles. "So, I actually heard about it on the Food Channel."

Angelina looks perplexed.

Guy reminds her, "Chinos. Always wanted to check it out. When I saw your address, I realized I was close to it, so decided to try it. Ever watch the Food Channel?"

"Yes, I do sometimes, but ..."

"It was on *Diners, Drive-Ins and Dives*." He begins fumbling in his coat pocket. He pulls out a small dog-eared spiral notebook and then begins looking in another pocket. "I know I have a pencil here somewhere."

"Here, let me get you one," she says as she walks back into the kitchen. Is this bumbling part of his Columbo act to appear naive or is he truly an absent-minded detective?

"I appreciate your taking time to talk to me." He flips open the notebook, turning the page with extra authority as if he means business, so much so that he rips the page in half. Myra fails to suppress a chuckle. As if he were someone trying to play tough cop.

He gives a little self-conscious laugh. "Don't make notebooks like they used to. My wife always said I was a bull in the china shop." With the mention of a wife, his voice sounds softer, more tender. Then his manner becomes more official. "I guess we should get into it. How long have you known Myra? Myra Anderson, the deceased."

What other Myra they would be talking about? "About eight years. I met her at the community center. They needed a fourth player for Mah Jongg the day I walked in and we've been playing together ever since that day. June and Clara are the other two players."

"Mah Jongg?" he asks.

"Yes, it's an ancient Chinese game. You play with ivory tiles. It can be quite challenging You have to make these combinations of hands and . . ." Angelina catches herself. "I guess you don't need to know the rules of the game now," she apologizes. "I tend to digress."

"Quite all right," he says. He gives her the same sort of sweet smile he did at the door. She notices the silver streaks in the temples of his dark hair and wonders how old he is, although that has nothing to do with . . . well, with anything.

"Do you know anyone, and I hope this isn't making you uncomfortable, but do you know anyone who disliked Myra? For example, the ladies you mentioned. Did you all get along? And please understand I'm not suggesting anything. Trying to understand the world Myra lived in, so to speak."

"Oh, we all get along. I mean we rarely agree on anything, but I don't think we've had a serious disagreement in eight years. We're very different and have our definite opinions, but it's never interfered with our friendship. Now that I think about it, you might say our differences are what have kept us together so long. And, of course, our love of Mah Jongg."

He says, "The daughter gave me your name and number. I believe I saw you at the gravesite. Those must have been your Mah Jongg friends with you?"

"Yes, we went together. Moral support." She goes to her desk and retrieves the black-and-white speckled notebook. When Guy notices it, she says with some embarrassment, "I made a few notes. Wanted to be prepared. My friends say I read too much Agatha Christie." She releases a nervous giggle.

"I'm impressed. I'm a notebook case solver myself. Stenos. I have hundreds. I'll transfer these notes into one tonight," he says as he waves the little tattered notebook. "Sadly, some of the old

Stenos contain notes on crimes still unsolved. You never know with DNA tests now. Maybe I'll need them again."

"Are they in safe storage?" Angelina asks with total fascination.

"Well, my metal file cabinets are fireproof. I guess that doesn't protect them against robbery. Guess I shouldn't be telling you that. Forget what I said. Yes, they're in a sealed vault. Like Fort Knox."

Angelina laughs. "Don't worry, Detective. I won't divulge your secret files any more than Henry would."

At the sound of his name, the fat cat opens one eye and twitches a yellow ear.

Guy says, "Her daughter told me you were one of her closest friends. Would you agree with that?"

"Well, she was a dear friend . . . and I'm flattered." Angelina feels her eyes moistening at the word dear. "Perhaps Myra and I had more in common than with the other two Mah Jongg friends. She was a widow when we met, but I was even a more recent one. I leaned on her a lot. How to make it through the first year and all."

"I'm sorry to hear that," he says and the look in his bluish-grey eyes conveys such sincerity she feels he means it although he hardly knows her.

"I went through it myself three years ago. We would have been married thirty-eight years last week. That first year can be rough."

Once again, Myra feels the beginning of tears burning her lids, catching her off guard. It shouldn't have surprised her, as the unexpected kindness of a stranger often does that to her. She takes a sip of water, trying to avoid his eyes, but when she sets the glass down, he's still looking at her kindly. She hasn't fooled him at all.

"I'm sorry. I didn't mean to upset you. Let's get back to Myra. Did you know her daughters well?"

"Not really. I've seen them at holidays and some family occasions through the years, but mainly my knowledge comes from what Myra told me about them. She was so proud of them all."

Angelina pauses a moment to look at her notebook. "Here's what I wrote. You probably already know most of this."

"Perhaps not. Please, go on."

"The oldest is Janet. She has political ambitions. Didn't always, but something about blocking a highway bypass in her neighborhood turned her on. Ran for some office. And then someone above her was appointed to Obama's cabinet and everyone moved up a notch. I think now she's running for Secretary of State but has even higher aspirations from what Myra said.

"Then there's Debbie. Married to the dentist, Randy. Two adorable little girls. The youngest daughter, Roxanne, they call her Rocky, is married to an accountant. Can't remember his name. They live in Texas with two boys."

"Did Myra like her sons-in-law?"

Weird question but perhaps he knows about Randy's constant requests for loans from Myra. She hesitates in her answer. *Should I mention that? Would it be disloyal to Myra who placed her confidence in me or would it be disloyal not to mention anything that might uncover what happened to Myra? Would it cause problems for Debbie?* Angelina isn't sure what to say.

Lucchino seems perceptive to her hesitation. "Is there anything else you want to tell me? You do know our conversation will remain confidential, don't you?" he asks gently, the way a teacher often asks a child what other children were responsible for the naughty words on the blackboard in her absence.

"Yes, of course. I don't want to create any embarrassment for Debbie, Randy's wife. What I mean is, I don't want to give an opinion because, well, that's just my opinion. It may not be relevant. Isn't that what they say on TV in the courtroom dramas? Opinion is hearsay, or not relevant, or something like that."

"We're a long way from court, Mrs. Popoff, so say what you're comfortable with for now. We'll have other chances to talk, if need be. You can always call me if you think of something after I leave. Most people do." Again, that sweet shy smile that was beginning to tug at Angelina.

"Well, Myra was upset each time Randy asked her for a loan because he never told Debbie he was doing it. Once he said he needed to remodel the office to be competitive with other dentists who had high-definition TV, cappuccino coffee and children's video games in the reception area. Then after he did all that, business dropped off with the economy slump. Myra said Debbie once told her, 'If it comes to braces or food on the table, kids are going to have to eat that food with a crooked bite for a while longer.'"

"Do you know if he ever paid Myra back?"

"I don't think he did. Then he asked for another loan. This time for some new equipment. Myra said he was losing patients due to companies downsizing and people moving."

Henry, who normally ignores people, walks to Guy and sniffs at the hem of his trench coat. Guy gently scratches the top of Henry's head between his ears.

Angelina continues. "This recession has created a whole new vocabulary, hasn't it? Downsizing. I saw a billboard the other day that read, Job Search Boot Camp. I thought boot camp was for the military. Guess it is a battle out there these days." Angelina shakes her head. "Here I go digressing again."

"That's fine. Say whatever comes to your mind. I appreciate your comments."

Encouraged, Angelina continues. "I think Randy knew Myra would never tell Debbie because then she would be worried about the money too. Myra wouldn't upset her that way and Randy, in my humble opinion, took advantage of his mother-in-law's generosity and kind spirit." She winces. "But I don't think he's the type to off his mother-in-law."

At the word *off* Guy chuckles. "So, you watch crime stuff on TV?"

"Not so much. Mostly I read mysteries."

"Me too. You'd think I'd have enough of it all day, but I spend a lot of evenings reading too. Or watching Kevin Bacon movies. Who's your favorite author?"

"I'm reading a Louise Penny now. Her stories take place in a little village called Three Pines in Quebec. The main character is Gamache, the Chief Inspector, as they say in Canada. You might like him. He . . ." and she stops. "I'm digressing again." She nods to the coffee table where the paperback, *Still Life*, lies with a bookmark in it. "I guess I'd have to say my all-time favorite for suspense was *A Kiss before Dying*. By Ira Levin. Have you read it?"

Guy squints his eyes and thinks a second. "I don't think so."

"It's old. Written in the fifties and there was a movie. You might know Levin better from *Rosemary's Baby* and *Stepford Wives*."

Angelina walks to the bookshelf above her desk and pulls out a thin brown hardcover book that looks like it has passed through many hands.

"I'd be happy to loan it to you. A masterpiece. You know right at the beginning who the killer is and yet you're on the edge of your seat for the entire book. Or at least I was. The way his mind worked was so fascinating." Angelina hands him the book like a treasured gift.

"Most killings are. Fascinating, that is. If we could get into the killer's head, we'd solve the crime every time." Guy takes the book and says, "I'd love to read it. I'll be sure to return it. So, getting back to Myra. But first, would you mind if I had another glass of water?"

"Of course not."

When Angelina returns with the water, Guy points to the bookcase against one wall and says, "Quite a mystery collection you have here." Then he nods to an overstuffed chair beside the shelf. "I bet this is where you solve your literary mysteries."

Angelina blushes as if she has been caught. "Oh, not sure about that, but what you said about getting into the killer's mind. That's what I love about Agatha. Her books seem to be more about human nature than the crime itself. Someone said, 'No one knows the human heart like Agatha Christie.'"

He takes another long drink, sets the glass down and turns the page of his notebook. "Myra seemed well-off. Do you know by chance what her husband did for a living?"

"She'd been a widow for several years when I met her, but I think he was an engineer and invented some kind of widget," and now Angelina laughs a bit. "For Porta Potty door handles."

"Really?"

"Really." Myra said. "You'd be surprised at how many Porta Potties are used on any given day, what with all the sporting events, outdoor concerts, walks for breast cancer, Alzheimer's, Gay Pride. You name it. And then construction sites. Quite a booming business. Who would have thought?"

"So, anything unusual, as if Porta Potties aren't unusual enough, come to mind about her husband? Did he have family she was involved with?"

"She never mentioned that. I think he had a sister in California, but they weren't close. That's where Myra and Richard met. At a small college in California. I think it was Claremont. She said she was so happy when his first job offer was in Phoenix. She grew up here and her parents were still here. And then the babies came right away. Three little girls, one each year."

"Did she ever have a career?"

"She was mostly a stay-at-home mom. She did mention teaching kindergarten one year after college. I remember a story about a box of chocolate candy she received one Valentine's Day. A big heart-shaped box that a little boy had proudly presented to her. When she opened it, there was a bite out of each piece."

Angelina takes a tissue out of her pocket to dab a tear. "Myra had the best stories."

"You've been very helpful, Mrs. Popoff." He smiles when he says this, and she notices his teeth are so white she wonders if they are his own. She decides they are when she notices the space between the top front teeth. False teeth would be more perfect. She finds this imperfection and his shy smile appealing and smiles back. He stands and somehow seems taller than when he arrived.

He pulls his wallet from his back pocket and starts thumbing through it. She guesses he is looking for a business card, which she suspects he won't find any more than he did the pencil. But he surprises her and pulls out a card. It isn't dog-eared as she thought it would be. He starts to hand it to her and then turns it over, writing something on the back.

"I'm going to give you my cell number, so you don't have to go through the switchboard. My partner's name is Bill, by the way, in case he should call you. But you can call me anytime. If anything else comes to mind or seems important."

"I take it Bill is the bad cop?"

"Bad? Oh, you mean good cop/bad cop?"

"Yes, you're too nice to play bad cop," Angelina says, surprised at how easily that came out.

He smiles and hands her his card. When his blue grey-eyes meet hers, they hold them for what seems longer than necessary.

"Thanks for your time, Mrs. Popoff. And the water. You really should try Chino Bandito sometime."

"Maybe I will. And you can call me Angelina."

"Angelina." He repeats it softly. "That's a beautiful name."

Angelina feels herself blushing and briefly at a loss for words. He stands at the door as if waiting for her to say something.

"It's rather an old-fashioned name. Makes me feel older than I am sometimes. But then I think grief will age a person too, don't you?"

"Oh, no question. I feel much older since Monica passed."

"Monica. That's nice. My husband was Peter. He was quite a bit older so that made me feel younger too, I suppose."

"Yeah, losing your life partner can age you quickly. You . . ." he starts to say more but stops. "I'll leave it at that."

They look at each other for a moment, and he speaks first, "I've taken enough of your time. Thanks again. Please call me if anything else about Myra comes to mind that you think I should know."

"I will." Angelina answers. She has the urge to ask him if she might fix the button missing on his coat and then catches herself. She obviously doesn't have enough to do in her life if she's considering taking in mending.

After he leaves, she returns her speckled notebook to her desk and realizes she forgot to ask him if he had leads he's pursuing. He probably wouldn't have told her anyway, but still, she should have asked. She wants to impress the detective with her own investigative skills. And to let him know she could possibly be a help to him.

In the days that follow Guy's visit, something stirs inside her when she thinks of him. And she does think of him often at odd moments. She sees a commercial for Alka-Seltzer and thinks of his indigestion and his boyish enthusiasm for the restaurant menu. And there's that urge again to perhaps take care of him, find his pencil, sew the button and assure him that he's not a bother. After many years, it's the first stirring of feeling, similar to a schoolgirl crush. It feels strange, but it's a good strange.

Chapter Seven
Present

Guy leaves Angelina's home feeling good. He isn't sure why but knows it doesn't have to do with Myra's investigation. It has quite a bit to do with Angelina. She's attractive and witty. And a widow. He's not had a desire to see anyone after Monica, although he's been the recipient of what his coworkers call the 'Casserole Crusade.' The entire station waits eagerly in the lunchroom for what leftovers Guy brings in.

"After all," his partner Bill so wisely notes, "If the way to a man's heart is through his stomach, they aren't going to send second-rate meals. Only their best."

Some attractive female opportunities have presented themselves to Guy, but no one's captured his interest. The one attempt to date in the past year caused him to miss Monica more than ever. Even after the raw grief subsided, it was replaced with what he called the numbness grief.

Tonight, for the first time he feels a stirring of wanting to spend more time with someone. Angelina seemed naive in some ways, with her cute black-and-white speckled notebook. He could tell she fashions herself an amateur sleuth. Normally, those people were annoying and troublesome, but maybe she could be a good sounding board. Then he reconsiders. Probably not a good idea since she knew the victim—if there was a victim.

In the days following his visit with her, he thinks of her often. Waiting for a red light to turn green, he smiles as he sees an older couple crossing the street holding hands. Or when he glances at the book she loaned him, now on his bedside table. What a kind gesture. *Should he invite her to lunch? No, that probably isn't a good idea, working on the case of her good friend and all. And what if she says no?* Although he is still numb at times, he tells himself numb might be better than rejection.

Chapter Eight

Six Months Prior to Myra's Death

Rhonda Feder unlocked her front door while juggling the cardboard box she salvaged from her mother's apartment. She dropped it on the footstool of the one comfortable chair she owned. She muttered, "From her entire life of forty-four years, only one friggin' box worth saving."

The other six boxes of trash were squeezed into Rhonda's Dodge Dart for a Goodwill drop-off. They probably won't even take the stuff. Such a pile of crap.

Rhonda raced to her mother's as quickly as she could when the paramedics called, but it wasn't soon enough to say goodbye. She was at work in the middle of doing a color application and scrambled to find someone to finish the client with foil twists in her hair, looking like she stepped off a spaceship. The paramedics couldn't save Dottie Feder who waited too long to call once her asthma attack escalated.

And that crappy landlady, Rhonda recalls, the screaming bitch who couldn't even wait for the ambulance to leave before she said, "If you don't get this stuff out now, you'll have to pay another month's rent." Like anybody was on a wait list for this stinking rat trap.

Rhonda poured herself a glass of Two Buck Chuck, which was actually $2.99 in Arizona, but still within her budget. It did the trick as well as the expensive wines she ordered on dates. Guys needed to realize that friends with benefits don't come cheap.

Rhonda pulled a handful of photos out of the box she salvaged. The first photo was familiar to her. An elderly couple standing beside her highchair as she squished her chubby baby hands into a frosted birthday cake with one candle. Rhonda didn't remember her grandparents, her mother's family, who both passed before she was four but was told repeatedly that Momo and Popo, as they wished to be called, adored her.

No dad photos. Any discussion of him was pretty much off-limits other than the fact that he was the smooth slow dancer her mother discovered at a local dive near the Phoenix Luke Air Force Base. She did remember her mother saying once, "his uniform was irresistible." Obviously irresistible, since she was born exactly nine months later. Dottie said she never had any regrets—that Rhonda was the best thing that happened to her.

Rhonda started to pull open a legal-size folder from the box but felt too drained and tired. *Screw it. It can wait.* Unlikely her Mom would have any important papers. Her life had been reduced to nothing but chain-smoking cigarettes despite the doctor's warning, black coffee for daytime soap operas and beer for nighttime reality TV. Her mother's daily beer consumption was the reason Rhonda never touched a beer. Her wine was cheap, but it was a step up from guzzling beer, out of the can no less, like a redneck truck driver.

Rhonda rose to refill her glass, going for the oblivion that would lull her to sleep off the depression of her mother's death. Or was it her mother's life that depressed her? She didn't know which was worse. Now exhausted, she stumbled and tipped the box over. Papers and photos scattered. She haphazardly started throwing them back in the box when the heading on one paper caught her eye. Adoption?

Who was adopted? Was she adopted? No, it couldn't be. No one would have given her single mom a child. Not on her meager income and no-ambition lifestyle.

Now wide awake and alert, she spread out the papers frantically looking for more information. Lots of legal mumbo-jumbo that she glazed over. She felt a familiar wine throb starting at the base of her head, and her hands were shaking when she saw the year 1967 and the name on the adoption papers. It wasn't her name. It was her grandparents' names. Were they the parents who adopted? Was her mother adopted? How could this be? Why wasn't she told? The grandparents Rhonda resembled were not really her grandparents? Impossible. She had Momo's blue eyes, Popo's dimples. They always said so.

None of this was making any sense and there was no one she could ask. Everyone who would know was dead. Momo, Popo and now her mother. No way to find Mr. Irresistible. Maybe he was a lie too. How could she believe anything now if these papers were true?

Rhonda lowered her head into her hands and sobbed for the first time since the paramedics called. Was she crying for the loss of her mother or for the big family she never had? A family like the ones on TV sitcoms with a dad, aunts, uncles, and cousins to have sleepovers with. She loved hanging out with friends who had big families, but it never lasted. After a few months, her girlfriends did something that ticked her off. Now she cried for all she missed. Big gulping sobs for everything she wanted but never had.

She stumbled into bed. *If this is true, then my mother does have another family besides Momo and Popo. That means I have a family somewhere. And I'm going to find them if it's the last thing I do.*

Chapter Nine

Prior

The following morning, Rhonda's car with the finicky starter took three attempts to turn over. The bronze Dart was older than she was. The odometer read 160,000 miles, which probably wasn't the first revolution. It was all she could afford, and since it hadn't fallen apart yet, she kept driving it. She could live with the mechanic's warning—brake fluid required weekly.

She was still reeling from the adoption discovery. She had a restless sleep with snatches of weird dreams. Something about an old-fashioned baby carriage. An old lady who looked like Momo was pushing the carriage. Rhonda peeked in to see the cute baby, but there was no baby. In its place was the box of yellowed legal papers from her mother's box. In the dream Momo screamed and Rhonda woke up, thinking maybe it was all a dream. She stumbled, still groggy, to the living room. But there they were, although quite faded, in black and white. Adoption papers.

Her car was still packed with the other six boxes from her mother's apartment that were hardly worth salvaging—chipped saucers, mismatched cups, pots and pans that needed a good scouring. She should have thrown them all in the dumpster. But there was Todd, the college hottie who worked at the Goodwill loading dock on a work-study program. As a sexually experienced twenty-two-year-old, she liked giving the twenty-year old an occasional treat. He was so easily aroused and could perform all night. Someday his future wife would thank her for the lessons she taught him on how to please a woman. None of that was important to her this morning, and now she regretted that she hadn't thrown the boxes in the dumpster.

As she drove, she thought again of how pathetic her mother's life had become. Her apartment was a desolate place for anyone to spend their last days on earth. That wasn't the only dreariness. Pain, worry over medical bills, constant apologies to Rhonda for not having been a better provider. Dottie Feder's later years were not golden, not even bronze. Perhaps more like the rust on Rhonda's Dart, which undoubtedly spent many days somewhere in the Midwest rust belt. Each time she noticed the rust, she was reminded that time was running out to change the plates from Illinois to Arizona.

As bad as Dottie's surroundings were, they could have been worse, as in a jail cell. Only through an upstart ambitious court-appointed public defender had she been acquitted of a reckless endangerment charge. She ran the curb several years ago and hit the little girl walking with her father that rainy night. At least she didn't leave the scene. All for a beer run. A run she shouldn't have made since she'd already consumed a six-pack, which caused her to register a .09 on the breathalyzer test. The little girl escaped with minor bruises. The news media, however, used Dottie as a scapegoat for every drunk driver who didn't serve a more punitive sentence.

Shortly after the incident, Rhonda placed an ad on Craig's List to sell the bucket of bolts her mother drove that night. She was glad she salted away the nine hundred dollars it sold for, so now she could at least pay for a cremation. With no gravesite to put flowers on maybe there would be enough left over for a bottle of wine she could toast her mother's life with. *Thanks Mom. Thanks for nothing.* That thought was followed by guilt the second it was conceived. The emotional seesaw went on even after her mother's death. Love, disgust, guilt, love.

Rhonda vowed not to make the mistakes her mother made. She squirreled every cent away to build a life that was just the opposite.

Rhonda had a plan far more ambitious than driving to the Goodwill where she was headed now on her way to work. She knew the route well as she had furnished much of her apartment with cheap finds there.

As she drove to the drop-off door, Todd came out, and a big smile spread across his face when he saw her.

"Hey, beautiful. Nice way to start my day." He leaned into the car window she had rolled down.

She had no desire to play the flirting game this morning. Even Todd's toned biceps bulging out of his white tee shirt couldn't shake the melancholy she felt.

She forced a smile. "Hi, Todd. Can't hang around. Running late for work. I'll call you later?"

"I'm ready anytime," he said with a big grin. "I'm always ready for you. Anytime."

Time. Had she given her mother enough time? She felt so empty. A week ago, she had a family, small though it was. Now she was truly on her own.

Rhonda tried not to let her mother see how much she secretly envied friends who had dads and huge extended families—siblings, cousins. She had no aunts or uncles growing up. No cousins. She hoped that one day she'd have her own big family, but first she needed the big bank account.

But maybe now, just maybe, she could have that big loving family while she was building her account. All she had to do was find them.

In Mah Jongg the East player is dealt fourteen tiles while the other three get thirteen. East discards the extra tile to start the game. A winning Mah Jongg requires the fourteenth tile with no discard.

Chapter Ten

The next Monday the Mah Jongg Mavens meet at Angelina's for their weekly game session. It's their first game without Myra, and their first time not playing in her retirement center.

"I thought it would be nice if we had a little lunch first," Angelina says, as she sets an informal kitchen table. "Change up our routine a bit."

"It will be a change all right. Only the three of us," Clara says as she and June arrange the Mah Jongg tiles on the card table set up in the living room.

"I'm not sure I remember how to play with only three of us," June says.

"It's easy. We create the fourth wall and do the Charleston with it like it's a real person. The back of our card rules say we should skip the Charleston with only three players, but I don't think we'll go to Mah Jongg jail if we do it." Angelina says. "But let's have a bite—lunch is ready."

She places a steaming casserole in the center of the table and begins to spoon a stuffed pepper on each plate. Big green peppers filled with ground beef and pork, rice and tomatoes. A few yellow hot banana peppers are nestled in for a spicy flavor, seasoned with paprika and a few red pepper flakes.

"Honestly, Angelina, you can stuff anything," June says. "Stuffed cabbage, stuffed cucumbers. You should teach a cooking class at the community center."

Clara, between mouthfuls, says, "Yeah, call it 'Stuff It.' I know some of those biddies I'd like to stuff it to." She alone laughs at her own wit as she often does.

"No, then I'd have to write out the recipes. Too much trouble. I have them in my head the way my mother did." Angelina takes a listless bite. "These don't taste as good without Myra here, do they? She loved them."

"What's not to love?" Clara says. She uses a chunk of crusty Vienna bread to sop up the juice in her bowl. "I have some recipes in my head. One is for Ding Chicken."

"Oh, is it Chinese?" Angelina asks.

"Hmm. Not exactly. You place a chicken breast on a plate in the microwave. When it goes ding, it's done."

"Oh Clara, you and your corny jokes," June says. "I still can't believe it."

"June, it's a joke."

"I'm not talking about chicken Clara. I'm talking about Myra. I can't believe she died. She looked perfectly healthy to me. How can you die overnight? With no ailments to speak of?" June sips her tea and shakes her head. "Besides her arthritis and finicky gall bladder, the only thing she ever complained about was heartburn when she ate Mexican food. Can a spicy burrito kill you?"

Clara says, "I've had some Mexican food that I thought would kill me. Especially late at night. So not a good idea. Myra did have that issue with her renal glands. Too much adrenaline or something like that. I don't remember it as being a recent problem. Didn't you talk to her daughters, Angelina? What are they saying really happened?"

"I called them but keep getting voice mail. I hate to be a pest at a time like this, but I'm concerned too, and curious, I guess." Angelina brushes bread crumbs off the table into the palm of her hand and then onto her own plate which she managed to clean.

Clara carefully pulls a piece of translucent skin off a green pepper. "Angelina, you are absolutely the world's best cook, but aren't you supposed to peel this skin off the peppers before you stuff them?"

"Some people parboil them and peel the skin. I roast them the way they come. If someone wants the skin off, it peels easily once it's baked and charred."

"I heard all the vitamins are in the skin," June comes to Angelina's defense, trying to soften Clara's comment. "My mother always said green peppers make your hair shiny."

Clara gives June one of her deadpan expressions. June's wispy blonde hair seems to be thinner each week. Tiny spots of scalp are beginning to peek through like they do on the plastic dolls her granddaughters play with.

Clara is tempted to comment with her quick and often thoughtless tongue, saying something like, *Obviously, you didn't follow her advice,* but since June is often overly sensitive, she decides not to take a chance of offending her. She'll save those comments for a tough-skinned person like the lady behind her at the supermarket yesterday who had the nerve to comment on how many items she had placed on the fifteen-or-fewer counter checkout. Well, she hadn't really said anything, but Clara caught her glaring at her items and felt she needed to justify the six cans of soup making it close to twenty items.

But first Clara checked into the lady's cart, doing a quick count to see if she herself was observing the rule. It was a very quick look because it didn't take long to count to five. "Damn," she muttered to herself.

"I don't know about you," she said to the lady who was now leaning over the handle of her shopping cart with an expression on her face that clearly implied, "You can count, can't you?"

Clara tried to justify her cart. "See, when you have multiples of one item, they count as one because they don't have to ring them up separately. Just one ring times six. Isn't that right, Carolyn?"

Carolyn, the check-out clerk, was another reason Clara wanted to go through her line. Carolyn usually asked about her grandson in Iraq. She took time for old-fashioned courtesies.

Remembering the incident, Clara now speaks out too loudly to June and Angelina. "I don't know why everyone's in such a hurry these days."

"Whatever are you talking about, Clara?" Angelina asks. "What does that have to do with green peppers?"

"Oh, nothing. I was thinking of something else."

Angelina looks at June and rolls her eyes. Clara has a way of going off on tangents, but since in most cases they are often interesting, they rarely discourage her.

They play two games of Mah Jongg, rather listlessly naming the tiles as they discard. Two bam, one crack, red dragon, west wind.

June finally declares Mah Jongg, and the other two dig into their little coin purses to give her the fifty cents she wins from each of them. June smiles and says, "A bird in hand is a penny earned."

As they are putting the tiles away, Angelina says, "Maybe we should ask one of Myra's daughters to play Mah Jongg with us. That's what they did in *The Joy Luck Club*. Remember? When one of the mothers died, the daughter took her place."

"Do any of the daughters know how to play?" June asks as she drops the quarters into her little Hedgehog coin purse.

"We could teach them," Angelina says.

"Speaking of daughters," Clara says, "Is there anything new with you and April? Have you spoken lately?"

Angelina shakes her head sadly. "No, but I'm not giving up. In fact, I think I'll call her again. This afternoon. Maybe she would like to be our fourth sometime. I taught her how to play many years ago."

Angelina perks up with a smile. "Yes, maybe April and I will come to an appreciation of each other like they did in *The Joy Luck Club*. This will give me a good excuse to call. Thank you, Clara."

"I can't take any credit. I just asked you . . ."

"It's a perfect solution. Really."

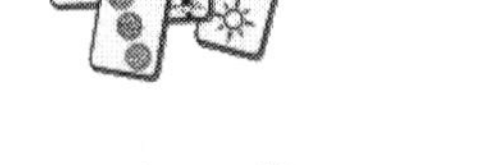

When Clara and June leave, Angelina goes to the den where one bookshelf is devoted to her favorites. The "keepers" as she calls them. The ones she might read again when she's in her rocking chair. If I can still see, she often tells herself. She pulls down *The Joy Luck Club*, and a receipt from the bookstore dated 1989 marks a page where she highlighted a quote from one of the Asian mothers. "American daughter swallows more Coca-Cola in her life than sorrow."

I need to fix the sorrow I have caused April. And soon.

Chapter Eleven
Prior

When Rhonda arrived at work, no one would guess that she had a toss-and turn night. Her blond hair billowed beautifully as always. Once a salon customer said she reminded her of Kyra Sedgwick with the flowing mane and quirky smile. She even had the dimples. But the more frequent comparison, especially from older ladies, was that she had Farrah Fawcett hair. The third time someone said that, she rented a DVD of an old season of *Charlie's Angels* and then considered the comments a compliment. Her lovely mane gave her job security when the owner of the salon often had her fill in for the receptionist. "You're the first person our clients see, and your beautiful hair assures them that they are in the right place."

The day dragged on for Rhonda. She wanted to begin the adoption search for her true grandmother, her mother's birth mother. Throughout the day she gave herself negative self-talk for not getting up early enough to do some online searching at home. She rationalized that the events of the previous day had wiped her out. It wasn't every day your mother died and you found out that same day your grandparents were not for real.

She hesitated to use the computer at work for her search in case one of the stylists peeked over her shoulder to check an appointment. One receptionist was fired when a manager discovered the websites she was searching all day between clients. That meant those bitches checked website histories. Talk about big brother watching. In this case, big sister. Another good reason not to work for anyone else. To be her own boss. The day dragged on forever with endless cups of coffee.

At home, she went straight to her computer. Then she sat there not knowing where to begin. With Google, of course, but what to type in first? She googled adoption search. She clicked on the first listing which was simply *Adoption Search*. The homepage displayed an emphasis on people wanting to adopt or people placing a child for adoption. How relevant was any of this in the 21st century going to be to an adoption in the 60's. Where would those records be?

She poured a glass of Two Buck Chuck and started over. This time she clicked on *Adoption in Arizona*. Again, so many mind-boggling choices. Then in the sidebar, she found *Search for Birth Family*. Yes, that's what she wanted. That led her to a site called *The Adoption Specialist, Inc.*

As she scrolled down the page, she found an inquiry form called, *To Request a Free Search Quote*. "Good," she thought. "Free is good." When the form appeared, she became discouraged when she realized how little information she had to work with. She left most of the columns blank. She stared at the adoption paper she found the night before intently, as if glaring at it would cause more information to appear. As if it would seep through an old typewritten document where the print was now faded in places.

The Superior Court of the State of Arizona, County of Maricopa, Juvenile Division was written across the top, followed by *In the matter of Sonja Mae Joforsky, a person under the age of eighteen years*. What the heck? Who was that? Was that the birth mother, her real grandmother? How old was she when she gave up the baby? Rhonda was so confused.

She read on. *COMES NOW, Robert Bobson, Maricopa County Attorney*, blah blah blah, *respectfully requests that the Court approve the communication agreement between the adoptive parents and birth mother. Pursuant to Ariz. Revis.Stat.* Blah blah blah. She skimmed down to *Thomas Bruce Feder and Beatrice Mae Feder*. That was Momo and Popo—*respectfully request the Court to approve the attached Contract and Communication Agreement entered into with the birth mother, Myra Mae Joforsky, regarding the above-named child.*

Rhonda blinked. How did she miss this last night? The birth mother's name. Right there. Then whose name was that on top, the person under eighteen years of age? Was that her mother's original name, the name given to the newborn baby by the birth mother, Myra, at birth? It must be. Sonja Mae Joforsky.

But this Myra Mae Joforsky, how would she find her now? Forty-three years later. Undoubtedly, she had married. What if she had moved away? Possibly a different last name and fifty big states to search. And what if she had left the States?

Overwhelmed, Rhonda refilled her wine glass and sank into the armchair and into despair. This wasn't going to be easy. Nothing in her life was easy. Why did she think this would be? She felt like throwing the wine glass across the room but still had enough presence of mind to know she didn't want wine stains on the carpet and glass shards under her bare feet.

Rhonda looked again at the computer screen. The promo for *Adoption Specialist* read, *...release to you, at the conclusion of your search, the most current name, address and other detailed information about the person you seek.*

The word current jumped out at her. Of course, that's why she needed a specialist. That's why this company existed. There had to be thousands of people looking for relatives under different names. The specialists had ways and means to find them. They were exactly what she needed. She returned to the form and added two more lines of information—the mother's maiden name, Myra Mae Joforsky and the baby's name, Sophie Mae Joforsky. Her fingers were trembling. Her hopes were high again with possibility. She had been so tired last night. No wonder she missed this vital information. And a bit too much Chuck?

She took out her wallet and credit card and filled in the information for the $39.95. It struck her funny, like an infomercial. For only $39.95 you can find your family. But wait, there's more. Call now and we'll throw in a few long-lost cousins.

The bottom of the form read, *we will respond within 24 hours.* That didn't mean they would find someone that soon, did it? Or was that to let her know they received her request? *Hell, what was another twenty-four hours after all these years?*

Chapter Twelve

Prior

The first thing Rhonda did as soon as she walked in the door each night was check her e-mail. As promised, within twenty-four hours, she received a response from Adoption Specialists. They would begin the search for the current name and address of the birth mother. With the information Rhonda provided, they felt confident they could help her, as they had a high success search ratio. Rhonda imagined her joyous reunion with aunts, uncles and cousins.

A week later she received an e-mail from Adoption Specialists, Inc. *We have successfully located the person you requested in your recent inquiry. Due to the number of hours required in this search, we will require an additional payment of $49.00. As soon as we receive the additional funds, we will forward our findings to you. Thank you for using our services.*

Rhonda's emotions boomeranged again. She was excited at the prospect of finding her grandmother but furious that they wanted more money. They didn't say anything about additional funds up front. What if the grandmother they located was dead? What good would that do her? But she couldn't stop now. She scrolled to the bottom of the form once again with her credit card information.

As she hit the send button, she muttered to herself. "This had better be worth it or they're going to be sorry. I'll post a comment on their website that will teach them to lead vulnerable people on. They'll be sorry they messed with me."

Feeling hunger pangs, Rhonda opened the refrigerator. A wheel of Laughing Cow cheese triangles. A container of hummus.

A few slices of shaved turkey breast. Some Healthy Choice dinners in the freezer. Nothing appealed to her.

Then a thought struck her. *This calls for a celebration. A little early perhaps, but I know it's the first step to finding my family. The family I've always wanted. I know it. I need to share this excitement with someone and I need to work off this nervous energy if I'm going to get any sleep tonight.*

She remembered Todd's offer and his big smile. *I can put another smile on his face.* She made two calls. One for a pizza delivery and one to Todd.

When he answered, she said, "Hey, I know it's a school night but how about sharing a pizza with me? I feel like celebrating."

"Sure," he answered. "What's the occasion?"

"Oh, nothing I can talk about yet, but trust me. I feel good and if you come over, I think you'll be feeling good too. Real good."

"I'll be right there," he answered. She could hear the eagerness in his voice. She loved young men's hormones.

Rhonda pulled cash out of her wallet for the pizza deliveryman and checked the time. She had fifteen minutes to get into something naughty that Todd would love taking off piece by piece. She knew exactly what turned him on. He liked her pink thong and see-through lacy bra. Far more titillating than a sorority girl's cotton tank top. She covered it with her plush blue bathrobe in case the pizza arrived first. She primped for the mirror, fluffed her big blond mane and smiled. "Maybe I should have waited to check out the pizza guy. Could have saved Todd a trip."

After pizza, wine, and a hot and heavy session with Todd, Rhonda slept deeply, making up for the hours she'd lost since she discovered the adoption papers.

Chapter Thirteen

Present

Guy sits at his kitchen table and opens a Steno notebook with notes to date on the investigation. As a young cop, he learned that the notebook was his best friend in solving a crime. Guy reviews the medical examiner's autopsy report of Myra again. *Cause of death: Anaphylactic shock. Swelling of bronchial passages. Airway constricted and blocked. Often brought on by allergic reaction to a drug or substance.*

As soon as Guy procured the report, he obtained a warrant for medical records from her family physician. At first reading, it appeared fairly routine for someone her age. Her last visit six months ago was for flu symptoms. No allergies to penicillin or antibiotics. He reads *history, January,1999: Sleeping pills prescribed following her husband's death.* Not unusual. *Gall bladder surgery 2005. June, 2009, patient complaining of frequent headaches, dizziness, and fatigue. Blood pressure high 180/110. Ordered cat scan of internal organs and blood test. No tumors found, but further blood testing shows excess adrenaline being produced from adrenal gland. Prescribed synthetic corticosteroids. Advised patient to avoid any anesthetic with epinephrine. Could produce a fatal reaction.* The word *anesthetic* triggers a thought for Guy.

He turns back a page in his Steno book and reviews Myra's schedule the day of death as far as he could piece together. *Dentist appointment at 1:00 p.m. Courtesy van at Friendship Acres gave her a ride at 12:30 to son-in-law Randy Moore's dental office eight miles away. Courtesy van returned to dentist for pickup at 2:15 and back to Friendship Acres at 3:00. Van made one additional stop on way back to pick up another passenger, Diane Robertson, at Southern Medical Plaza.*

According to interview with driver, Louie, Myra seemed in good spirits coming and going. Commented about wishing she were going to the mall instead of the dentist. Noted nothing unusual.

Interview with the passenger, Diane Robertson. First time she had met Myra and thought she seemed very personable as she joked about possibly having a crooked smile after local anesthetic.

Myra was seen in the lobby gift shop about 4 p.m. Volunteer Mary Marotz working that shift remembered that she purchased a sympathy card because they talked about how she sold more of those than birthday cards. As Guy thanked Mary for her time, she said sadly, "I had no idea I'd be getting a sympathy card for Myra's daughter the very next day."

Guy studies the autopsy report again. *Time of death: Between 7 and 9 p.m.* His notes: *Tenant below Myra, Apartment 123, called maintenance at 9:17 p.m. to report lack of hot water for her bath. Maintenance man George noted, on master control panel, continuous running water in unit 223 above. Went up and knocked on door. No answer. Called tenant on phone number listed in his directory. No answer. Knocked again. Was going to get the emergency key in the director's office when he tried the door. Surprisingly it was unlocked. Found Myra lying in tub with shower running. Called paramedics immediately. Myra pronounced dead at the scene.*

When Guy checked her apartment, as they always did in the case of an unattended death, the sympathy card Myra bought that afternoon was on her desk, not yet addressed. Because his training taught him not to overlook any detail, he wondered who she was sending the card to, although it probably wasn't relevant. But it was his nature to be curious. His wife always said his curiosity about things others considered normal was what made him such a good detective.

Once on an especially challenging case that kept hitting dead ends, Monica splurged. It was during the holidays and she bought him the top-of-the-line—a bottle of Johnnie Walker Blue.

Although it blew the budget, she felt the time was right. Her card read, *The best for the best. I know you'll crack this case and this might help along the way. Also, a great way to celebrate when you do . . . and you will.* Although the bottle was now empty, he couldn't bear to part with it, and it remained on the top shelf of the liquor cabinet.

The first year she was gone, he found himself pouring more than one drink each night. The night he fell asleep at the table and knocked over a whole bottle of Johnnie, spilling it on his notes, was a wake-up call, not to mention a waste of good Scotch. He had seen too many of his coworkers take that rocky road and he didn't want to join that exclusive club. He decided then that work and staying busy, not retirement, was essential.

He looks over his Steno page on Myra Anderson one more time. Activities of her final day. *Myra called daughter Debbie, married to dentist Randy, about 4:30, saying she liked the new artwork in Randy's outer office. Cannot find anyone else who saw or talked to Myra after gift shop visit. Autopsy report indicates she had a light dinner about 5 p.m. One glass of wine on the kitchen counter with wine left in it. Bottle of Riesling still half full. Bottle not corked. Had she planned to drink more? No fingerprints on the bottle. Did she wipe it down with a towel after pouring? Why?*

Guy hopes the challenge of solving the puzzle will absorb him until he crawls into bed alone at night. He still pats the pillow next to him as he does most nights. *Good night, Monica.*

Chapter Fourteen

Prior

Rhonda still couldn't believe that the search for current information led her to a neighborhood in the same city, only twenty-two miles from her work.

There were no other cars on the wide street with mature trees on either side shading the large homes spaced a distance apart. It didn't look like the typical Phoenix neighborhood of cookie-cutter homes with red tile roofs and front lawns of desert landscaping of rocks and cacti. This was an old, established neighborhood, now dubbed historic district. The word *historic* automatically added $100,000 to any real estate property. It was a neighborhood that subtly said, *we have arrived.* Like that phrase she'd heard, *old money*. Old money didn't need to prove anything like the new-money subdivisions where each home vied to outdo the other with Southwest adornments or trendy lawn décor. Perhaps a javelina, the wild boar look-alike or a Kokopelli, the fertility god—something to show their constant visitors from the cold country that they now appreciated the Native American culture. This neighborhood was what one might call comfortable in the highest sense of the word. She drove slowly, admiring each home, their addresses displayed in fancy Mexican tiles.

A familiar feeling started in the pit of her stomach. It was one of intimidation and inferiority She felt it each time she was around signs of wealth. It was the same feeling that arose when she saw large families gathering, laughing, showing signs of affection.

When she saw 2153 W. Mayberry Lane, she pulled over to the curb. She didn't want to call attention to herself, so she backed up, observing it from an angle. It was lovely. If this was indeed her mother's birth mother's home, it was the house Dottie should have grown up in. Feelings of sadness arose.

Dottie should have played on the front lawn and rode her tricycle down this shaded sidewalk. She should have had her little girl birthday parties with a rented Disney princess in what was undoubtedly a beautiful, manicured backyard with flowers and maybe a swing and a flagstone patio with a built-in barbeque grill. Dottie should have spent her last days on a comfortable chaise lounge in the screened porch, called an Arizona room, that Rhonda saw on the side of the house. And Rhonda should have come here as a grandchild to run through the sprinkler on the back lawn and chase butterflies and have tea parties for her little friends too.

As Rhonda imagined all this, she felt her resentment growing. A resentment for all her mother was denied and for herself too. If this was her real grandmother, why did her mother die in a one-bedroom apartment where you could hear the neighbors squabbling or smell the cheap cut of meat they were cooking for dinner? And why was Rhonda driving a rattletrap with a faulty starter that leaked brake fluid? For a minute she was sorry she began her search. What had she hoped to find? Would she have felt better if her real grandmother lived in a hovel?

As she sat there trying unsuccessfully to squelch the negative thoughts, a car pulled up from the other direction and turned into the driveway. Obviously, a realtor's car with the logo on the side panel. *Re-Max. We sell more homes than anyone*. A lady carrying a briefcase walked briskly to the front door. Rhonda couldn't tear her eyes away as the woman rang the doorbell. Quickly she leaned across the front seat and rolled down her passenger window, cursing the handle that always stuck. She wanted a clear look at whoever answered the door.

An older lady with tightly-curled white hair framing a round face smiled at the realtor. The lady of the house wore powder-blue slacks with a beige shell and a matching beige cardigan as well as a single strand of pearls. She looked like Barbara Bush. She looked like someone's grandmother. And she was. Myra Anderson was her grandmother.

Chapter Fifteen
Present

Angelina can't decide when and where to call April. She doesn't want to bother her at work, but if she waits until she gets home, Gary might be there, and she may not feel free to talk. Perhaps at the end of her work day. Whenever that is.

At 5:30 she calls April's cell. She answers on the first ring. Her hello sounds cool. But then again with caller ID, if she didn't want to talk to her, would she have answered?

"April, are you still at work?"

"Yes."

"Do you have a few minutes or are you busy?"

"I just shut down my computer, so I'm fine to talk."

"I won't keep you. Just wondered if we could set a lunch date this coming week."

"Mother, I . . ." She could sense her resistance crackling through their connection.

"This is not about Gary. I have an idea to run by you."

There is a pause. "Let me check my calendar."

Angelina feels a sense of hope. Th*is was a good idea*. But the hope is fleeting.

"My work schedule is ridiculous. Let me call you when things are not so hectic."

"Sure."

Angelina hangs up wanting to believe it's truly April's busy schedule that is keeping her from meeting. She will try again. Better late than never. Or as June might say, "You can lead a gift horse to water, but never look it in the mouth."

Is she trying to lead April to water she doesn't care to drink?

Chapter Sixteen

Prior

Rhonda drove to Mayberry Lane at least once a week. She was careful not to park in the same spot for fear the neighbors might notice her junker of a car, one that didn't exactly fit in this neighborhood, unless it belonged to the domestic help. She considered attaching a fake sign to her car door, like Merry Maids, so she could park it on the street each week. The second time she went, she noticed the For Sale sign on the front lawn, and it was only a few weeks later that a Sold banner was placed across it.

Rhonda had heard the real estate market was terrible. This property must have been priced below market to sell so quickly. Then she had a moment of panic. Now that she had found her grandmother, where was she going? And what did it matter anyway where she went? Not like Rhonda was going to be invited for a visit. No, she hadn't been invited for any visits, nor had her mother and why not? Why were they not entitled to some of this wealth? She felt angry and then hopeful. Maybe all that would change now.

Rhonda started driving through the neighborhood at different times. She was amazed at what one could find out about a person through observation. Or, as she called it, downright spying. One evening a Lexus SUV was parked in the driveway. When she circled back thirty minutes later, an attractive lady, she guessed in early forties, with two little girls, stepped out of the front door along with Myra. Under the floodlights of the front entry, she saw the girls give Myra a big hug and then skip to their car, holding what looked like identical dolls. Probably a gift from Grandmother. Grandmother with deep pockets.

Rhonda drove away from Myra's house that night with tears running down her cheeks. Tears for the grandmother gifts missed in her life. She was too old for the dolls she felt entitled to, but she also cried for the hugs she'd missed. She wasn't too old for them.

The next time the Lexus was in the driveway, she waited and followed it when it drove away. When it made a stop at Safeway, she climbed out of her car and slowly walked through the grocery aisles with a small shopping basket on her arm behind the lady and two little girls. She wanted a closer look at her *aunt.*

At one point the mother stopped to talk to another shopper, and Rhonda got as close to them as she could without being obvious. They were in the salad dressing aisle, and Rhonda turned her back to them and scanned the shelves of Honey Mustard, Italian, Poppy Seed, Balsamic, as if she couldn't decide which to choose. All the while she listened to their conversation.

"Debbie, the girls are so cute and how they've grown!" the lady said to Myra's daughter. "How old are they now?"

"Seven and nine. Can you believe it? Seems they just started school and now one is almost ready for middle school. How about your boys? They're probably in high school."

So this daughter was Debbie. Rhonda's research told her Myra had three daughters. She handled a few bottles of salad dressing, as if reading the labels but didn't want to get out of earshot of this conversation.

"Yes, a freshman and a junior. Scary to think of college tuition around the corner. Say, how's Randy's business doing? I read that even doctors are being affected by this rotten economy."

"It's been hurt a little. I think dentists are more susceptible than doctors. People can't help getting sick, but they can choose to skip their six-month tooth cleaning. It's a shame but that's the way it is."

She's married to the dentist. She probably met him in college, some pricey school that Rhonda could never afford. A school her own mother might have attended if anyone had cared.

The little girls started squabbling over something and Debbie said, “I’d better get going. Hey, it was good to see you. Say hi to Jim.”

Rhonda left the salad dressing aisle and hung around the checkout stands browsing at some of the end-cap specials. She studied the myriad of gift cards now available at grocery stores from iTunes to Applebee’s. When Debbie went in the checkout line, Rhonda dropped off her empty handbasket and exited the store. She waited in her car to see where their next stop was.

They drove a few miles to a gated community. Rhonda followed but not too closely. She thought she could get into the neighborhood if she were to tailgate Debbie’s car, but what if the gate started to close on her? She drove past the entrance and realized once again that she was excluded. No code, no password, or whatever it was wealthy people had such easy access to. She was still an outsider, but that was about to change. Soon.

She pressed her foot to the gas pedal and narrowly missed a rabbit scurrying across the road. Then in anger, she veered to the right and hit it. Her anger had to be directed at something. One desert bunny more or less wouldn’t be missed.

Chapter Seventeen

Present

Before Guy sets up a meeting with the dentist son-in-law, Randy Moore, he calls his own dentist, Walter Rap.

"Need a favor, Wally. Do you have a few minutes to answer some questions?"

"Sure. Do you want to come by or meet after hours?"

"Wouldn't mind buying you a beer," Guy says.

They agree to meet at Teakwood Grill in the same strip mall as Wally's office the following day.

Walter has been both his and Monica's dentist for years. He always razzed Guy about how he found a girl as classy as Monica. When Wally referred the orthodontist for his daughter's braces, Guy then grilled him good naturedly about how much of a percentage was his for the referral and said, "I paid him enough for both of you, I'm sure."

"Well, those beautiful smiles don't come cheap," was Wally's response.

Their beers arrive, and after Wally takes a long drink out of his sweaty bottle of Michelob, he says, "So what's on your mind, Buddy?"

"Do you know of any medication you use in routine procedures that could cause an anaphylactic shock?"

Wally takes another swig of beer, sets it down and squints his eyes as if the double Jeopardy question was on the board.

"People can be allergic to many things, but I think you're asking for commonly known ones, right?"

"Trying to learn more about its causes."

"I have this one patient. An older lady. Can't think of her name."

"I don't need her name."

"I couldn't give it to you anyway, but I was thinking we could go back to the office and I could pull her file to describe her condition.

"So, what's her story?" Guy asks patiently.

"She had some kidney problems, an adrenal gland issue. It produced too much adrenalin. You have to steer clear of epinephrine in that case. Not a good combination. It could cause a severe reaction. Darn, I can see her face and the molar I was working on. Number 22."

"So, how would you know this? Know not to use the epinephrine?"

"In this case, she told me. I guess her physician advised her of the seriousness of it and she was to tell anyone who would have reason to give her an anesthetic. I think he specifically mentioned dentists, as some people forget we use anesthetics." Wally shakes his head and rolls his eyes. "God help us if we didn't."

"So, epinephrine is in the anesthetic?"

"In most cases, local anesthetic contains epinephrine."

"What would you use then in its place?"

"You'd use an anesthetic without it. There are several. Still numbs the area but takes a little longer to do the job. The purpose of the epinephrine is to reduce the blood supply to the area, to constrict it. But local anesthetic can be administered without it."

"What would the reaction have been if you had given it to this patient?"

"It could have been mild as in hyperventilation or hives, or severe as in bronchial and throat swelling. Blockage of air passage."

"Could it result in death?"

"It could if it were a severe reaction and not discovered and treated immediately."

"I think that's all the information I need for now. You've been helpful."

"Glad to help." Wally downs the rest of his beer.

"Like another?" asks Guy, who these days has plenty of time with no one waiting at home.

"No, I should get going."

"You go ahead. I'm going to sit here a few minutes and make some notes. By the way, how's your golf game?"

"Golf? You know there's a reason it's a four-letter word." Wally smirks, slaps Guy on the back and leaves.

At home Guy checks the yellow pages for dentists. A younger detective would look on-line but old habits are hard to break. He finds a Randolph Moore, DDS.

Guy calls the next day and endures a thorough grilling from the receptionist as to the nature of his call. He's tempted to say something silly like, "It's about teeth, okay?" But he learned long ago to make friends with receptionists, secretaries and frontline people. To patiently answer their questions as they are doing their job, and because there was no getting around them.

When Randy picks up the line, Guy explains he has a few questions about his mother-in-law, Myra.

Randy says, "Is there some sort of problem?"

"Just routine investigation."

"Fine. I'll send you back to reception to see what time is available."

The receptionist returns to the line and Guy writes in his notebook. Tomorrow. 9:15 am. And adds, Randy sounds defensive.

After the tiles are dealt and before play begins, the Charleston exchange is performed. Three to the right, three across, three to the left. Reverse. An additional pass of up to three tiles with the person across from you is then optional.

Chapter Eighteen

Present

"If it's Monday, it must be Mah Jongg," Clara says as she opens the door to Angelina and June.

As they settle at the card table, June says, "It's not just Myra I miss." She flips the Mah Jongg tiles facedown."I miss all those people at the retirement center we used to see every Monday in the dining room. I miss singing Happy Birthday to someone older than me for a change."

"I think everyone there was older than Myra. Said she was tired of rattling around alone in her big house and she loved the activities offered at Friendship Acres." Angelina helps June shuffle the tiles.

Clara pulls tiles to build her wall. "You know why there's joy in their birthday singing? They're thrilled they made it through another year." As usual, she alone snickers at her humor as she pops a piece of red licorice in her mouth.

They read somewhere that red licorice was served at Mah Jongg games in the twenties when it became the fashionable game to play. In addition, Clara set out a bowl of Gummy Bears, June's snack of choice.

June says, "I liked it when the grandkids showed up. Remember that little girl in the purple tutu who came from her dance lesson to help her grandfather blow out his birthday candles?"

Angelina smiles at June's memory.

"I miss all the delicious cakes they served for each birthday," Clara says, lining up two rows of nineteen tiles. "That lemon butter cream frosting was to die for. Did they make those cakes there? I wish I had asked Myra that, but who expected her to check out so soon?"

After they roll the dice, Angelina announces that she is East and pushes out her wall of tiles. "I miss all the romance gossip in the retirement center. Who would have thought?"

"My favorite story is Bob and Diane," June says, as she takes her turn pulling four tiles off the center row.

"Which one was that?" Angelina asks.

"Remember? Bob is 94, Diane's 92. Both widowed. They want to get married in the Catholic Church because Diane's Catholic. Devout. The priest tells Bob he has to go to six weeks of instruction because he isn't."

"He isn't devout? How did the priest know?" Clara asks.

"No, Clara, because he isn't Catholic." June continues. "Bob, I was told, scratched his old bald head and said, 'With all due respect to your religion, Father, I'm not sure I have six weeks left.' So they sashayed—well, with Bob's walker, I'm not sure sashay is the right word. Maybe they shuffled across the street to the Methodist church where they were pronounced man and wife."

Clara says. "And I think theirs was the cake with the lemon crème filling and strawberries. Delicious."

Clara arranges her tiles into suites on her rack, sorting all the bams, dots and cracks together. Winds and flowers on the left, discards on the right. "Did you hear what happened at last week's funeral?"

"It seems there is one a week, doesn't it?" Angelina remarks, as she scrutinizes her tiles and tries not to reveal her pleasure in getting three jokers.

"You know Scott, the one who's married to Tracy?"

"You mean Scott and Tracy Wilson?" Angelina asks.

"Yes. Did you know that Scott's first wife's name was also Tracy?" Clara asks with the air of someone who has top secret CIA information.

"Was she dead or alive?" June asks.

"Of course, she was alive. He wasn't a widow. They were divorced."

June answers, "How was I supposed to know that? I don't keep track of men's marital status. I'm happily married."

Clara huffs. "Never mind. Anyway, if you can believe it, they actually called them Tracy One and Tracy Two."

"Really? Who's they?"

"People, June, just people. Now let me tell this story. So, Tracy One dies."

"I thought she was alive," June says.

"She was alive. Till she died, okay? So when she dies, the obituary in the paper says, "Tracy Wilson died." A friend of Tracy Two reads about it in the paper and goes to the funeral home thinking it's her."

"Which her? One or Two? June asks.

"Tracy Two, June. Pay attention."

"Who's on first?" Angelina asks.

"What?" Clara glares at Angelina.

"Never mind. Keep going, Clara. Finish your story."

"I'm trying. So this friend of Tracy Two, who doesn't even know there's a Tracy One, goes to the funeral home all grief stricken, looks in the casket and sees it's not her friend, and practically screams. First out of surprise and then relief, I guess. She runs out of the funeral home like a banshee."

"Really, Clara, most people make a long story short. You certainly can make a short story long," June shakes her head and reaches for another Gummy Bear.

"Clara, how do you hear all these stories?" Angelina asks as she discards a red dragon.

"You have to pay attention. There's a lot going on and it's quite interesting."

"We could join the group that plays on Fridays at the Center," June suggests.

"Absolutely not," Clara responds. "They are such sticklers for the rules. I heard they call the Mah Jongg League in New York at least once every session to get a ruling. I mean, seriously?"

"Really?" June's eyes are wide. "What do they ask them?"

"Once I heard they asked, 'If a player has announced a discard but has not placed the tile on the table, may she change her mind?'"

"Can she?" June asks.

"The answer was 'once you announce a tile, it is considered a discarded tile and you must lay it down.'" Clara says.

"Oh my, that means we have been fudging a little a few times." June frowns.

"That's not the point, June. I mean we're playing for mere quarters. Does that warrant a call to New York?"

"Well, I guess it's good to do it right," June says.

"And I guess it's good to stay in our own group."

June attempts a compromise. "Maybe we can invite one of the Friday ladies to join us here on Mondays. Or better yet, have her reserve a Monday table for us at the retirement center. Then we'll have a foursome and all those wonderful birthday cakes."

Clara seems to be considering the suggestion but says nothing.

In Angelina's mind, it seems disrespectful to replace Myra so soon.

Chapter Nineteen

Prior

The following week Rhonda sat in her car on Mayberry Lane watching the house, hoping there would be some activity. The Christmas décor wasn't as splendid during the day. She recalled her one trip to Las Vegas. How the strip sparkled at night but didn't look so inviting the next morning.

The garage door opened and Myra's car started backing out. Rhonda's patience was rewarded. She followed the sensible Buick sedan, not as ostentatious as the daughter's but not exactly a rattletrap either. She thought of her mother's last pitiful car. Like Rhonda's, the odometer indicated it had been around the block a few times. She didn't tell the kid who bought it about all the things wrong with it but told herself that's the risk when you buy used goods. It wasn't like the previous Dart owner had clued her in on anything.

Rhonda continued to follow Myra. She drove slow like most old people, but not bad for a senior citizen. Rhonda had become quite adept at finding vital statistics online. Point here, click there. A person could find out almost anything they needed to know. She considered any money spent for that information not so much an expenditure but an investment in her future. She now knew Myra's age, her birthday, her birthplace and the day she became Mrs. Richard Anderson. She knew the birthdays of all three of her daughters. Three in rapid succession, starting in 1974, a few years after her own mother's birth. She assumed Myra was a senior in high school when Dottie was born. Obviously, Myra, although pregnant, finished high school as Rhonda's point/click search also listed the date Myra graduated from college.

Myra made one more turn and pulled into a well-manicured circular driveway with a sign that read Friendship Acres Retirement Center. A sign so elegant it was subtly screaming Money Acres. Nice subliminal image. If you live here, you'll have acres of friends. What they don't say is they have to replace all the ones who die.

Myra parked the car in a space reserved for guest parking. Rhonda checked her watch. She didn't have much time left. She waited ten minutes, but Myra didn't return. Rhonda drove back to start her shift at Fuchsia Spa. She just might pay Friendship Acres a visit on her day off.

Chapter Twenty

Present

While Guy waits in Dr. Moore's dental reception office, he notes the plush furnishings, the high-definition TV Angelina had mentioned and the artistic wall hangings she referred to. He can't help but wonder if Randy will expand or decorate even further once his wife receives what he assumes will be a substantial inheritance from Myra.

The receptionist escorts him down a long hallway with several examining rooms. Randy's office is small and although tastefully furnished, it's not elaborate, which tells Guy the borrowed dollars have been spent mainly where clients could see them. The brochures for cruise lines sitting on the corner of the doctor's desk don't escape Guy's attention.

"First of all, my condolences in the loss of your mother-in-law," Guy says, which Randy acknowledges briefly with a nod.

"A few questions as I trace Myra's activities of the day she passed."

"I understand."

Although Randy seemed a bit defensive on the phone, he appears now to be calm and poised. After years of reading body language, Guy surmises that the questioning is not making him uncomfortable.

"Was Myra a patient of yours for many years?" Guy starts with general non-threatening questions.

"Ever since Debbie and I became engaged, so that would be about thirteen years."

"How many times a year did you see Myra? As her dentist, I mean."

"Of course." Randy refers briefly to a folder he has lying on his desk. "I pulled her file this morning. Normally once a year for cleaning and checkups. Once every two years, we did an x-ray."

"Any serious dental problems?"

"Not really. I replaced several fillings over the years that had worn thin. They were the older kind with silver. Such better materials are available today. Made to last a lifetime."

Then he winces and fidgets with his pen, as obviously Myra's lifetime ended shortly after the filling.

Enough for generalities. "Her last visit…it was routine?"

"She had her routine checkup two weeks prior and this was a follow-up. I recommended a filling replacement. Nothing urgent, but I told her it should be done soon. She could possibly lose the filling before the next checkup."

"So she scheduled the filling visit after her checkup?"

"Yes, on her way out. My receptionist schedules the next appointment."

"And did the procedure go well? Anything unusual?"

Randy opens the folder on his desk again, glances at it. "Not that I can see. It was a simple filling."

"Did it require an anesthetic?" Guy attempts to sound casual, although this answer is critical to his investigation.

"I would never attempt a filling without one."

"Do your notes show the type of anesthetic used? And the dosage?"

Randy's back seems to stiffen and his body posture changes to a familiar mode Guy recognizes from years of questioning, best described as guarded.

"What are you suggesting, Detective?"

"Not a thing. Routine questioning."

Randy looks at his notes again. "Actually, I had to be very careful with Myra. A few years ago, she had a renal condition. Her renal glands tend to produce excessive adrenalin. Sporadically. Her family physician advised her to be careful and avoid any anesthetics with epinephrine. It could cause a reaction resulting in anaphylaxis."

Guy was surprised that both Randy and Walter would have a patient with a similar condition. Perhaps it wasn't as uncommon as Wally led him to believe. Although Guy was aware of anaphylaxis from the medical examiner's autopsy report and his conversation with Walter, he asks Randy, "And what would that be—this anaphylaxis?"

"It's a serious allergic reaction. It can affect different people different ways. From something as simple as hives, annoying but not serious, to severe anaphylaxis, which can be fatal if air passages become blocked due to swelling of bronchial passages."

Guy didn't know how much information Randy and the family had received after the autopsy, but as if the doctor read his mind, he said, "Detective, I know Myra's death was caused by something very similar to anaphylactic shock. As a doctor and family member, I demanded the results of her autopsy as soon as they were available. If you're implying in some way that I was careless . . ."

"Of course not, Doctor. No implication. Merely checking her activities prior to her death.

I'm sure you took every precaution with your mother-in-law. I'm just curious, however. What does a dentist use for the patient who cannot have epinephrine? If that's a major ingredient in local anesthetics."

"Did I say it was?" Randy asked, once again defensive.

"Perhaps you didn't. Perhaps I implied it from your previous comment." Guy realizes he revealed more than he had let on.

"You merely use a local anesthetic without epinephrine. It's not as effective and takes a little longer to work, but the patient doesn't feel any sensation."

"I see," Guy said. "Is it common? This avoidance? Do you have other patients who cannot use epinephrine?"

"Not too common. I can think of one other patient offhand. I'd have to check my files. If you're wondering if any of them died following my visit, I hardly think so." Randy's demeanor was now cold.

"Not at all, not at all. I guess that answers my questions," Guy flips his notebook closed and begins to stand.

Then he opens it again. "So that I don't have to take any more of your time later, would it be possible to make a copy of Myra's last visit? Your notes. Procedure and dosage of anesthetic used. I didn't bring a warrant but could..."

"Not necessary at this point."

"I appreciate that. My partner is rather anal about those things. I try to keep him happy. You don't want him coming around. He's a real talker. Would really waste your time."

Guy points to the little ceramic golfer on the desk corner holding business cards. "I see you're a golfer. My partner would bore you to death about how he's trying to correct his slice."

Randy's shoulders lose their tenseness. "I'd much rather talk about that myself than anesthetics."

Guy nods to the brochures on Randy's desk. "Planning a cruise? I've heard it's a great way to travel. Haven't tried it myself."

"I've been promising my wife a nice vacation for the past two years."

Guy stands and extends his hand across the desk. "Thank you for your time and again, my sincere condolences."

Randy shakes his hand and closes Myra's folder.

Guy turns toward the door and then pauses. "Did I ask you if you saw Myra for any reason after her visit with you?"

Randy scowls. "How could I have seen her? She died that night, didn't she?"

"I meant later in that day, or perhaps that evening?"

"Of course not," he replies curtly. "Why would I have done that?"

"I thought perhaps you and your wife stopped by for some reason." Guy flips through a few pages of his little notebook. He feigns an apology. "Sorry, I did talk to your wife about that evening. She said she hadn't seen her mother for a few days. In fact, according to my notes here, your wife was at a school function for the girls that night. Did you attend with her?"

Randy blinks rapidly and his jaw tightens. "No, I wasn't able to attend. I had a dental meeting. We have a local group that meets once a month at Keegan's. Very informal. We shoot the breeze mostly."

"Sounds good." He closes his book and asks, "So, your receptionist will be making that copy of Myra's last visit?"

When Guy leaves his office, Randy looks at his desk calendar. On the night in question, he has the dental meeting penciled in and underneath it, he has the initial, M-7 p.m.

Guy calls Wally again. He's with a patient, but when he returns the call, Guy asks if by chance he's a part of the dental group that meets informally at Keegan's. His practice isn't far from Randy's.

"Yes, we get together mostly to share war stories. Worst patients. No names, of course."

"Do you by chance recall if Randy Moore was at the last get-together?

"Hmm, let me think a minute. It was a small group that night. I think only four of us showed up. No, I don't think Randy was there. In fact, I know he wasn't because Rick joked that Randy didn't show because he owed him five bucks on a bet they had about who had the most cancellations last month. You can see we are a very serious and professional group." Wally laughs.

"Thanks, buddy. I owe you another beer."

"Anytime."

Guy makes a note in his steno. Randy lied about where he was. Why?

The following day, the receptionist walks to Randy's office to tell him the detective is here again. No appointment this time but wants a few minutes.

Randy sets aside the brochure.

The receptionist says "So, are you and Debbie finally going to take that cruise? It's been a long time since you've had a day off."

"God knows I can use a vacation. Something nice without worrying about the budget for a change. Go ahead and send him in." Randy stuffs the brochure in his desk drawer as Guy enters.

"Sorry to trouble you again, but you probably know why I'm back."

Randy doesn't answer.

"I happen to know one of the dentists in your shoot-the-breeze group. He tells me you weren't at the last meeting. Do you want to tell me where you were that night?"

"I don't know why I need to account for my whereabouts. Am I under some sort of suspicion here? I can assure you . . ."

"Just doing my job, Dr. Moore. We just need to determine what actually caused your mother-in-law's death."

Randy scowls and then says, "I was with a friend. A lady friend. Just a casual dinner, but I'd rather my wife didn't know about it."

"I see. If I called this casual dinner friend, would she verify you were with her?"

"Of course, she would."

"May I have her name and number?"

"Marilyn. Do you need a last name?"

"Not at this time, but I do need a contact number."

Randy opens his cell phone and scrolls for a minute.

Guy has his steno book open. He jots down the number Randy gives him.

Randy says, "If you don't mind, I'd like to give her a heads-up that you'll be calling."

"Sure, do you want to call her now?" Guy asks. He wants to hear just how much of a heads-up Randy gives.

Randy presses one button on his phone and in a few seconds, he says, "Marilyn, it's me."

A slight blush appears on Randy's cheeks. Guy assumes Marilyn said something that caused it. Also, "it's me" vs. "this is Randy" indicates she's familiar with his voice.

"Uh . . . I'm giving your number to a detective named Guy. Guy…" He looks up.

"Lucchino."

"A Guy Lucchino. He wants to verify where I was the last time we had dinner together. I hope you don't mind that he calls you?"

Pause. "Thanks, Marilyn. I'll explain later."

Guy knows she will verify, so he asks Randy where they had dinner

"A little place in Gilbert. Travitta. We didn't want to stay in the neighborhood. Marilyn is also married, and you know that's how rumors get started."

"Sure, I understand," Guy says. *I understand totally. How rumors start and how marriages end.*

"Thanks. I'll give Marilyn a call. In fact, I'll do it right now and be done with it." Guy decides to call her right there before the dentist can call her back with the name of the restaurant.

She confirms that she was with Randy and gives the same name of the restaurant.

"Thanks, Doctor. I appreciate your time and cooperation."

"I'd, of course, appreciate if you didn't mention this to Debbie. I could be in big trouble for missing a school event."

"No need to mention it." Guy says, knowing Randy would be in big trouble for more than a missed school meeting.

Guy leaves feeling like he has to wash his hands. Although he's seen many seedy things in his line of work, he's still surprised by the number of men who are unfaithful. Having had a good marriage with no thoughts of straying, he wonders why men do. He is reminded of the Paul Newman saying, "Why go out for hamburger when you have steak at home." Monica was definitely steak.

Dim sum, a small fried or steamed dumpling, is a traditional Mah Jongg snack. Literally it means "small hearts" in Chinese. Red licorice is also a favorite snack at the Mah Jongg table.

Chapter Twenty-One

Present

"So, when are you going to tell us, Angelina?" Clara asks.

"Tell you what?" Angelina rearranges her Mah Jongg tiles with all the discards on the left end of her rack. She loves being dealt three green dragons but assumes a poker face to hide her pleasure.

"What the detective wanted. What did he say?" Clara pursues.

Angelina feels a slight blush to her cheeks, hoping neither of them detect it any more than they detected her lucky dragon deal. "He didn't say much of anything. Mostly he asked me to talk. Lots of questions. Like cop shows on TV. You watch those, don't you?"

June pipes in, "Not anymore. They're too violent. I like the old-fashioned ones like Perry Mason. You remember how Della Street always came into the courtroom at the last minute with the missing clue?"

"Speaking of missing, where are all the jokers in this hand? I didn't get a one," Clara complains.

"Yeah, Della always whispered the last clue in Perry's ear," June says almost dreamily.

"You think they were sleeping together?" Clara asks.

"In real life or the TV show?" June asks, popping a green Gummy Bear in her mouth.

"Well, if they were on TV today, they would be. Sleeping together on the show, I mean. They certainly don't leave anything to the imagination these days, do they?" Angelina declares.

"Can't be any worse than the Viagra commercials." Then imitating a deep announcer's voice, Clara exaggerates the commercial, 'If you have an erection that lasts over four *years*, please call your doctor.' Like a guy is going to complain about that."

Angelina and June chuckle.

"What kind of questions did he ask?" Clara is relentless.

Clara's persistence would make her a better investigator than Lucchino. "I guess the usual ones. How long did I know her? Was there anything unusual going on in her life? Did I know anyone who didn't like her?"

"What? What did you say to that?" Clara asks, almost knocking her rack of tiles into her glass of iced tea.

"I said the only one I could think of was a lady she played Mah Jongg with. Her name is Clara Strong." Angelina tries to keep a straight face but laughs and ruins the charade.

Still Clara looks appalled. "You didn't!"

June's eyes open wide and her eyes dart back and forth at her friends as if she's at Wimbledon.

"Of course not, Clara. I'm just funning with you." Angelina tells them that Detective Lucchino asked if the four of them—-the Mah Jongg Mavens—all got along. "I told him that we rarely agree on anything but that's what keeps our group so interesting." She looks at each of her friends in turn. "How would you answer that question?"

"Yes, it's like we agree to disagree, with no hard feelings," June says. "I belonged to a book club once where if you didn't agree with the person who chose the book, you were made to feel like a dodo bird or like you considered Archie and Jughead fine literature. So, I stopped going."

"Really." agrees Clara. "What's the point of discussing something if someone has already decided what you should be thinking?"

"My point exactly," June says, which surprises Angelina. That June and Clara agree on something. The planets must be aligned.

"You know," Angelina says, "Our backgrounds are so different. I mean, look at religion. I know you're never supposed to discuss religion or politics, but we seem to respect our religious differences. I for one love hearing about your customs, June, in the synagogue and the traditions you were brought up with."

"I was thinking about the mass they had for Myra, being Catholic and all." Clara says. "I think Catholics believe that her soul cannot get to heaven until she's forgiven for her sins. The soul is hanging out in purgatory or something like that." Then Clara adds in a rare weak moment of admission, "Actually, I don't know what I'm talking about."

"Isn't that like eternal damnation—people who stay in purgatory forever?" June asks.

Clara adds, "Kind of like the week we spent in El Paso. It was the longest vacation I *never* had. I still haven't forgiven Frank for that one."

Clara complains about her husband each week, but it's obvious to Angelina and June that her stories are exaggerated. She says she plays Mah Jongg to have a few hours away from him now that he's retired.

Angelina recalls how Clara ranted once he was underfoot all day. "He's telling me which laundry detergent to use. Like I haven't done it alone for years. And the first week he was retired he said 'Hi' to me each time I walked into the room. Scared me to death. Not a little 'Hi,' but a loud one like he was surprised I lived there too. 'Lordy,' I thought. 'If this keeps up, I'm going back to work.'"

Angelina picks up the north wind tile that June discards and displays it with two others on her rack. "I thought Catholics wiped the slate clean every time they went to confession. You know, it used to annoy me. Sort of like they were cheating. I had a girlfriend in high school who went to confession every Saturday morning. Sometimes I'd walk with her to the neighborhood church and wait on the steps while she confessed her sins and came out all smiles. I thought of some of the mean, gossipy things she said during the week. Like all that was okay because she could wipe the slate clean on Saturday morning. Then she'd turn around and gossip again the next week."

"We have Yom Kippur. Jewish holiday of atonement. We do it once a year." June picks up the three crack and displays another one with a joker.

"Do what?"

"Ask for forgiveness."

"Oh, my gosh. If I waited all year, it would take me half of the next year to say it all." Clara discards a five bam.

"No, you specifically ask your family members. It's a good feeling."

"Do you still do it?"

"Of course."

Angelina peers at June. "Junie, I can't imagine you needing to ask forgiveness for anything. Especially in your family. You treat them so well."

"But sometimes it's not the way I feel. Sometimes I harbor jealousy and resentment. You know, in my heart."

"Oh, like Jimmy Carter and his lusting. I He said it wasn't a sin if it was only in his heart. Something like that," Angelina comments.

"Well, getting back to Myra," Clara says, "Honest to a fault. She seemed nice to her daughters, wouldn't you say? And hardly said a bad word about that no-good son-in-law, who wanted to tap into her bank account like it was his right. Myra said he had a third request for money, and she didn't want to do it."

"Then what happened?" asks June.

"I don't know. Then she died."

"Sadly, so she did," Angelina remarks.

"See, that makes him even more suspect. He had to get that money somehow," Clara says.

Angelina picks up the south wind that Clara discards. "At the funeral lunch, I heard him talking about taking a cruise. Something about going first class."

"There you have it. Poor Myra. Barely buried and he's spending his inheritance."

"I was thinking of going on one of those Mah Jongg cruises," June says. "Wouldn't that be fun—playing Mah Jongg all day?"

Clara turns to June, her eyes wide. "Surely you jest. They would eat you alive."

June discards a flower and says, "Birds of a feather hang out together."

"They flock, June, not hang out. Flock. And what does that have to do with a Mah Jongg cruise?"

"Well, it's obvious. All those hanging out on the ship play Mah Jongg."

Clara rolls her eyes, Angelina discards a three bam and the game goes on.

After another hour of playing, Clara and June leave. Angelina clears the coffee cups and dessert dishes and pulls out her speckled notebook. She was going to jot down something Clara said, but now it eludes her. Darn. She should have done it right away.

Angelina leaves the book on her bedside table in case the idea comes to her in the middle of the night.

The talk of forgiveness reminds Angelina of her goal to meet with April. She checks the time, dials her number and leaves a message on her voice mail.

"It's your mother. Clara and June keep insisting I call you to run their idea past you. I'd love to do it over lunch if your schedule is better."

April always liked Clara and June. Maybe she'll call if it's at their request. It's a cheap shot, but she justifies her action with the thought that desperate times call for desperate measures. Or as June might say, actions speak louder than people who live in glass houses. Or something to that effect.

At two a.m., Angelina pops up and switches on the bedside lamp. She rubs the sleep from her eyes, opens her notebook and scribbles a note before it eludes her sleepy brain. Myra's confession. Shortly before she died, Myra told Angelina she desperately needed to go to confession.

Chapter Twenty-Two

Prior

The following Monday, Fuchsia's slowest day and her day off, Rhonda drove to Friendship Acres and parked in the same visitor spot Myra had the previous week. She entered and fabricated a story to the receptionist that she was checking out retirement homes for her aunt. While waiting she looked around and noticed the tasteful décor and art displays. No Dollar Store items here. Everything looked like it came from an upscale floral shop or an exclusive boutique.

In a few minutes, she was led into an elegant and tastefully furnished office. The nameplate on the desk read Kathleen Donahoe, Director. Kathleen entered a few minutes later, all smiles. *Of course, a warm welcome. I represent potential dollars.*

How many dollars? From the looks of the lobby furnishings, this place wasn't for folks who depended solely on their social security checks. Rhonda's money radar knew how to spot wealth every time. The other thing she noticed immediately, as she did with all women she met, was the stylish cut and style of Kathleen's hair. Surely something done in Scottsdale or Paradise Valley.

"I'd love to show you around. Do you have a few minutes? I could give you a mini-tour that takes about fifteen minutes."

"I'd love it." Rhonda replied enthusiastically to mask the inferiority she could feel rising in her as it often did in the company of finished-looking women.

"I don't have a vacancy now to show you a typical apartment." Kathleen came from around her desk and stood before a wall showing architectural drawings of floor plans. "I don't know your aunt's time frame, but you can't get her name in too early. Our waiting list is quite long. I can show you a typical floor plan here on our board."

She pointed to the wall display. "And, of course, it's in our brochure." She handed Rhonda a piece of literature with glossy, colored photos that looked like covers of *Better Homes and Gardens*.

"We have three models, one with one bedroom and two with two bedrooms. Most people at this stage in their life don't need more than two bedrooms. And I should mention that we do have guest quarters on the property for those who might have overflow visitors for those special occasions. I'd show that to you, but I believe Wendy Henes' son from Michigan is still visiting here with her grandson."

Rhonda smiled and said, "Of course," once again feeling the familiar pang when people referred so casually to large families as if they were something everyone had. She found herself not liking Kathleen for her cultured ease and confidence. And for rubbing it in about large families.

"Let's take a quick tour." Kathleen led the way out of the office. Rhonda found herself mimicking the way Kathleen walked for a second as she followed her, the way she used to in junior high when a teacher reprimanded her. Of course, then she might have made an ugly face and stuck her middle finger in the air to make her classmates laugh. Which she maturely refrained from doing today.

"We'll start here in our dining room, near the lobby. So many of our residents have guests for lunch or dinner. It's easy for them to find the dining room near the front entrance. You might notice too that every guest must check in with our receptionist. Our residents' safety is very important to us."

She took Rhonda to the dining room, the library, the game room, the TV room, the workout room, the pool area, the craft room, and the music room.

"It's like summer camp for adults, isn't it?" Kathleen flashed her polished smile. They circled back to the gift shop near the lobby where they began.

"Many of the items for sale here are made by our residents and sold on consignment. It's not that our residents need the money," she quickly explained. "It's being recognized for their artistic ability. I think that's important, don't you? So many talented people here; you wouldn't believe what comes out of that craft room. Our instructor is a Martha Stewart clone."

Kathleen had even given Rhonda a peek into the kitchen where gleaming copper pots and pans hung from the ceiling rack as if it were a five-star hotel. "Honestly, the food is so good I think I gained five pounds the first few months here." Her laugh derived from someone who obviously never gained a pound, or she wouldn't have found it humorous. Dressed in a well-tailored knit suit, Kathleen looked ready for an afternoon wedding or corporate board meeting.

"Are the apartments furnished?" Rhonda asked, feigning a genuine interest for her aunt.

"No, but we can furnish them. We work with the Ethan Galleries that supply us with furnishings and give us a choice of four different styles. Most of our clients, I mean residents, are scaling down from larger homes and want to bring a few of their favorite pieces. A chair, a desk, their own bed. Or we can mix and match—fill in what they don't bring. As you can see, we're quite flexible at Friendship Acres."

Kathleen flashed that professional smile again. "We pride ourselves on our staff, the way they make our clients feel like they're family. That's our main goal—to make everyone here feel like they belong to a big family. Of course, they can have all the privacy they want or can be as active as they want."

The schedule of posted activities made Rhonda feel she was at summer camp. Except she'd never gone to summer camp. Another sore spot. But enough of her friends had that she imagined what it was like.

Her sore spot was agitated now. Bet Myra's kids went to summer camp. The pangs of jealousy she felt each summer surfaced like new, her friends telling about their cabin mates, suddenly their new *best* friends, sporting suntans from hours at the pool, doling out handmade lanyards in bright colors. Rhonda still had the yellow and green one her friend Nancy made her in fourth grade. She'd kept the key to her mother's house on it.

They were almost done with the tour when Kathleen said, "Oh, I forgot one very important room." She emphasized *very*. "We have our own barber shop and beauty shop."

She opened the door to a room resembling a professional salon with a few polished ebony sinks and two styling chairs with large mirrors. In one corner was a barber chair.

"It's closed Sundays and Mondays, but we're open enough days that there's no trouble getting scheduled. We also have a minivan that takes our clients to their doctor appointments and shopping. Some women prefer their own hairdresser, but it is nice to have an in-house option, don't you think?"

Rhonda couldn't agree more. A lovely option. Lovelier than she could have imagined. As she drove away that afternoon, she thought of just how lovely it might be for her personally. Perhaps she could work at the salon one day a week. What better way to get to know her grandmother than to see her each week? She might even give her a modern hairdo. An easy way to get a strand of hair for DNA. How much would a DNA test cost? It would be well worth it, whatever the price.

A guy's face came to mind. Eddie. On their first date, he bragged about his work in a crime lab that did DNA testing, trying to impress her. At the time it didn't impress her enough to accept the second date. Something about his hair. Greasy. Bad hair on a guy was one of the biggest turnoffs for her. But maybe she could overlook the greasy hair one time. One time might be enough to trade what he wanted for what she wanted.

She learned early in life why it was called the oldest profession in the world. Although she worked on women's hair, she discovered at a young age that good work on men's heads also opened many doors—men's small heads, that was.

Chapter Twenty-Three

Present

Angelina starts to recall little incidents when Myra did seem bothered at times. She wasn't herself on several occasions. For example, she bristled every time we said her hair looked nice after her visits to the new hairdresser. It wasn't like her not to be gracious after a compliment.

Angelina makes a few notes in her book. Is it worth a call to Guy? Or is it an excuse to see him again? She feels a stirring in her chest at the thought. Maybe her ability to feel didn't die with Peter as she thought it had. Her love for Peter would never die and no one could ever take his place in her heart, but she forgot how good a flutter could feel.

Angelina takes Guy's business card out and sets it next to the phone. She starts to dial and then hangs up. No, she doesn't have enough to say to warrant the call. However, he did say call him with *anything*. She pours herself an iced tea and decides she'll give it some thought.

Later that evening while watching TV, she sees the aspirin commercial. The one promoting heart attack prevention. It shows an older lady, actually one her age, even though she still doesn't think of herself as the age of the silver-haired actresses in commercials. This lady and others her age are saying the things they still want to do in their lives. "I want to play golf with my grandkids." Another one says, "I want to walk the dog without leg aches and pains," and then the last one with an implied promise of heart attack prevention and a longer life says, "I want to fall in love again."

Angelina pictures Guy's shy smile. Is this really about Myra or is this about Guy? She tells herself it could be both, and so what if it is? Glancing at the clock over the hearth, she decides to do it now before she loses her nerve again.

Should she use her house phone or cell phone? All of a sudden it seems like a monumental decision. *This is silly. I feel like a teenager.* Picking up the house phone in the kitchen, she misdials the first time and starts over, punching numbers slowly and deliberately.

"Lucchino," says a voice that sounds gruff and more official than the one she remembered at her house. It causes her to hesitate. She hears the television in the background.

"Hello?" he asks.

"Hello," Angelina says trying to control the jitter in her voice. Does he detect it? "Detective, it's Angelina Popoff. Myra Anderson's friend? You said I should call if . . ."

He jumps in, "Yes, Angelina. Good to hear from you." His voice changes to a tone that is friendly. And softer. Or is that her imagination? And the television sound she heard earlier is gone as if muted.

"I've been thinking a lot about Myra since your visit and I'm not sure I have anything new, but then again, maybe it's something. You said to tell you anything."

"I did say that. And sometimes the littlest things lead to bigger things. Important clues. Discoveries."

"It's not anything specific. I'm not even sure how to put it into words. It's a feeling I have."

"Angelina?" he interrupts again, a question in his voice.

"Did I catch you at a bad time? It is rather late to be calling."

"Not at all. Just hanging out with Kevin."

"Kevin?"

"Bacon…getting my nightly movie fix."

"Oh," she answers, not sure how to respond. "Well, I'll be brief."

"No, no need to. Say, have you tried that restaurant yet?"

"Restaurant?"

"Chino Bandito?"

"Oh no, not yet." That was the furthest thing from Angelina's mind.

"Well, how about we go there, and you can tell me what you're thinking? I haven't had any indigestion since the night we first spoke. Been eating boring bland food."

"Well, if you're up for torture again, I'm willing to try it. "

They agree on the following day.

"I'll bring the Tums," Angelina says.

Chapter Twenty-Four
Prior

That night when Rhonda returned from Friendship Acres, she threw a Lean Cuisine in the microwave, set it on five minutes and sipped her Two Buck Chuck while she waited. She was feeling good about the potential of seeing her grandmother on a weekly basis if she could work in the beauty salon while formulating a plan to reveal their connection. But something about Friendship Acres nagged at her.

She ate her sesame chicken dinner out of the microwave container. Probably not something Myra would approve of. She thought of Myra's elegant home. Bet no one ate out of plastic containers in that dining room. Fine china, sterling silver, crystal.

A picture flashed through her mind of the cheap pastel Melmac plates she had thrown in the Goodwill box from her mother's cupboard. Most of them with cigarette stains. A miracle she hadn't burned the house down.

The resentment built again. She would avenge her mother's pauper's death. She would claim the life her mother should have had. Someone said living well is the best revenge. She planned to live well.

She threw the empty Lean Cuisine container in the overflowing kitchen trash can. By spending so many hours tracking Myra's neighborhood and movements, she'd neglected her own home. She always vowed never to live in squalor as her mother had, and here she was picking up garbage that had fallen on the floor. The irony of it all.

Walking out through the laundry door past the key rack, she saw the old green and yellow lanyard with her mother's house key.

The lanyard her friend Nancy had made for her at summer camp. Then it clicked. The earlier nagging thought surfaced. When Director Kathleen said, "It's like summer camp here," Rhonda had pushed aside a memory, but now with the Merlot flowing through her melancholy veins, the memory surfaced. In living color, sound and smell.

She pictured Nancy DelDuca, her best friend in fourth grade. Nancy had the family Rhonda wanted, so she tried at every opportunity to be a part of them. She never missed a chance to eat at their home when invited, to sleep over, to endear herself to Nancy's mother by helping around the house so she would be invited back. Mrs. DelDuca praised Rhonda constantly for her efforts and her cheery disposition. Rhonda spent so much time with Nancy's family that the two weeks Nancy was at summer camp were the loneliest of the summer.

Although she missed Nancy, she also missed being at the DelDuca home, having a dad to tug on her ponytail or play checkers with her. She wished she could hang out there in Nancy's absence. In fact, not having to share Nancy's dad's attention would have been wonderful. She couldn't even offer to babysit the younger brother, Ricky, who was shipped off to a cousin in Ohio, so the parents could take an anniversary cruise in the Bahamas.

When Mrs. DelDuca called the day before they were to pick Nancy up at camp, she asked if Rhonda would like to ride along. Of course, she wanted to be a part of Nancy's welcome-home family greeting. But through the years, she regretted that day many times.

When their car pulled into the campground gates, Rhonda was sitting on the edge of her seat in anticipation. Two hours north of Phoenix, the campground near Flagstaff was nestled in tall pines. At an altitude of seven thousand feet, the air was cool and crisp. The sky was the color of her then favorite blue crayon—azure. They parked the car and went into the large rustic log-cabin lodge with long knotty pine picnic tables and benches. The high-beamed ceiling with tall windows showed patches of the blue sky and allowed bright sunlight to fill the room.

It was a buzz of activity with both joy and tears. Happiness of families reuniting and groups of girls crying in huddles who were saying goodbye to each other. When Nancy saw her family and

Rhonda, she ran and hugged them all. Then she said, "I'll be right back. I have to say my goodbyes."

"Rhonda, why don't you go with Nancy and meet her cabin mates?" Mrs. DelDuca said.

Rhonda turned to follow Nancy who was already running back toward her group. Nancy hadn't suggested Rhonda tag along, and she almost lost sight of her in the crowded room. When she reached Nancy on the long front porch with the rockers and gliders, she witnessed something she wished through the years she had not.

It was painful to see her best friend hugging her new-found friends. Only two weeks and they'd replaced Rhonda, whom Nancy had known for two years. Not only hugging them but crying as she said goodbye. Nancy hadn't cried when she left Rhonda for two weeks. Then they all joined hands in some secret handshake like a football team in a huddle, sang a little song and threw their hands up in the air with a shout, giggling like only ten-year-olds can. The little group broke up, but one girl with freckles and the reddest hair Rhonda had ever seen, clung to Nancy. Holding each other close, they spoke with the intimacy of lovers.

Seeing this vivid memory again, Rhonda understood why she hated doing the hair of redheads. Although she made them look good, she often sabotaged her work, unbeknownst to them, with a chunk cut out of the back or a perm that was a tad too frizzy, not discovered until they were home doing their own hair.

Rhonda tried to stifle her jealousy of the new friend and of the whole camp experience. And jealousy for having a mom and a dad and a family who could afford to send her to camp. Rhonda consoled herself. After all, she was a part of Nancy's family, wasn't she? As much as possible.

In the backseat of the car on the way home, finally alone with Nancy, she tried to forget what she'd witnessed. Nancy dug into her backpack on the seat between them and pulled out the green and yellow lanyard.

"I made this for you, Rhonda. I missed you a lot." Nancy's words caused Rhonda to forgive her infidelity with little Miss Redhead, whose name she didn't want to know. She had her friend and her family back, but later that year in fifth grade, when Nancy's family moved to a nicer subdivision and a different school, they drifted apart. They stayed in touch for a while, but soon Nancy's phone calls were less frequent.

She was invited to one sleepover at Nancy's new house, but it felt strange and different. The girls there talked about boys Rhonda didn't know and experimented with eye shadow and lipsticks Rhonda couldn't afford. Rhonda didn't belong and was never invited back. She couldn't invite Nancy to her house. Too shabby. Nancy probably returned to summer camp the following year where she continued the friendship with other girls who could afford to go. Nancy and Red probably became college roommates at some high-tuition university.

It was strange that she had kept the lanyard all these years, but now that she knew of her real family—what might have been—the lanyard represented all she had missed. When Rhonda returned from taking the garbage out, she removed her mother's house key from the lanyard and threw it in the trash. Then took the lanyard and twisted it as hard as she could, but it was stubbornly durable, even after twelve years. She found a match, went out into the backyard and tried to light the lanyard. The damn thing wouldn't even burn. How she wanted those painful memories to go up in flame, but all it did was smolder and blacken. Finally, in desperation, she threw it in the garbage can, thankful to be rid of it forever.

After all, Rhonda was about to embark on her own family adventure. People who would welcome her. Tell her how sorry they were that they missed her childhood. And they would make it up to her every way possible. Yes, Myra was her new lanyard, holding the key to her long-desired family happiness.

She fell asleep that night picturing the joyous scene when she told Myra. She'd be the guest of honor at the party Myra hosted, inviting all her aunts, uncles and cousins to meet her—and embrace her.

Chapter Twenty-Five

Present

Angelina tries on several outfits. Three of them are strewn across her bed before she decides on the aqua pantsuit with a crème-colored shell and a simple gold chain. Everyone tells her aqua is a good color with her dark complexion. She applies eye shadow and mascara, which she rarely uses anymore. Should she add a touch of rouge? She dabs it on, looks at herself from several angles in the bathroom mirror and then wipes it off with cleansing cream. No, she won't be one of those old women with two red spots on her cheeks like Bozo the clown. Then she has to repair her foundation again, which she'd wiped off with the cleanser.

I'm acting like a schoolgirl. Yet it feels good to have butterflies. To have feelings at all. What will she say to Clara and June if they find out? She hopes the long shot of them being anywhere near the restaurant is truly that—a long shot.

Although Guy offers to pick her up, she says she can find the restaurant easily after her morning errands. She has no errands, but somehow his coming to her place seems like a date and that thought makes her nervous. She isn't ready for a date. Or maybe she's ready but not ready to admit it.

When she arrives a few minutes early, Guy is already inside the entry.

"They have a table for us. Right here." He cups his hand under her elbow and it feels comfortable and natural.

He's wearing the rumpled raincoat even though the spring day requires no jacket, and she can't help but notice the button is still missing. He slips it off revealing a blue plaid, button-down shirt, all buttons intact, and neatly pressed khaki trousers. A slight middle-aged paunch pokes out at his waistline, and she thinks perhaps he wears the rumpled raincoat to hide it. It certainly isn't unattractive enough to warrant that. In fact, it makes him seem huggable. The feelings he arouses in her are a sweet surprise.

He sits across from her and opens one of the two menus lying on the table and spreads it open between them so they can both see it. He goes into an elaborate explanation of how Chinese is on one side and Mexican on the other.

"Here's what did me in last time," he says, pointing to a photo of a burrito. "Probably too spicy for you anyway."

"Oh, I love spicy," Angelina says. "I grew up on spicy. My parents were from Bulgaria. Hot peppers were a staple at every meal. Even at breakfast. No better way to start the day than scrambled eggs with cheese and hot peppers. Kinda jump-starts your metabolism."

"Really?" his eyes get wide. "You cook like that now?"

"To be honest, I don't cook as much as I used to. Hardly seems worth it for one person."

"That's for sure," he agrees.

They gaze at each other with an unspoken understanding.

"How long have you been alone?" Angelina asks.

"Monica passed away three years ago. Breast cancer. She went through surgery, chemo and radiation seven years ago. We thought we had it beat. Then it returned with a vengeance."

"I'm sorry. I've heard that happens. How many years were you married, if you don't mind my asking?"

"We met in high school. Started dating the end of our senior year. She went to nurses' training. Me? I had no clue what I wanted to do. I fell in love with her, but sure I would lose her if she compared my no-ambition life with all the brainy interns she would meet. There was no doubt in my mind they'd discover how sweet she was. Then I was drafted and sent to Vietnam. Probably the best thing that could have happened to me."

"How's that?" Angelina asks.

"I matured, I guess. Seeing your friends die will do that to you. When I came home, I chose the police academy. Monica wrote to me often in Nam, but I wasn't sure if she loved me or was bolstering the spirits of a soldier in a war no one approved of."

"So you beat out the brainiacs?"

"One day, years later, I finally expressed to her the jealousy I had of the med students. She said my fears were groundless because she found them too cocky. They vainly assumed all student nurses were in love with them. Or else they were so wiped out from the clinical hours they couldn't stay awake long enough to go on a date. I felt like I dodged two bullets. One there and one in Nam."

He fiddled with the menu. "I thought I was a strong man. Tough cop. Police work prepares you for the worst. But nothing was as bad as losing her. I didn't even want to get out of bed in the morning." He shakes his head and peers at Angelina, "I'm talking too much."

"No, not at all. I felt the same way. Although I stayed busy with activities without Peter when he was alive, once he passed there was such an emptiness. The days seemed to go on forever. I even found myself missing his little habits that were sometimes annoying," she sheepishly admits.

"And you can only do so much with your kids." He rolls his eyes.

She realizes they have much in common. "I do love to cook for my family, and I have them over once a week. Making my son and grandkids' favorites makes it all worthwhile." She doesn't mention that April hasn't been to a family Sunday dinner for several months.

"And then I have the Mah Jongg Mavens. They love to eat. But if you can handle spicy, I'd love to cook a Bulgarian meal for you." She couldn't believe she said that. So soon and so easily.

"You would?" His eyes light up, and she notices how his eyes change colors. Sometimes the blue is deeper, other times the grey. Peter's eyes were the color of caramel candy. She's glad for the difference in the color of Guy's and Peter's eyes, although she doesn't know why.

"I guess we should order," he says.

"I'll try the shrimp tacos," Angelina decides. "And a cup of hot and sour soup. I'll give each country equal time."

"I'll give the Mexican another shot. See if the beef tacos can outdo the killer burrito. Hey, wanna share?" he asks, the glimmer of a little boy he might have been rising to the surface.

"Sure, why not?"

"Let's get some egg rolls too," he suggests.

While waiting for the food to arrive, Guy rests both arms on the table and leans forward. "Do you want to tell me about Peter?"

"I do, but let's save that for another time."

Guy nods. "Tell me about these Bulgarian parents. Were they born in Europe?" His warm eyes bore directly into hers and she has his full attention.

"Yes," she takes a sip of her iced tea as his intimate gaze makes her feel warm. She can feel the traces of a little mustache on her upper lip and hopes her perspiration isn't making it show. It's been years since she worried about her *mustache*. For a second, she pictures the blue jar of Nair hair removal she tried in high school that left her skin blotchy and swollen. On prom night no less.

She continues, "My parents' marriage was arranged by two aunts who were friends. One aunt of my mother's and one of my father's. After the introduction, their courtship was rather short—ten minutes alone in a room to check each other out, or whatever they called it in those days. To get acquainted."

"You're serious about the ten minutes for your parents? Really?"

"True story. Who could make that stuff up? At our ages, we both know truth is stranger than fiction. Especially in your line of work."

"Oh yeah." He takes a drink of his coffee.

Angelina makes a mental note that he drinks his coffee black and continues, "The story goes like this: My father was a thirty-something bachelor and my mother was a naive twenty-two-year-old who had been in America only six years. Her mother died in Europe and her father, who came to America years before her to earn her passage overseas, had remarried. When her father brought her to America at age sixteen, she was now living with a stepmother only a few years older than she was. A second wife and a daughter close to the same age? You can only imagine how that scenario played out. Also, in the six years that followed, my mother became the caretaker for the three babies her father and stepmother had, plus she was working long hours in the father's bakery.

"The two aunts wanted to save my mother from that Cinderella-stepmother existence and my father needed a wife. They spoke the same language and the families knew each other. What more could a matchmaker hope for?"

"Maybe another ten minutes?" Guy says.

Their food arrives, and Myra stops talking long enough to take a sip of the hot and sour soup. "Delicious."

"So they married after a ten-minute introduction?"

"The story goes that when they were alone in the private courtship room, my dad asked my mother, 'Do you think you could marry me?' She answered, '*Prepostavavum*,' which translates to 'I suppose.'" Angelina smiles. "How's that for enthusiasm and affirmation?"

Guy laughs. "Well, I guess it's better than *nessun modo l'uomo*.

"Which is . . .?"

"Italian for 'No way, man.'"

Now Angelina laughs. "You speak Italian?" She feels a giddy sense of pleasure. An attractive man who speaks Italian.

"Oh, I remember a few phrases from my parents." Then he adds sheepishly, "Not many I could use in front of a lady, however."

"Was your wife Italian?" For some reason Angelina is hoping he'll say no. She pictures the glamorous actress, Sophia Loren. How can she compete with a wife like that? And why is she trying to compete with a dead wife?

"No, but my mother, bless her heart, spent years trying to convert her to Italian. Wanted her to cook all the old family recipes."

"Did she?"

"Uh…sort of." He takes a big bite of his beef taco and a dollop of melted cheese stays on his chin. Angelina has the urge to reach across the table and wipe it off gently with her index finger as she often did for Peter. But the thought of touching Guy's face seems way too intimate. Then again, you can't let people walk around with cheese on their face or spinach in their teeth. Still, she refrains.

Guy is oblivious to his cheese schmear and goes on, "She mastered a few of the favorites, but they still didn't taste as good as Mom's."

"Oh, I hope you never said that." Angelina eyes are wide.

"I'm not as stupid as I might appear, but . . ." He takes his napkin, evidently now aware of the cheese, and wipes his chin. "but I am a sloppy eater."

Angelina tries to make him feel less conspicuous. "Me too. I usually wear my lunch on my blouse. Such a hurry to get it to my mouth."

The kind look on Guy's face communicates that he knows she's only saying this to make him feel better.

"But getting back to your wife. Even if she were Julia Child, rarely does anyone stand a chance against childhood favorites made by Mama. I think we give our food memories far more credit than they deserve, don't you?"

He takes another big mouthful as she says this, so she doesn't wait for his reply.

"I know I've spent a lifetime trying to capture a taste from childhood, but it's elusive. Like the first time I had a chocolate milkshake or some American food we never ate at home. Someone told me we have more taste buds in childhood, so everything is sharper, sweeter, saltier, whatever."

He nods while continuing to chew. The man obviously loves to eat.

Angelina takes a bite of her shrimp tacos and they both chew for a minute.

Angelina continues, "Our Italian neighbors made pizza on a paper-thin, crispy crust with just cheese and fresh tomatoes. With no air-conditioning and windows open all summer, you could smell what everyone was having for dinner. My friend Francie always brought me a piece. I can still taste it and would give anything to find it again. Dinners on those summer nights were usually followed by a game of stickball in the street or kick the can."

She smiles. "There, now you know how old I am. Really, I can't believe I said stickball in the street."

Guy smiles in return. "You seem young to me. You have the spark and enthusiasm of a young girl. It's refreshing."

Angelina feels her cheeks growing warm and her eyes moisten. Something twitches inside her chest. It's been so long since a man has paid her a compliment. A young girl? And a man with such a sweet smile. He seems bashful when he says it, which makes it more endearing.

Guy says, "Did you see the Food Channel segment when they visited the Heart Attack Grill? I think it was on the Guy Fieri show. Can't believe I like that guy with the crazy hair."

Angelina laughs. A man who not only watches the Food Channel but admits it. "Don't tell me your secret ambition. I know. You moonlight as a chef."

"Oh no, this job creates enough weird hours without moonlighting. But I have to admit, I like the cooking shows," he says in a tone somewhat sheepish, like he should be watching the NBA finals instead. "It's amazing what you can find on TV when you have insomnia."

"I do know. After Peter, I went through a spell with the old movies, but they were such sappy romances I felt even sadder than before I started."

They glance at each other with yet another unspoken understanding and then Guy eyes the last shrimp taco on Myra's plate.

She pushes the plate toward him. "Please try it. They're delicious."

Guy takes a bite and smacks his lips in approval, then continues his story. "So, one of my favorites is when they go across the country visiting dives and diners. There's one right here in Arizona I've been wanting to check out. It's called Heart Attack Grill, and the waitresses are dressed as nurses with stethoscopes around their necks. Instead of— listen to this—instead of a salad bar they have a French fry bar with unlimited visits." He says *unlimited* like he's discovered a gold mine.

"Oh my, sounds like a sure visit to the emergency room," Angelina says.

"Wanna go?"

"To the emergency room? No thanks."

"No, the grill. Let's go there next time."

He wants a next time? She's not surprised that she's hoping for one too.

Then he seems to realize what he said.

Oh, my gosh, was he actually blushing?. Ka-ching! More points for him.

He finally pushes his plate away. "*Abastanza.* Enough."

"*Dosta,*" she responds and pushes her plate aside too.

"Bulgarian?" he asks.

"I'm not sure if it's Bulgarian or Macedonian. We spoke both at home. The countries border one another, give or take an ethnic cleansing. And the languages are similar. Then you throw in the English I was picking up from my brother who started school before me."

Angelina sees her four-year-old self, anxiously sitting on the front porch stoop each day for her brother to return from school with his new words. "It was an international experience at our house. A sentence could be a mixture of three languages, but we all understood exactly what we meant."

He nods as if he totally gets it.

She continues. "I remember a funny story about the word *dosta.* If you'd like to hear it."

"Funny is good. Bring it on. There's not much funny in my line of work."

"I suppose not." A reminder to Angelina why she called this meeting in the first place.

"Okay, I'll tell this. Maybe it's more cute than funny. And then we need to talk about Myra."

"Oh yes, Myra."

"Okay, so this family in Bulgaria has five daughters and no sons. They are so desperate for a son that they name their last daughter, Dosta." Angelina waits for his response, but Guy gives her a blank look as if he's waiting for the punchline.

"And so?" he asks tentatively.

"Can you imagine a child in America being named Enough?"

Guy laughs. "I get it now. *Dosta.* Enough." He pauses a second and then says, "And then the middle name could be ... are you ready for this?"

"I have a feeling it's going to be awful."

"If the first name is Enough, how about a middle name of Already?"

Now Angelina laughs with him and thinks again how nice it is to hear the resounding sound of a male laugh. She didn't realize she missed it. Not that June and Clara and her grandchildren don't provide laughs in her life, but this is different. And Better.

When the waitress clears the dishes, it's a signal to Angelina that it's time for Myra.

Chapter Twenty-Six

Prior

As Rhonda continued to cruise Mayberry Heights on her lunch hour, she spotted what she had been suspecting since she saw the SOLD sign. The moving van in front of Myra's house could lead her to Myra's new home, which she suspected was Friendship Acres.

After work, she gathered her tote bag from under the counter at work, reviewed the appointment book quickly with the evening shift receptionist and hurried to her Dart, hoping she wouldn't have trouble with the starter again. It started on the second try, and when she arrived at Myra's, she breathed a sigh of relief to see the van still in front of the house. Of course, it would take hours to load that mansion of goods.

She arrived with few minutes to spare. In the doorway stood a man in blue coveralls with a clipboard, handing it to Myra for a signature.

As they stood there, another car pulled up and a man took a large sign out of his trunk which he hammered into the front lawn. Estate sale Saturday and Sunday. Did that mean there were enough possessions to move some and still have a sale? Of course.

Rhonda felt her heart race and her palms moisten. She would have a chance to walk through the house. Would Myra be there also? Maybe she could even purchase a trinket or two. As if she could afford it. And once again the anger built. Why should she pay for something that was rightfully hers to begin with? No, Rhonda thought. I think Myra owes me a little bauble or two.

Rhonda followed the moving van, and as she suspected, it turned into Friendship Acres and pulled behind the back-door unloading zone. An upscale place like this couldn't disturb the ambience with scruffy movers going in and out the front door.

The estate sale was scheduled for a weekend. Rhonda knew she couldn't take Saturday off. It was Fuchsia's busiest day, so she traded her Sunday afternoon shift easily with one of the girls who wanted to be at her daughter's weeknight school program. Rhonda didn't care which day she went to the sale. It wasn't like she was going to buy anything. She wanted to snoop and see Myra's affluent lifestyle. Perhaps even the grand dame herself would be there, so she could get a closer look at her. Would her eyes be the same shade of blue as Rhonda's? Might she have the same pug nose as her mother's?

When she pulled into Mulberry Lane, there were so many cars she had to drive past the house to find a parking spot. She entered and was greeted by a young lady who gave her a number and asked her to sign the guest register. Rhonda hadn't been prepared for this and felt a moment of panic. For some reason, she didn't want to leave her real name. What did it matter what she wrote down? She wrote the first name that came to mind—that of her high school English teacher, Yvonne Brooks. She'd heard from a client the other day that Ms. Brooks had passed away, so it would be a fitting tribute to her memory. Ms. Brooks always encouraged her to be creative. She was doing her memory proud.

As she walked through the furnished rooms, she noticed sold tags on many items. She decided that Myra's taste was a bit outdated as many of the paintings on the walls looked like they belonged in museums. Or was that the sign of good taste? There was a staff person in each room, milling around. Evidently, visitors were not to be trusted on their own.

Rhonda briefly entertained the idea of slipping something into her purse unnoticed. Her shoplifting days as a teen often came in handy. What started as a friend's "I dare you" turned into a rewarding pastime. Today, she wasn't going to pay for anything she already felt was rightfully hers, her birthright. But with such tight security, she might not "acquire" a trinket from Grandmother after all.

When she overhead a woman saying, "That's a hideous color," referring to a small boudoir chair, Rhonda realized Myra would stay away, so people could speak freely about their choices or non-choices. And it was obvious from the lack of items on the tables that many personal items had been removed—the very things Rhonda was hoping to see. It was foolish to expect Myra to be present or to leave family photos out for public viewing. With all the weirdos in the world now, who would do that?

She saw that one bedroom was furnished as a little girl's room, obviously for the granddaughters' overnight visits. Pink and lavender bedspreads on twin beds. But she saw only green again, as the jealousy arose in her and she couldn't stuff it down. Not that she ever longed for a pink dust ruffle on a bed with a frilly canopy, but she thought of her twin bed with the threadbare quilt she slept in until she left home, her resentment deepening.

While she stood there gawking, two women came in. They looked like mother and daughter. Same chins. The older of the two walked to the dresser, picked up a snow globe with a winter scene. A horse-drawn carriage in a forest. She shook it and turned the key at the bottom. Snowflakes filled the globe as a tinkling version of "Lara's Theme" filled the room.

"Look, Roxanne, isn't this charming?" It's playing that tune from *Dr. Zhivago*, 'Somewhere My love.' Shall we get it for Isla?"

The daughter picked up the music box and checked the price tag. "Mother, it's silly to pay so much for a music box. Isla's too young to appreciate it. She'd probably rather have something from Hello Kitty at the mall."

The older woman looked perturbed. "You know, Roxanne, you need to expose her to nice things at an early age. It will develop her taste to appreciate more than junk fads."

"I'm sure you're right, Mother, but that music is too dated for her. Perhaps I should buy it for you?" Roxanne held the globe out to her mother as she smiled at her.

The older women said, "Let's move on."

Rhonda inched toward the table and picked up the globe. The price tag on the underside read $50.00. That was pricey for her budget, but suddenly she wanted it. Not only wanted it but felt a desperate need to have it. If Myra really was her grandmother, she wanted something that belonged to her. The globe was probably going to be the cheapest item in the house, and for some odd reason, it appealed to Rhonda. Maybe it was the song, "Somewhere My Love." Yes, somewhere, Myra, somewhere you had a daughter and a granddaughter you could have, should have loved.

Now her dilemma was how she was going to pay for it with her credit card or checkbook showing a different name than the one she signed in with. She took the music box to the young lady guarding the room's possessions. Her name tag said Cheryl.

"Cheryl, I'd love to have this but I'm a little short of cash. Would you please hold it for me while I find an ATM?"

"Certainly, let me write your name on it." Once again Rhonda lied as she said, "Yvonne Brooks."

Rhonda drove to the nearest ATM and withdrew $50.00 plus a $2.00 transaction fee since it wasn't her bank's ATM. *Damn, why am I doing this? I am not normally a frivolous impulse shopper.* She had a financial goal and rarely took money out of her account, but she was driven by something deep inside she couldn't control.

She returned to the estate sale, paid cash and left with a music box wrapped in lovely tissue to protect it. The ledger now showed Yvonne Brooks, shopper number 86, as the proud owner of Myra's snow globe music box.

Before Rhonda fell asleep that night, she turned the key and listened to the tinkling melody.

Somewhere a hill blossoms in green and gold. And there are dreams—all that your heart can hold.

When would she let Myra know that she too had dreams. Dreams all during her childhood for a large, loving family.

While Rhonda was looking for an ATM, several other guests registered. One signed in as shopper number 93. Randy Moore.

He walked slowly through the house, stopping periodically to pick up an item. To turn over a price card.

He couldn't understand why some of the pieces were for sale that could have been given outright to him and Debbie. He circled back through and out the door. *What does it matter? It will come to us one way or another. Hopefully, sooner rather than later.*

Chapter Twenty-Seven

Present

As the waitress clears their plates, Angelina reaches for her notebook, which has been lying on the empty chair between them. She places it on the table and opens it with an efficient school teacher demeanor. "Now, about Myra."

She sees the smile on Guy's face and is embarrassed. "I brought it in case I forgot what I wanted to tell you."

"Oh, no, don't get me wrong. I love your notebook. Really. It's a good thing." Guy reassures her.

"Burrito insurance," she says.

"What?"

"In case I went into a burrito coma like you did and forgot everything," she teases. "Seriously, I started thinking that there were a few times recently when Myra seemed distracted and fidgety. I can't quite put my finger on it, so I'm not even sure what I'm saying." Angelina looks at Guy apologetically, but he appears interested so she continues.

"When she first moved into the retirement center, she was so excited and proud of it. Then I remember she made a comment like, 'I wish I'd never seen this place.' I was taken back a bit and said something like, 'I thought you loved it here.'

"She acted surprised I had heard her, like maybe she was thinking out loud. Then she said, 'I mean the food here. It's so good. I think I'm gaining weight. All my clothes are feeling snug.'

"I told her she should sign up for the WII fitness bowling. Maybe it would be a senior Olympic sport. We both laughed, and the moment passed."

Angelina glances again at her notebook. "Then there seemed to be other times like that. Fleeting moments. I thought maybe she was worrying about the son-in-law. And she said something one day about not having been to confession for some time, and she felt the need to go. I think she said she needed to go desperately. Do you think you could talk to her priest?"

"I could, but they are bound to keep confession confidential."

"Would he say if he personally thought anything was disturbing her?"

"I doubt it, but it was a good idea, Angelina."

Angelina senses that Guy is humoring her.

"Perhaps I could visit him? As a friend of Myra's?"

"On what pretense? I know you mean well, but…"

"You're right," she says but knows in her heart she's going to go despite what Guy says. *What can it hurt?*

She continues, "Now that we've shared salsa and egg rolls, I guess it's okay to ask you this, but I understand if you can't answer. Do you suspect foul play with Myra's death?" She watches his face intently for a hidden sign, but he gives none. She wonders if they teach a class in poker face at the Police Academy?

Guy looks down and folds his napkin carefully and sets it beside his plate. When he looks up he says, "You know I can't discuss that with you. I feel that you're trustworthy, but believe me, it's easier for you not to know something than to try not to repeat it if you do. Or to guard your conversations with friends. Let's say whenever there is a large estate and money involved in a death with no apparent cause, the family is always under investigation, as well as the retirement center."

"As in liable for her accident?"

"Could be that, but also there are cases where a person dies with no heirs listed and the retirement center sells their totally paid-for unit to someone else. It's a double dip, so to speak."

"Oh my, is the family suspecting the retirement center?" Then she adds, "Of course, you can't comment on that either, can you?"

"No, I can't, but I appreciate so much your observations and reflections. Would you do me a big favor?"

"Of course," she answers way too quickly.

"Keep that speckled notebook handy, and when you think of anything, anything at all, jot it down. Maybe even on your bedside table. Those middle-of-the-night thoughts can be fleeting and hard to recapture in the morning. I think writing them down causes our subconscious to dig deeper. It seems once I do that, other details of the same scenario begin to replay and expand. I solved one case where the clue appeared in a dream."

"Really?" Angelina says with the awe a teen might show a rock star. "Oh, you've done this a few times. I can tell."

"You might say a few." He chuckles. "And I won't mention the times I look at something I scribbled in the night and can't read a word of it in the morning."

When the waitress brings the check, Angelina reaches for her purse, but Guy says, "Please, this is my treat."

"Oh, let's go Dutch. I asked you to meet."

"I think we have enough countries in this lunch. Italy, Bulgaria, Macedonia. We don't need Holland too. Let's say it was a working lunch."

When they step out of the restaurant, the Phoenix sunlight is almost blinding, even though the fierce summer heat hasn't yet arrived in the desert. It's a perfect temperature of sixty-nine degrees with a slight breeze. Guy doesn't bother with the raincoat as he slings it over his shoulder.

He says, "I suppose we should enjoy this weather. We know what's coming our way very soon."

"Yes, hot and hotter. It must be so boring to be a weatherman in Phoenix. How many ways can you say hot?"

Guy speaks Italian. "*Caldo. Caliente*."

Angelina responds in Bulgarian. "*Gores, Toplo*."

They both are smiling as he walks her to her car. She pushes the open button on her key ring, and he deftly sidesteps her to open her door.

She's glad her passenger seat doesn't look like the pigpen it often does with the usual piles of library books, store coupons, grocery lists, and dry cleaning.

"Oh, I forgot to give you something." She digs into her purse. "Here," she says, handing him the roll of Tums.

He gives her a half smile. When he takes it from her, their fingers touch briefly, and their eyes meet.

"Thank you," he says, and she senses he is saying thank you for more than the Tums. "It feels kinda good to be taken care of again."

"Well, then you'd better just hand over that raincoat of yours and let me sew on that button. Or is that part of your blundering cop M.O. to make people feel comfortable? So they can tell you everything? I will admit now that Columbo came to mind the first time we met."

"I hadn't thought of it that way, but if that works, here, let me rip off a few more buttons. Maybe I'll get signed confessions."

"I'm serious," she says as she reaches for the coat. "Let me have it. You'll hardly need it in this nice weather."

"What if it rains?"

They both chuckle at the preposterous notion of rain in a place that averages eight inches a year.

"You and I both know the chances of that are slim to none. I promise it won't take me long. In fact, I'll do it as soon as I get home. You'll have it back before monsoon season."

"And then . . .?"

"And then you can come and get it."

"And would it be possible if I could come on a day you're cooking a Bulgarian meal?"

Did he just invite himself to dinner? "Yes, I'll fix you some Bulgarian stuffed peppers. How's that?"

"How's that? That's great. That's how that is."

She likes the wrinkles, the laugh lines in the corners of his eyes.

He says, "It seems like I'm getting all the perks. What can I do for you?"

She peers into his eyes, now greyer than blue in the bright sun, and says, "If anyone deliberately hurt Myra, you can find him."

Chapter Twenty-Eight

Prior

Once Rhonda knew that Myra had moved to Friendship Acres, she came up with a plan to become better acquainted with her grandmother. She called Director Kathleen for an appointment.

As the receptionist ushered her into Kathleen's office, Rhonda's first words were, "I wanted to thank you for the lovely tour. Unfortunately, my aunt won't be moving to Phoenix after all. She decided to move to San Diego with another niece because she was worried about the excessive summer heat here in Phoenix.

"I'm sorry to hear that," Kathleen replied. "Yes, it can be a problem for many people."

"However, I was so impressed with. . . well, with everything here, and I was wondering if I could be of service to you in the hair salon. I am a licensed hairdresser and am hoping to open my own salon someday." *No need to mention that I am low on the food chain, doubling as the receptionist and shampoo girl at this point.*

"Well, you certainly are a good advertisement for your business. Your hair is lovely. I noticed that immediately the first time we met. I know I'm dating myself, but you remind me of Farah Fawcett."

Rhonda smiled and graciously accepted the compliment she'd grown accustomed to receiving. "Do you employ hairstylists or are they volunteers? I'd be glad to volunteer one afternoon a week. I can't afford to take too many hours away from the salon. I thought perhaps on my day off?

"Well, aren't you the sweetest thing? We wouldn't think of not paying you for your services. You've probably noticed we have an affluent clientele."

"Yes, I had noticed they seem quite . . ." She almost slipped and said rich, but instead she managed to blurt out, "quite comfortable."

'Well, Miss Feder. Your timing is perfect."

"Please, call me Rhonda."

"As I was saying, Rhonda. We have one hairdresser whose husband wants to move to the Northwest. Quite an avid fisherman who thinks there aren't enough fish in Arizona, or so he says."

"There is one little problem. Mondays are my day off and I believe you said the salon was closed on Mondays."

"What a shame. I think you would have been a good addition to Friendship Acres." Kathleen's smile was complacent. "You might call us if your day changes. And leave your phone number in case something opens up here."

Rhonda left the building feeling defeated. Maybe she could change her day off at the salon but that was unlikely. It was the slowest day of the week. She drove off, her foot so heavy on the pedal she cut off several drivers in her frustration.

A good Mah Jongg player will not throw a dangerous or obvious tile at any time. Every pick and discard should be a challenge to the very last tile. A discarded joker can never be picked up nor can a joker ever be used with a pair.

Chapter Twenty-Nine

Present

"We're sitting around here moping about Myra. Let's skip Mah Jongg this week. How about a movie? A comedy," Angelina suggests.

"How about the new casino that opened last week? The one with the big billboard signs on every highway." Clara suggests.

"Great idea. I've heard they give away thousands each day." June's face lights up.

Clara rolls her eyes in June's direction. "You are so gullible. Of course, the casino ads are going to say that. Do you know anyone who actually won?"

"Well, they haven't been open that long. I'm sure everyone we know hasn't been there yet," June says in self-defense.

Thirty minutes later, they turn into the large parking lot of the sprawling casino.

"Well, June," Angelina says, "the parking lot is packed. Evidently you're not the only one who believes the thousands of daily dollars giveaway."

June smiles at Clara as if to say, "I told you so," but says instead, "I think this is a good change for us. You don't have to think about bingo. They call a number. Either you have it or you don't. It's not like Mah Jongg where you have to rack your brain along with your tiles."

They join the queue for bingo cards. June steps up to the teller cage. The lady in front of her leaves with a fistful of papers. June eyes them and has no clue what to ask for.

"I'd like to play bingo," she says to the attractive Native American woman behind the teller cage.

"That's good," the woman responds, "Since you *are* in the bingo parlor. Do you want the regular pack or the jumbo pack?"

June stares at the beautiful turquoise pendant resting on the lady's bosom. "I don't know. What's the difference?"

"Ten dollars," the pendant answers.

"I mean what's the difference in the game?"

"More chances and more money. The double pack pays out double."

"Then I guess I'll get a double pack," June says.

"There's also a bonus pack."

"Oh, how much is that?"

"Five dollars."

"Okay, I might as well," June says, afraid to refuse anything for fear it might be the lucky one.

"How about the early bird game? It's a warm-up game," the pendant says.

"Well, I'm early so I might as well get it," June says and adds, "Early bird gets the silver lining."

The attendant peers at June, her expression unreadable. Then she methodically gathers up packets of paper sheets and slaps then down, sliding them toward June.

Clara and Angelina have gone to other cashier windows, so June doesn't know what they are choosing.

She mumbles, "I wish I knew what my friends were getting. We should have all stayed together."

The teller takes her money and yells, "Next."

When June sees Angelina and Clara, she breathes a sigh of relief. They too have purchased the double pack, the bonus pack and the early bird. They'll know what do with this hodgepodge of paper. At first, bingo sounded easy but now she's not so sure. June remembers childhood carnivals where all she had was a little cup of popcorn kernels and one card. The biggest challenge was making sure the kernel didn't roll off the number they already called.

She sits, spreads out her sheets and stares at them. There's no way she can find that many numbers across the board in a short amount of time.

Angelina pulls out the colored dobbers she's bought for each of them.

"What color do you want?" she asks.

Both Clara and June call out "Red" at the same time.

"There's only one red. June. How about a nice green? You're wearing green today and green is the color of money."

Clara smiles and says, "I like that money symbol. I'll take green."

Without another word, Angelina hands Clara the green, June the red, and takes the blue for herself.

The PA system comes on and welcomes them to Early Bird Bingo with the enthusiasm of Ed McMahon announcing, *Here's Johnny*! He says, "We'll be playing with the grey card. Pull out your grey sheet. The first one in the early bird packet."

Clara and Angelina easily lay out their grey papers with three bingo squares in a vertical line. June's packet is out of order and she scrambles to find grey. Her chin starts to quiver.

Angelina notices. She calmly pulls the grey card from the pile. "Here, Junie. You're all set. Dob the free spaces to start. Then he'll call the number and it will also flash on that big board." Angelina points to the wall and June peers up to see a large board with B I N G O horizontally and the numbers vertically. At the top, Early Bird is flashing in bright neon letters.

The caller starts slowly, but as they progress into the other larger packets, he calls the numbers faster and the designs they are looking for are not merely simple straight lines. Make a kite. Make a postage stamp. Four corners count. Four corners don't count.

By the time the break comes around, June's face is flushed and she says, "Who said bingo was easy compared to Mah Jongg? I have never worked so hard. We've hardly had a minute to say a word."

"We can talk now. We have a fifteen-minute break." Angelina says. "But first, I'm going to find the ladies' room."

"Did you see the size of those burgers people are getting for only two dollars? I love it here!" Clara exclaims.

She leaves and returns shortly with enough food on her plate to feed a third-world country. "Look at the size of this lemon meringue pie. Only fifty cents."

After the break the announcer says, "The pattern we're looking for on the blue sheet is the letter P in the upper left-hand corner. P for Pet. On the stage are four large stuffed animals, each one containing a dollar amount prize. Whoever makes a P for Pet bingo first can choose one stuffed animal. They can keep the animal AND whatever dollar amount it contains. Here we go. The first number is I-23."

They dob furiously, heads down for several minutes.

"I think I only need one more," June nudges Angelina.

Angelina glances over and sees the P on June's card that is almost all filled in, all except B-7, but the B-7 on her own card had been dobbed.

She quickly looks at the neon board and sees that B-7 has been called.

"June, B-7 has been called. Dob it. Quick. And yell bingo."

June looks startled. She dobs it but is tongue-tied.

Clara stands and screams loud enough for the entire parlor to hear, "Bingo. She's got bingo!"

"Clara, shush, it's my bingo," June says.

"Well, speak up, June, or you won't get it." Clara replies

"I was about to say it," June replies.

The roaming attendant appears at Clara's side.

"It's her card, not mine," Clara points to June.

The attendant glares at Clara and picks up June's card, calling the numbers out loudly to the announcer.

"Ladies and gentlemen, we have a legitimate bingo. One winner. Please come to the stage and select your pet. Prizes range from one hundred to a thousand dollars."

June springs to her feet and says,"I can't believe it. She hurries to the stage to face a four-foot panda, an equally large tiger, a five-foot spotted Dalmatian, and a huge furry pink pig.

Clara's says, "You know they probably hid the big money in the pig because no one would choose something so ugly."

Angelina says, "Didn't Myra have a pig collection?"as June strides toward the pig and wraps her arms around its pink furry pot belly.

The attendant says, "Our winner has chosen the pig." He opens the envelope and hands it to the announcer. "Congratulations, you've chosen the $1000 pet." As they leave the casino, Clara grumbles about the green dobber. "So much for the color of money."

On the way home, June's in the back seat with the pink pig propped up beside her. She smiles and says, "I picked the pig because of Myra's collection. I wish she had been here to see this."

"Maybe she did see it, June." Angelina says. "Perhaps she guided your decision."

"Clara, I told you they give away thousands every day." June pats the pig's snout beside her and says, "You should never look a gift horse in the nose."

Chapter Thirty

Prior

The next day Rhonda was thrilled to get a voice mail from Kathleen asking her to come in discuss working on Mondays.

"I thought the salon was closed on Mondays," Rhonda said as soon as she entered Kathleen's office.

"It has been in the past, but we decided to try Monday and see what happens. Maybe it would be a good way to start the week. Our days aren't cast in stone New week, new do. Perfect phrase for our newsletter."

Kathleen had Rhonda fill out an employment form, and when Rhonda saw the salary, she was surprised at how her little project wouldn't only satisfy her need to see her grandmother but would make a nice addition to her bank account. Mad money—a luxury she'd never had before.

She was frugal, rarely allowing herself a treat. Now her bank account might grow in an unexpected way. Grandmother would surely be generous. Rhonda's first goal was to observe her grandmother—check for common characteristics she and her mother might have inherited from her. Discover if mannerisms were truly in a person' s DNA.

On the first Monday Rhonda worked at Friendship Acres, she arrived at noon. Kathleen was anxious to have her residents meet the new stylist with the beautiful hair. She started with introductions to people having lunch in the dining room. Then, "Let's go up to the game room. I think it's busy today."

It was easy to recognize Myra with her white hair and pearls. She sat at a table with three other ladies. They seemed intent on the game as they laid the little ivory tiles in the center of the table with comments like green dragon, west wind, four dot.

Kathleen approached their table. "I'd like you to meet our new hairdresser, Rhonda Feder. Aren't we lucky to have someone with her talent in our salon? Look at her lovely hair." She said this in the same tone nurses use when they say, "it's time for our sleeping pill."

"She'll be here every Monday afternoon."

"I'll be ready for a new perm soon," Myra said, "but I couldn't possibly give up my Monday Mah Jongg. We've been playing on Mondays for eight years. It's my favorite day." The other three concurred with smiles and nods.

Rhonda stared at the tiles on the card table. "That looks so fascinating," she said. "What time do you finish your game?"

"Well, we play until three. Sometimes we talk until four," Myra said.

"Or five or six," June said with a little giggle.

"I wouldn't mind staying late on a Monday if you would like me to," Rhonda spoke directly to Myra and looked into eyes that were a shade of blue, almost purple, that she knew well. The same blue she looked at every day in the mirror.

"Really? How nice of you. I've been going to the same hairdresser for fourteen years, but it would be so convenient to have someone right here. Since I've moved, I'm over ten miles from her. That might be out of our van's service range?" Myra looked at Kathleen for confirmation.

Kathleen agreed. "Other than the airport, we do try to limit the van to a ten-mile radius."

Rhonda touched Myra lightly on the shoulder. "Please stop by the salon this afternoon. If I'm not busy, we can talk about what you'd like done with your hair, and I'll be sure to get the right products. I could call your hairdresser and find out what she uses, if you don't mind my calling her."

"Oh, my goodness, that would be so nice. I'll call her myself and explain the challenge the miles present for me now," Myra replied.

As they moved to the next table, Clara said, "She's quite accommodating."

"A pretty girl," Angelina added.

"She reminds me of the girl on television with the long blond hair. What was that show? You know, those angels," June said.

"Charlie's? Yes, *Charlie's Angels*." Angelina replied.

"That's it. The girl with the big hair, Farrah Fawcett. That's who she looks like." June added.

"I think she looks like Kyra Sedgwick. Do you watch that show, *The Closer*?" Angelina asked.

"Never heard of it," June answered. "Too current for me. I'm in a time warp. I'd rather watch *Happy Days* reruns."

Chapter Thirty-One

Prior

"Janet, I am so proud of you," Myra said as she folded her napkin across her plate. They had finished lunch at the cafeteria in the Capital Building where many people stopped to speak to Janet.

"Oh Mom, it's not so much a big deal as you might think," Janet answered, although she seemed pleased.

"I'm still so surprised you chose politics. Not that I don't approve, dear. I thought you might do something like nursing or teaching. You were always sticking bandages on your dolls or rounding up the neighborhood kids for a spelling bee or a bug field trip." Myra smiled as she recalled the memories.

"I guess it surprised me too. When I became involved in stopping that truck bypass around our subdivision, it was such a rush when it was defeated by our grassroots effort. No budget or funding. Just old-fashioned, door-to-door knocking."

"I read that this election is very close. I have all my friends in the retirement center pumped up to vote for you. They say they will or maybe they're humoring me. When you came and spoke to them about senior citizen concerns, they were impressed."

"There's such a fierce battle between party lines right now. I have people supporting me who don't even know me—so long as I oust the Republican. One thing I forgot to mention." Janet leans in closer to Myra. "Someone in my party did some background snooping on my opponent, Nelson, and came up with some juicy skeletons. Maybe you've seen the news. I had nothing to do with it, believe me. I actually feel sorry for him. Trying to convince your followers or would-be voters the rumors are false is almost impossible. That's the sacrifice you make in the public life. You have no private life."

"What was the scandal? I hadn't heard."

"He had some DUIs in high school. Not a big deal, but another report claims that he skipped out on child support for a pregnant girlfriend he never married. I don't know how they found the girl, but she's screaming paternity suit and demanding back support for the past fourteen years." Janet took a sip of coffee.

"Then going way back, something about his father serving time for driving a getaway car in a robbery when he was a teen. Hardly Nelson's fault. It's not fair to be blamed for your parents' mistakes, but in politics everything is fair game, or I should say unfair game. And blown out of proportion."

"Character defamation is a hard one to overcome," Myra agreed. She started to feel an uneasiness in the direction the comments were going.

"If you deny it, you're calling people liars. If you don't, it's like an admission of guilt. It's a no-win situation."

"Sounds like it might be a win for you, Janet."

"I'd rather win on my own merits—people voting for me rather than against someone else, but I'll take the votes any way I can get them. It won't change what I'm going to do when elected. I do pride myself on my ethical standards and hope to keep them high once in office."

Janet checked her watch. "Come on, Mom, let me get you back home. I have a three o'clock meeting."

As Janet pulled out of the circular driveway of Friendship Acres, Myra cheerfully waved goodbye, but her smile faded as her daughter's Honda CRV left the grounds. The words *closet skeletons* remained with her. What if someone started looking into Janet's past? How far back would they go? Would they discover Myra's past? She shuddered at the thought. Her imagination ran wild. *The adoption was under my maiden name. It couldn't be traced or connected to Janet. It was all so long ago. And so what if*

I gave a baby up for adoption when I was a high school senior? That was an admirable thing to do . . . to find a good home for a child. That couldn't hurt Janet in any way, could it? Myra hoped she'd never have to find out.

She took the elevator to her second-floor apartment and changed into a loose cotton shift she often wore in the evenings at home. Myra had planned to watch a few of her favorite TV shows but found herself fidgety and unable to sit. She walked into the bedroom and pulled open the file cabinet that was designed to look like a nightstand. Most of her important documents were in a safe-deposit box at the bank, but she kept some personal files at her bedside. There wasn't much. Mostly sentimental things. When the house sold, she spent an entire day shredding papers no longer of importance.

Myra reached into the back of one folder labeled in handwriting, *High School Reunions*. Although she didn't finish her senior year with her class, and the embarrassment of her pregnancy kept her from attending reunions, she did have a booklet mailed to her each time her class met.

She also contributed a bio that was not only positive but purposely glowing. Her last one was something to the effect of "Myra Anderson is enjoying retirement as the mother of three daughters and several grandchildren. She travels extensively throughout the world." Well, she did take that Caribbean cruise a few years ago. It wasn't as if she kept in touch with anyone from high school to deny the story.

As the class sizes shrunk, the alumni committees combined several graduation years for the reunions, and she wanted to be sure that if Mark read it, he'd be impressed. Likewise, she was kept informed of Mark Cook's successful life in Washington, D.C. through his blurbs in the reunion booklet. Had he ever told his wife about the baby he fathered in 1967? Did he think of the baby as often as she did through the years?

Myra confided her past to Richard before they married. She wanted no secrets between them. He said he loved her for telling him.

She had, however, kept one secret from Richard. It was in an envelope between the pages of reunion booklets. Her only secret was that she still couldn't bear to part with Mark's faded black-

and-white senior photo—the same photo that was in her yearbook, but this one had his signature on it. On the back he'd written, *To Myra. I hope you will always be MY Myra.*

It was amazing how, despite many years of marriage to a wonderful man whom she loved dearly, the senior class photo of Mark never failed to stir up the feelings she'd had for her first love and the boy to whom she'd surrendered her virginity.

The summer before her senior year was a time of passionate discovery. If she so much as heard a song from that summer, such as the Beatles' "I Want to Hold Your Hand," she pictured Mark. Or Bobby Vinton's "Blue Velvet." Mark always said her eyes were like blue velvet. Even today, in a crowd, if she caught a whiff of the Old Spice shaving lotion he wore, she was instantly back on the gym floor, wearing her purple miniskirt and white go-go boots, dancing with him. And once in a while, the taste of Juicy Fruit gum made her think of his kisses. If she closed her eyes, she remembered the taste of his lips. She could with little effort evoke those memories at any time, as she did now. Instead of fading with the years, it seemed the memories were magnified.

On the night before he left for the Air Force Academy, Mark had thrown a rock at her bedroom window. When she snuck down in her flimsy baby-doll pajamas for one more goodbye, they succumbed to their teen passions with an urgency and a lack of care.

Seven weeks passed before she could speak to Mark. Freshmen at the Air Force Academy, or doolies as they were called, were not allowed any phone calls the first three weeks of training. Then one call to their parents followed by another three weeks in the field with no phones. When Mark was finally able to make a personal call by waiting an hour for the dorm pay phone line to be free, she told him how much she missed him. Then she began to cry as she told him what else she had missed. Her period.

She was heartbroken when her parents accepted the money Mark's parents offered if she agreed to give the baby up for adoption and never disclose the father. Her parents consoled her saying now she would have money for college. They sent her to a fine private school in California—a chance to start over.

Only when she met Richard her junior year did she begin to heal. Marriage after graduation, a job offer for Richard in Arizona where her parents still lived and then the three little girls in quick succession. Whenever she marveled at her beautiful daughters, she felt she had been both forgiven and blessed.

Now with Internet genealogy searches and DNA tests, she wondered if her adopted daughter ever looked for her. Perhaps one day she'd get an e-mail or a call. *Are you my mother?* Myra thought of her so often, but that chapter of her life was closed, and it was best to remain that way.

Only today did she feel a page opening in the book. A sense of foreboding. Politics was a dirty business. What if someone wanted to hurt Janet? How deep in the past would they go? Was it possible to find out about Myra's past? She shuddered at the thought but realized there was nothing she could do at this point but hope it would stay in the past. And giving up a child for adoption was no crime. It was admirable. That's what she told herself.

She placed Mark's photo back in the envelope. That's where he and the baby belonged. In the past. A distant memory.

Chapter Thirty-Two

Prior

With Rhonda's encouragement, Myra began getting a weekly wash and set following her Mah Jongg game each Monday. At each appointment, Rhonda attempted to find out more about Myra's life, her family, her friends, and her interests. She begged her to bring in the quilt she was making and then raved about it. When she discovered Myra had a fondness for ceramic pigs, she brought her one she found while browsing at Goodwill. Rhonda wanted so much to endear herself to Myra.

"Everyone loves my new hairdo. I even received a rare compliment from Clara," Myra said.

"I'm so glad." When Rhonda and Myra discussed coloring her hair, she asked Myra to bring in a photo of herself in younger years to see what her natural color had been.

Rhonda almost gasped when she saw the photo. A grainy Polaroid photo of the sixties with the date on the white border. Although faded, the resemblance to her mother, Dottie Feder, was unmistakable.

Myra said, "I can't remember what year I started going white. I was going to touch it up, but it progressed so quickly I decided to let it go. White isn't as bad as grey."

"That's true," Rhonda agreed. "It's actually a lovely, shiny white but a soft blond or light brown would take years away. I've seen some handsome widowers here at Friendship Acres," she teased her.

Myra laughed. "I'm not much interested in romance any more. My family provides all the love I need right now."

And you're about to acquire one more family member to love. The music of the snow globe played in her head. *Somewhere my love . . . all that your heart can hold.* Rhonda couldn't wait to tell Myra, but she wanted to do a test run on the adoption issue itself first.

The next time Myra came in, Rhonda faked tears behind a tissue. She even went so far as to blow her nose loudly. The slight sniffles she had the last few days made it all the more credible.

Myra responded on cue as if she had a script. "Rhonda, whatever is the matter, dear? Why are you crying?"

"I'm fine, but I feel so bad about my friend, Sue. Sue Ellis. We've been friends since junior high, and it breaks my heart."

"Why? What happened?"

Rhonda continued with her concocted story. "She's had this cad of a boyfriend forever. Adam. He's worthless and she doesn't see it. I actually had to tell her once, 'He's just not that into you.' Well, pardon my French, but he did get into her, if you know what I mean. Gets her pregnant, and of course, he doesn't want to marry her. Tells her to abort the baby and even arranges a visit to a sleazy place where they probably use coat hangers or something." Rhonda covers her eyes with her hands and shakes her head. "I'm sorry. I shouldn't have said that to you, Myra. Please excuse me. But he's such scum, and I'm so mad at him." Rhonda watched Myra's reaction.

Myra looked appalled. "So, did she go there?"

"Of course not. Sue's such a Pollyanna. She thought when he saw the baby, he would change his mind. So she went through nine months with no support from him, not financial or emotional. And when she delivers the baby, he's such a coward that he runs away. And takes his new girlfriend with him—a cute little thing who still has a waistline."

"Oh my, then what happened?" Myra asked, as if it were the next installment of her soap opera.

"That's the saddest part. She gives the baby up for adoption." Rhonda paused briefly to read Myra's reaction to the word *adoption*. Myra's eyes widened.

"Says she deserves a good family who can love her and provide for her. Sue has no family to speak of. Her parents are separated, and her mother barely has the means to support herself, let alone Sue and now a baby."

Myra said, "That was a very responsible and unselfish act on her part."

"But now that she's gone ahead and done it, she is so remorseful. So regretful. But it's too late. I feel so bad for her. I don't have any children. Heck, I don't even have a boyfriend, and guys like Adam are probably one reason why. Too many jerks out there. But what makes me saddest is, I can't imagine giving up a baby, can you?"

Rhonda studied Myra's face again. She saw exactly what she hoped to see. Was it her imagination or did a shadow pass across her face, causing her to age in mere seconds? Was that regret on her face? *Regret that I could reverse in one instance. Like what people say who have been in car accidents. One's life can change in a second. This could be such a positive change for Myra. It could undo years of wondering where her daughter is and whether she may have other grandchildren. Of course, she'd want to know this. Wouldn't any mother?*

A wall game occurs when all the tiles are used and no one has declared a Mah Jongg. Players generally expose their tiles then to show the other players which hand they were attempting to make. It is often difficult to declare Mah Jongg if two people are attempting the same hand.

Chapter Thirty-Three

Present

"I can't believe the clothes young girls wear to school these days. Or should I say don't wear. Short skirts, skimpy tops. What happened to dress codes, and where are the parents?" Clara says as she shuffles the Mah Jongg titles.

"What is sending you off on that subject today?" Angelina asks, knowing Clara usually has a hidden agenda.

"On my way here, I saw a group of young girls waiting for the school bus, all but naked."

"I think school uniforms are a good idea," June pipes in. "That way girls don't have peer pressure to have the latest fashions."

"I remember Myra's grandchildren wore uniforms when they stopped in after school. Don't they go to a Catholic school?" Angelina asks, building a dummy wall of tiles at Myra's empty seat.

"Angelina, on your suspect list, we forgot about the people Myra knew at church. Maybe someone there had a motive," Clara says.

"She was quite involved. Maybe she saw someone's hand in the till . . . or should I say collection plate?" June comments.

"Or caught the priest inviting little boys into his study."

"Clara!" June says. "That's a terrible accusation."

"I didn't invent it. It's on the news all the time." Clara stacks the tiles in two rows of nineteen.

"Hmm, if that were the case, the priest could have slipped something special in her communion wine? Special, like hemlock?"

June and Clara look at Angelina as if she has sprouted two heads.

"Going along with the gag here. Just thinking outside the box." Angelina says.

"You read too many mysteries," June says.

"Actually, that's out of Shakespeare," Angelina replies. "If you're a good detective, you don't rule out anything or anyone."

"Speaking of, has that detective been around again? I don't know why he doesn't want to talk to us," Clara says.

Angelina doesn't reveal that she has seen him again. She wants to keep it her little secret for now. "Maybe he'll still call. He probably has a lot of people to talk to." Angelina makes a mental note to mention to Guy that her friends are feeling excluded. And who knows? Maybe they have a perspective Angelina has overlooked.

They play one game, which Clara wins by completing a consecutive run hand. When they're reshuffling the tiles, Angelina says, "I wish we had worn uniforms in grade school. I always felt different than the other girls."

"How was that?" June asks.

"Well, for one thing, it seemed my mother never bought clothes that fit. Always ones I could grow into."

"At some point they must have fit you," Clara says.

"Perhaps, but of course, we only remember the bad things. Everything is so dramatic at that age." Angelina continues, "Our grade school girls' bathroom had no doors on the stalls and for years I had to wear long cotton bloomers, almost to my knees. I was so ashamed of them I learned to hold it in all day. I envied Judy Lee whose little silk panties said, Monday, Tuesday, Wednesday. Judy with her perfect banana curls and frilly dresses." Angelina gazes out the window. "I wonder where she is now."

"Oh, Angelina, that's a sad story. I had no idea your childhood was so traumatic." June says.

"Oh, I'd hardly call it traumatic. My brother and I figured out early that our parents had many hilarious customs that were different from American families. Thank goodness he was around so we could laugh about it. And our neighborhood was full of people of different ethnic groups who all had their eccentricities, or special weirdness, you might say."

"I'm sure you're a better person for it," June says and pats Angelina's arm as if she said she had cancer.

Angelina lets it slide and merely says, "Thank you."

"Your turn, June," Clara says.

June discards a tile distractedly. "I was thinking of things about my parents that embarrassed me. Maybe when my mother would say to me, "I love your face," in front of my non-Jewish friends. They all thought she was talking about my face."

"She wasn't?" Clara asks.

"Not really. What that means in the Yiddish culture is I love *everything* about you. When I see your face, my heart fills with love or something like that. It means all of you, not just your face."

Clara says, "And why is it that when someone is heavy, they always say, 'She has such a pretty face,' like that's some consolation for her big butt." Then she adds, "I don't remember my parents embarrassing me, but if Frank doesn't stop following me around Target or worse yet, waiting for me in the salon while I get a pedicure, I swear …"

Angelina laughs. "You complain, but you and Frank are proof that marriage is forever. How many years did you celebrate recently? Wasn't it forty-five?"

"Frank says the only reason we've been married so long is that neither one of us wanted a divorce at the same time."

June discards a white dragon and says in a sorrowful voice, "Speaking of embarrassment, If Myra were here now, she'd probably talk about her maiden name. How some people called it a hunky name, like Janokowski or Jabowski—something like that."

Talking about priests with June and Clara reminds Angelina to pay a visit to Myra's priest. Although Guy said it wasn't worth the time because of confidentiality, Angelina thinks it might reveal something. Nothing ventured, nothing gained. And what harm could it do? She doesn't need Guy's permission.

The next day she drives to St. Andrews. It's a small parish, and that's what Myra said she liked about it. Angelina goes to the church office and asks if she can speak to Father Thomas for a few minutes. The secretary speaks into the intercom. "There's an Angelina Popoff to see you, Father. A friend of Myra Anderson."

In a few minutes, Father Thomas bounds out with a sincere welcome and a handshake for Angelina. She recognizes him from the funeral. He's a burly man with white hair and a bushy beard, long enough that he could easily moonlight as Santa Claus. He seems cheerful enough.

In a more somber tone, he says, "I'm sorry for your loss," as he leads her into his office. "How can I help you today? Sit, please." He motions to the chair across from his desk.

Angelina sits and fumbles with the clasp on her purse. "To be honest, I'm not even sure why I stopped by except I feel so bad about Myra's death and I was wondering. . ." She's not sure how to continue.

"I was wondering if there was anything you noticed that was bothering Myra recently. I guess I'm trying to make some sense of it. It doesn't seem right that a healthy woman should die so suddenly. Not that anything you say will bring Myra back, but I'm thinking that perhaps there was something I could have said or done for her." Angelina squirms in her chair.

Father Thomas doesn't respond and shuffles a few papers on his desk.

Angelina goes on. "Perhaps I'm feeling that guilt of things unsaid. Thinking we have forever to tell our friends we care for them." She wasn't making sense, yet she didn't want to admit she suspected foul play. It seemed too preposterous to voice.

Father Thomas responds as Guy said he would. "Mrs. Popoff, I understand how badly you must feel, but of course I can't divulge anything Myra told me in confidence. I know the death of loved ones is hard to accept. I'm sure with the passage of time, your grief will subside."

"Of course." Then Angelina thinks perhaps she can leave him on a more positive note. "Was there a favorite cause here at the church that Myra cared about? Perhaps I could make a contribution. I would feel like I was doing something for her."

He clears his throat and places his hands firmly on the desk. "As a matter of fact, there is. She recently made a sizeable donation to the Orphan Fund of our sister church in Aqua Prieta, Mexico."

He pulls a black ledger out from under a stack of books piled haphazardly on his desk. "I have it right here." He opens the book and scrolls down a page with his index finger. "Yes, she made it in memory of a Sophie Mae Joforsky."

Angelina takes out her checkbook and writes a check. "Do I make it out to St. Andrews?" she asks. She also jots *Sophie Mae Joforsky* on a deposit slip in the checkbook.

"Yes," Father Thomas answers. "Thank you so much. A very thoughtful gesture."

As Angelina drives away, she thinks of the name. Joforsky. What did June say about Myra's maiden name? Something with a J? Was that it? She needs to let Guy know. He might be impressed that she found out something—anything.

Father Thomas closes the ledger after Angelina leaves and recalls Myra's last confession. No harm in letting her friend know about the dedicated donation. After all, Myra didn't discuss that in the confessional box. And Angelina's contribution will help the Orphan Fund.

Chapter Thirty-Four

Prior

Today. Rhonda felt certain the time was right. She placed the snow globe music box under the counter near the styling chair. Yes, Grandmother, today is the day. Our day to connect.

Myra would be arriving for her appointment at five. Rhonda couldn't decide if she should have the music box playing when she came in or after she did her hair. She wanted to be sure they were not interrupted but had no control over that. Maybe she could take Myra to the sitting area outside the dining room. There was also a private gazebo in the courtyard, or would that be too staged? Perhaps staying here was best. She could close the door to the salon to discourage anyone from popping in. Rhonda paced the small space in the salon, working at a snagged cuticle. Relax, she told herself.

Rhonda was glad that Christine came in and requested a wash and set prior to Myra. "Stay busy," she kept saying to herself. "Stay busy." She was adding the finishing touches on Christine's wispy white hair when Myra walked in. Rhonda's hands were shaking. She thought to herself, "Good thing this is only a set and not a cut, or Christine might leave with a crew cut."

Rhonda had played the scenario over and over in her mind. She envisioned that Myra would be quite surprised at first. Then Rhonda would see the joy in her eyes when she realized that at last, the longing she must have felt in her heart for her long-lost daughter would soon be filled.

Rhonda did Myra's hair as usual. When she finished, Rhonda gave Myra the hand mirror and swiveled her chair so she could see the back.

“Do you like it?”

“I do. Makes me wish I had somewhere special to go.”

Then Rhonda swiveled the styling chair so Myra was facing the big mirror. Now both their faces were visible side by side. She said, “I couldn’t help notice, from the first time you were in, how pretty your blue eyes are. Sort of like mine.” Rhonda placed her face closer to Myra’s in the mirror.

“My goodness, they are the same shade of blue. That’s amazing, isn’t it? It’s an unusual blue. Or so I’ve been told.”

“I think there’s a good reason for that,” Rhonda said, her heart beating so hard she was sure Myra could hear it.

“Now I’ve heard of little blue-haired old ladies, but you aren’t using any dye on my eyes, are you?” Myra chuckled.

“Maybe this will help you understand the reason.”

Rhonda reached under the counter and pulled out the music box. She shook the snow globe, so the snow would be falling on Lara’s coach as it traveled through the Russian countryside just like it did in *Doctor Zhivago*. She turned it on and “Lara’s Theme” played in a tinkling melody.

Myra’s hand went to her chest. “Oh my. I had a music box similar to that. It sold in the estate sale.”

“I know,” Rhonda said with a little corner of her mouth turned up.

Myra gave Rhonda a questioning look.

“I bought it.”

“You did? That’s lovely. That you found something you liked.” Then she looked puzzled. “But how did you know it was my sale? My house?”

“I’ve been doing a little research into my, or should I say *our* background, and well, what I discovered was quite fascinating.”

“Whatever do you mean, Rhonda? I don’t understand.”

“I’m trying to tell you, Myra, the reason that I have this music box and the reason our eyes are the same shade of blue. You must have an inkling why.”

Did Rhonda imagine the glint of fear in Myra’s eyes?

“Because, Myra, I wanted something that once belonged to my grandmother. My grandmother, whose eyes are the same shade of blue as mine.”

Myra rubbed her arms as if she had a chill, her eyes open wide but never leaving Rhonda's.

"You see, my mother was the baby you gave up years ago for adoption. Perhaps she never looked for you, but now that I have, I want to be your granddaughter. I *am* your granddaughter, but I want to be one in the real sense of the word. I've always wanted a big family with aunts and cousins, and now that I've found you, I want it more than ever."

Myra looked stricken. Her face became so pale Rhonda thought she might have to get the smelling salts from the first-aid kit.

Myra didn't say anything at first. Then a brief stammer. "But, but . . ."

"I'm sorry to shock you this way. I've wanted to tell you so often but didn't know how. It seemed the longer I delayed the harder it became. I couldn't wait anymore."

Myra shook her head slightly, a vertical line appearing between her eyebrows. "How do you know this, Rhonda? How can you be sure?"

"My mother passed away recently. I didn't know she was adopted until I found some papers in her belongings and then I started to search for the answers."

"And your father, where is he?"

"I don't know. I never knew him. He was in the service, stationed at Luke Air Force Base here in Phoenix. My mother raised me alone. The couple who adopted her, Momo and Papa, died before I was four. They must have been financially stable to be able to adopt, but I remember my mother saying something about their savings being wiped out later by medical bills."

"Do you have photographs of your mother?" Myra asked.

Was she asking because she really wanted to see her daughter or for proof? Rhonda couldn't tell which. "Of course," Rhonda said and scolded herself for not having them on hand for this special moment. "Would you like to see them"?

Myra mumbled something that sounded like Dear God. "Yes, of course, I'd love to see any photos," she answered. Then quickly added, "But not yet. I'm not ready."

"I could bring them next time," Rhonda assured her eagerly.

"I was wondering. How can you be sure? I mean . . ."

Rhonda interrupted her. Did Myra not believe she was telling the truth? She dug into her back pack lying in the corner and waved the yellowed adoption paper in front of Myra. "Would this help convince you? Does the name Sophie Mae Joforsky mean anything to you?"

"Oh, my God," was Myra's response, and her thin bony fingers gripped Rhonda's wrist firmly. Rhonda could see the blue veins in her hand protruding as she stuttered, "I..I believe you. And I want to hear all about your mother . . . and you. But until I have a chance to absorb this, could we please keep it between us?"

"Yes, but may I call you Grandmother?"

Rhonda couldn't make out what Myra's answer was. She was mumbling again. It sounded like, "Yes, I guess that would be…"

Rhonda chattered on about her mother, as if oblivious to Myra's confusion and discomfort. "I'm sorry to say my mother had a hard life. She was on welfare and died of asthma. She drank quite a bit, and one night she got behind the wheel when she shouldn't have. Hit a little girl."

Myra's face expressed horror. "Oh no!"

"Oh, the little girl was fine. Minor bruises. But Mom had to spend some time in jail." Rhonda seemed determined to disclose it all. Perhaps she longed for Myra's sympathy. When she knew the whole story, she would embrace Rhonda and try to make it up to her.

Myra bolted to her feet, holding the side of the chair as if to steady herself. "Please excuse me. I need to go to my room. I need to lie down."

"Are you going to be all right? Do you want me to come with you?"

"No, no, Rhonda, I need to be alone for now. You can understand that, can't you?"

"I think so," was her reply, but she didn't understand. Why wouldn't she want to be with her now? Why wouldn't she want to make up every precious moment that they were apart?

Myra reached for her purse to pay.

"Oh no, you can't pay today. We're family now."

When Myra left, Rhonda threw herself into the styling chair, her head in her hands and cried. Her stomach was knotted. This didn't go as she'd planned. Myra was supposed to be the one crying tears of joy. She was supposed to hug Rhonda and say, "I can't believe that after all these years I have found the piece of me that was lost." She was supposed to say, "I can't wait for the rest of the family to meet you. Those aunts and uncles you've been denied all these years. Rhonda, I'm going to make it up to you."

Instead Myra wanted to be alone. She needed time to think. What was there to think about? Rhonda felt the hurt turning to something else, a familiar feeling. Anger. More than anger. Rage.

She ripped her smock off and reached for her purse. Then as she was about to go out the door, she composed herself and looked around to make sure everything was in order and switched off the lights. It was after six. She slipped into the hallway leading to the lobby. Hopefully, Kathleen nor any of her hair clients would surface. No way she could speak nice to anyone. What she needed was to be alone like Myra. To come up with Plan B. Plan A didn't work.

As she drove home, she gripped the steering wheel tightly. *No, Myra, I didn't let you pay for your wash and set. I wouldn't think of charging you, GRANDMOTHER, but since you couldn't find it in your heart to welcome me after all these years, you will pay. Much more. It will cost you so much more.*

Chapter Thirty-Five

Present

Angelina changes her outfit three times, settling on the sage green broomstick skirt and matching top in a soft crushed cotton. *This is silly. He's going to be inhaling the stuffed peppers. Probably won't even notice what I'm wearing. Should I wear an apron? Then I'd have to change my outfit again. My best apron, the red one, would clash with this green outfit. I'll look like a Christmas elf. No, more like Mrs. Claus with those twelve pounds that refuse to leave me. But maybe I should change. The apron would be a nice touch. But too Donna Reed-ish?* Angelina fears she looks more like Aunt Bee in Mayberry than Donna Reed in the all-American town of Hillsdale.

She's putting on the second earring when the doorbell rings.

Guy is standing there with a small bunch of fresh flowers, looking sheepish as if he either stole them or was questioning whether they were a good idea.

Angelina smiles, thinking they're probably both shy about this meeting, further proof neither of them is experienced in dating. At least that's what he told her, and if she couldn't believe a police officer, who could she believe? But aren't the police trained to look believable no matter what they say?

"They're beautiful!" she says, a bit too enthusiastically.

"Smells wonderful in here," he says.

Good. Food talk. Their mutual comfort zone.

She says, "Isn't it funny how even if you're not hungry, the smell of something delicious can make you feel ravenous?"

"Yes. I don't know if you believe in heaven as a place, but if there is one, I think the favorite aromas of your life linger there forever."

Angelina grins. *I like a man who speaks of heaven and food in the same sentence.* "And what would those aromas be?" she asks as she walks into the kitchen for a flower vase.

He follows. "What I'm smelling right now would work. And . . ." he pauses.

"What?"

"Not to put a damper on this fine evening, but to be honest, I would have to say my wife's perfume, White Shoulders." His expression is a mixture of earnestness and skepticism, as if he crossed a forbidden line.

"I think that's a lovely thing to say." Angelina reassures him. "There are things about Peter I wish I could have bottled and uncorked when I needed him so much that first year."

Angelina breaks eye contact by retrieving a serving dish from the cupboard. "As for favorite food aroma memories, Sunday was the one day we ate our main meal at noon. You could smell the pot roast the minute you walked in the door after church. The delicious smell filled your senses and then that evening the leftovers would be shredded with sautéed onions and a little ketchup for a barbeque I've yet to find as good."

"You know, the Food Channel has all these shows on how to stretch one meal into meals for the whole week. They act like it's rocket science. Our parents did it all the time, didn't they?"

She offers him a choice of wine, beer, or a mixed drink. She hopes he doesn't choose the mixed. She isn't good at mixed drinks, which was Peter's forte. She only learned how to uncork a wine bottle after his death.

To her relief, Guy says, "Cold beer sounds good to me."

Angelina remembers something else from her childhood she hasn't thought of in years. She pictures her father drinking a warm beer with his meal on a summer evening, sitting in his usual place at the kitchen table in a thin cotton, short-sleeved plaid shirt.

"I never knew people drank beer cold till I was on my first date with a college man. My dad always drank it warm, European style."

In the center of the kitchen island is a traditional Bulgarian appetizer platter of feta cheese, black olives—the kind with wrinkly skin—and red peppers, which Angelina roasted, peeled and marinated in olive oil with a smidge of balsamic vinegar. They stand around the kitchen island talking and sipping their drinks while she slices crusty Vienna bread into hefty pieces.

While she goes to get a bread platter, he walks to her kitchen desk and picks up a photo of two teenagers, laughing on a sandy beach. A pretty girl with long wind-blown hair and a younger boy, ready to pour a bucket of water on her head.

"These must be your children."

"Yes, that's one of my favorites from a California vacation. We did the whole thing. Sea World, the zoo, Disneyland. I think they were ten and twelve then." Angelina feels a pang of sadness looking at April's laugh, which she hasn't seen for some time. She asks, "How about you? Children?"

"A daughter in law school."

"Here in Arizona?"

"University of Chicago. So brainy she received a scholarship." Then a sheepish smile. "I didn't mean to brag."

"Well, you should. Top-notch school."

"I have to give the credit to Monica. She didn't go back to nursing until my daughter was in junior high. She spent a lot of time with her. Definitely the homework Nazi."

Then he adds, "Tell me something nice about your kids, so I won't feel like such a boastful parent."

"I could pull out the home movies if that would make you feel better," she offers. Then adds, "I won't do that to you. Unless you have insomnia."

She nudges the appetizer plate toward him. "My daughter-in-law has always worked so my two grandchildren grew up in daycares. I was skeptical until I had to drop off little Sam one day. He was so happy to be there. Several friends ran to hug him, and the teacher greeted him by name as if he were the most important person in her life. I never felt bad about it after that."

"I see kids in homes where they'd be better off in daycare than with their parents," Guy says.

Angelina is reminded once again that he's a cop who sees a lot of seedy life but switches to a more positive note. "What I love most about kids on the playground is one minute they're bonking each other with a sand-lot shovel and the next they're hugging like long-lost friends."

"Yeah, it's too bad we outgrow that. Some people harbor every rotten thing that is said or done to them," Guy says.

"You don't strike me as that type," Angelina says. She brushes his elbow on the way to the center island and feels a sense of comfort, like they've been standing in her kitchen for years, fixing dinner and talking. Again, she is surprised at how natural it feels. How glad she is that they met. Then she thinks of Myra and feels sad that she is benefitting from her friend's death.

"I know it's a Saturday night, and you're off duty, but could I say one thing? No, two things about Myra before we start dinner and then we don't have to talk about it the rest of the evening."

"That's fine. We can talk about it as little or as much as you'd like. This is your party, so to speak. You're the hostess."

Angelina thinks about Myra, ready to speak, but when she glances up at him, she has the urge to brush the piece of hair that constantly falls across his forehead. She wants to push it up away from the eyes that tonight look bluer than grey, but she refrains from reaching out. "I know you said that talking to her priest wouldn't do much good. He couldn't reveal anything confidential, but . . ." She peers up at Guy and once again wants to touch his hair.

"But you went anyway, didn't you?"

Angelina can't tell if he approves or disapproves. She assumes the latter. "You must know, Guy, that I miss Myra." She continues to justify her visit. "I thought talking to her priest might make me feel better."

"Did it?"

"Actually, it did. And I found out something that could be important, but I'm not sure I should tell you since you didn't want me to go in the first place."

Guy laughs. "Out with it. You know you're dying to tell me. Or do I have to confiscate your speckled notebook?"

Angelina laughs too. "I don't know why I have to do all the legwork in this investigation and get no credit for it."

Guy doesn't react. Does she detect a small smile he's trying to disguise?

"Okay. Myra recently made a substantial donation to an orphanage in Mexico in memory of a Sophie Mae Joforsky. I think Joforsky is her maiden name, but I never heard her speak of a Sophie Mae. I mean it could be a distant relative. It's not like she had to tell me everything she ever did, but we did talk about a lot of things and that name never came up. So, of course, I wondered who she is or was."

"Did you find out?"

"That's your job, Detective."

"Yes, ma'am." Guy answers with a mock salute. "You said there were two things."

"Myra went to the beauty parlor at the retirement center each week after our Mah Jongg session on Mondays. A few weeks before she . . . before she passed away. . ." She still couldn't bring herself to say *died.*

"I normally leave the center right after our Mah Jongg game, but I had gone into the gift shop. They have the cutest things there. I bought this adorable..." She glances at him as if he might be interested and then stops mid-sentence.

"If you're thinking that because I watch the Food Channel I like to shop at cutesy boutiques, you've got the wrong guy," he says in his best imitation macho voice which fools neither of them.

"No, no, I wasn't implying anything. I mean sometimes even men need a foo-foo gift. Anyway, I shopped and then remembered I was going to give Myra a phone number she'd asked for. I went into the salon, and she and the hairdresser were the only ones in there. She wasn't working on Myra's hair, but they were both sitting in the little reception area in two straight back chairs talking very intently, it seemed. They stopped as soon as they saw me, but it looked like a serious conversation was taking place.

"When I said, 'I'm sorry I didn't mean to interrupt anything,' Myra became even more flustered and knocked herself out to convince me I hadn't interrupted. I gave her the phone number and left."

"I remember thinking on my drive home that her behavior was a little strange. Like 'methinks the lady doth protest too much.' You would think I would have remembered this the first or second time we talked. Again, it's probably nothing, but you said to tell you anything that seemed unusual."

"I did, and that's exactly what you should be doing. You have a keen sense of observation, Angelina. More than the average person."

"Really?" Angelina is flattered. "Why do you say that?"

"Well, what you just told me you observed. And there is the case of the missing coat button. Very observant."

"Oh yes, I'm going to set that out right now, so I don't forget." She leaves the room and returns with the rumpled trench coat, all buttons intact, leaving it on the side table by the front door.

When she returns to the kitchen, Guy is filling his appetizer plate again and says, "I owe you one."

"For…?"

"The button."

"Don't be silly. But if it makes you feel better, I'll think of something."

"Please do. Or might I suggest? A lot of people like to ride in a cop car with the red light flashing on the dome. Could I interest you in such a joy ride?"

Angelina laughs easily. "I'm not a seven-year old boy. And I thought detectives had unmarked cars."

"Right on both accounts," he says sheepishly. "Just trying to impress you."

"You already have, Detective. Shall we eat?"

Chapter Thirty-Six

Prior

Myra awoke in the night startled from a bad dream. In it, she was wearing the big cardigan sweater she wore constantly between Thanksgiving and Christmas of her senior year before she was sent to her aunt's house. The long, navy blue cable-knit sweater covered the skirt waistbands that no longer closed as a tiny baby bump started to show. She used the biggest safety pin she could find to keep the ends together. One day the pin popped open and left a red prick mark on her skin.

She thought, "I'm already a horrible mother. I'm hurting my baby before it's even born with pins and tight clothes I can hardly breathe in." The rubber Playtex girdle she wore each day cut into her waist leaving a red line in her skin. When she peeled it off each night, she could finally take a deep breath.

In the dream, her father and mother were standing over her saying, "Remember, Myra, you can never tell anyone. We're taking this money. That's the deal we promised." Her father held a big wad of multi-colored dollars in his hand—pink, green, blue and white, like Monopoly money—waving it around for emphasis. "This money will give you the opportunity to start over in a new place where no one knows. You'll have a fine education and a good life. But you must keep this secret."

This was her father speaking in the dream. Her mother, standing a few steps behind him, didn't say a word but wore the scowl Myra remembered. The perpetual scowl for no reason, and now that Myra had given her a reason, the scowl seemed deeper and angrier, along with a smug expression that said, "I knew it. I knew you would mess up."

As far back as Myra could remember, her mother always warned her, "Do not bring shame to the family." The first time Myra heard this, she was so young she wasn't even sure what shame meant. Like what? Don't steal or get bad grades or curse in front of your relatives?

Once she had her period, the shame conversation took on a whole new meaning, and Myra understood it meant only one thing. Do not get pregnant. What had she been thinking that night with the touch of autumn in the air? That she was immune? That it wouldn't happen? They had been having sex since the end of her junior year and then throughout the summer. Had she become complacent? Obviously.

She couldn't even blame Mark. She had encouraged him that night when they snuck into the toolshed and spread out the old Army blanket her dad kept in there. She remembered Mark's comment, "I can't use this Army blanket. I'm going to be an Air Force guy." She thought it was so cute. And he was so cute. And it would be their last night together until his Christmas vacation.

Even in her dream, the self- blame went deep, and she would pay the price. Mark would go unscathed. He'd have his fine education and marry someone after graduation in one of those beautiful military weddings where the couple walks through the raised and crossed swords. Mark, handsome in his blue and white uniform. The feelings were as real as they were back then. The fears, the shame, the sorrow, the regret.

It was the damp nightgown that woke her. She was perspiring. She hadn't done that since going through menopause. That was some fifteen years ago and now here she was soaked, due to hormones again. The hormones she couldn't control as a teen had come back to haunt her.

She climbed out of bed, changed her gown, wrapped her blue chenille robe tightly around her, hoping it would comfort her like a security blanket, but she still felt chilled and clammy. She headed for the kitchen and the tea kettle. A soothing cup of chamomile tea would help. She had to calm down.

What was she going to do about Rhonda? What would her other daughters say? How would she explain this to her young granddaughters? All of a sudden, out of nowhere appears another granddaughter? How about Janet's political aspirations? If she made this public, could it hurt Janet? Mud-slinging.

But if it were true, Rhonda was her flesh and blood. How could she turn her away? Then again, what if she wasn't hers? What if she was a little gold digger who happened to have the same shade of blue eyes? But Rhonda knew the baby's name. Sophie Mae Joforsky. In her heart, Myra believed Rhonda spoke the truth.

Of all the things at the estate sale, why did she choose the music box? Little did Rhonda know that the music box was a gift from her real grandfather, Mark, not long after they saw the *Dr. Zhivago* movie together in 1966. Their passion at that time rivaled that of Yuri and Lara in the movie. She remembered that after they watched it, they went to their special place and kissed until their young bodies were sated. It would always be their song.

Myra sipped the hot tea, but it didn't have the calming effect the advertisements claimed on the box. She returned to bed and tossed and turned, hoping for sleep yet fearful of the recurring dream. Her father's words echoed.

"We've accepted this money and you must never tell anyone about this baby."

Chapter Thirty-Seven

Present

When Guy takes the first bite of stuffed peppers, Angelina tries not to stare at him but hopes he loves them.

When he closes his eyes and gives a hum of satisfaction, she glances away to hide her pleasure, then back again. She has spent so much time looking at the blue-grey eyes that she hasn't noticed how attractive his mouth is. Full lips that form a perfect outline.

Without thinking, she asks, "Did you by any chance play a brass instrument in high school or college?" She doesn't even know if he went to college. Did the police academy have a marching band?

He looks at her and laughs. "First of all, these peppers are amazing. Secondly, how did you know I was first-chair trumpet? High school only. I never went to college. Just a dumb cop hanging out at the donut shop."

"First, college is highly overrated, I'd say. Second, I don't think dumb cops make detective. And third, my brother was a trumpet player and . . ." Now how was she going to continue this story without letting him know she was admiring his lips? "I'll just say it, but I'm sort of embarrassed." She fiddles with the salt and pepper shakers.

"Good. Now I really want to hear it." He smiles.

"Okay. As I've aged, I wished I played a brass instrument because my brother, even in his seventies, had the most beautiful, perfectly-shaped lips any girl would love to have. I always thought the trumpet he played had something to do with it. I should add that he continued to play the rest of his life. Army band, community band. I think it was that continued lip exercise on a mouthpiece. That's why his lips stayed so perfect."

"Hmm. An interesting theory. And you're telling me this now because . . ."

"Because," she pauses. "Okay, I'll confess. Because I was watching you take your first bite. I wanted to be sure you liked the stuffed peppers, and I noticed your lips were shaped as nicely as my brother's." She couldn't believe she actually said it.

Guy puts down the fork he's been holding suspended in mid-air for most of this exchange, as if he were waiting for a break in the conversation to start eating again.

"That's one of the nicest things anyone has ever said to me."

"Well…" She tries to brush it off.

"Not only are you a wonderful gourmet cook, but you are a charming and gracious lady."

Angelina feels her cheeks warm and a tickle in her chest. And it isn't from the flakes of red pepper she likes to sprinkle on her stuffed peppers.

The evening passes too quickly, and as they stand at the door, Guy says, "I had some reservations about seeing you while I was still investigating Myra's death. But I don't think there's any harm, do you? I would like to see you more often. Perhaps a movie, an occasional dinner?"

Angelina answers, "I see no harm at all in that. It sounds lovely and I'd like it very much."

When Guy says goodnight, he leans down and kisses Angelina's cheek. "Thank you for a lovely evening."

After he leaves, Angelina remains against the door for a moment, enjoying the cheek kiss and the thought of future meetings.

Angelina sighs. In her sixties and smitten. With a Columbo wannabe.

In the game of Mah Jongg, dragons are divided into three colors: red, green, and white. Reds match cracks, greens match bamboo and whites match dots. The sixteen winds have the initial of their direction in the upper left-hand corner-north, south, east and west.

Chapter Thirty-Eight

Prior

The following Monday, Myra fidgeted all through her Mah Jongg game. She would be seeing Rhonda afterwards at her standing five o'clock appointment. Having not heard from Rhonda during the week, she thought several times about contacting her outside of the salon. The agency who conducted the estate sale had given her a list of all purchasers. She scanned it quickly. Under Snow Globe Music Box was Yvonne Brooks #86, $50.00. That confused her further. She could have asked Director Kathleen for a contact number for Rhonda but didn't want to get into any explanations. So, she waited.

Prior to the Mah Jongg game, Myra poked her head into the salon to ask what time Rhonda normally arrived.

"She usually comes right after lunch," Kathleen told her. "I must say your hair is looking lovelier than ever, Myra," Kathleen commented. "That softer curl makes you look ten years younger."

A week ago, that compliment would have been welcome. Now Myra could only think that her hair looked good, but her face must have aged years with the stress of Rhonda's news. She had to see her. They had to talk. So many questions. Questions that required answers.

During the first hour of Mah Jongg play, Myra kept scanning the game room for signs of Rhonda, although she rarely came up there.

"What is wrong with you today?" Clara asked. She wasn't one to miss anything or be discreet in asking questions. "What do you keep looking around for? Did you lose something or someone?"

How ironic that comment was. Lose something? No, she found something. Or rather, something had found her. She answered with a white lie. "Looking for Andrea Harper. She said she'd like to learn to play Mah Jongg, and I invited her to sit and observe some Monday. I hope that's okay with all of you."

"That's a great idea," June said, always accommodating.

"Fine with me," Angelina said.

"As long as she doesn't keep talking about her dog's narcolepsy," Clara said.

"The dog's what?" June asked.

"Narcolepsy. You know. He has a sleep disorder."

"The dog has a sleep disorder?" Angelina asked.

"Yes, he falls asleep standing up. A deep sleep she can't wake him from."

"So, what's the problem? Let sleeping dogs stand . . . or sleep. It's not like he has to drive somewhere," June said.

"No, but she stumbled over him one night in the bathroom. He was standing there in front of the sink like a brick statue when Andrea went to get a glass of water."

"I'm sure my cat suffers from the same disorder," Angelina said. "Henry sleeps twenty-three hours a day."

"But is he standing?"

"Well, no . . ."

Clara said, "It's weird all right, but Andrea is obsessed with that dog's medical issues. I think he also has a hernia and she describes every symptom. But if she wants to learn Mah Jongg, I'm fine with that. We'll tell her it's bad luck to talk about animals while playing. Call it an old Chinese proverb."

Angelina and June both laughed, but Myra was feeling worse than ever. Here was a whole discussion taking place over something she just made up. Something that would probably never come to pass. Although Andrea had casually expressed an interest in Mah Jongg, she hadn't yet invited her to join them. This Rhonda thing was turning her into a fibber. No, a liar. She detested liars. Her hands were getting moist, and then she knocked over the entire rack of tiles with her elbow.

"Myra, whatever is going on with you?" Clara asked.

June helped her gather the scattered tiles. "No use crying over a stitch in time."

"Milk, June, spilt milk," Clara said.

Myra picked up her tiles and play proceeded. Three crack. North wind. Seven bam.

Myra was still so distracted she passed a chance to take a free joker off Angelina's rack, and the others groaned. Even though it was to their advantage that she erred, the lost opportunity was so great it always elicited a group sympathy groan.

Focus, Myra, focus. All she could think of was how was she going to tell Rhonda, blood or no blood, that she couldn't possibly include her in her life right now.

And she knew in her heart, as well as her gut, that wasn't going to sit well with this girl.

Chapter Thirty-Nine

Prior

In the salon, Rhonda was giving a cut to Linda Hazelwood. Although Linda's red hair was now faded, Rhonda could tell she'd been a beautiful redhead in her youth. Rhonda felt herself reverting to the old resentment pattern of clipping a piece off in back, but since it was so faded, she squelched the desire.

"Linda, women half your age would die for this hair," Rhonda said.

Linda beamed. Rhonda knew Linda's tip would be in proportion to how good she felt about herself when she left.

Myra paused in the doorway, and when Rhonda saw her, she gave a little start but answered calmly. "Hi Myra, are we on for five o'clock?"

"I was wondering. Could I perhaps reschedule?" She motioned with her index finger for Rhonda to come closer.

"Excuse me a minute, Linda."

Rhonda approached Myra who spoke to her in a whisper.

"How about we skip the hair today and instead, you come to apartment 223 about 5:00? We need to talk privately.

"Sure, of course," Rhonda said loud enough for Linda to hear. "We can reschedule that. No problem. I'll see you at 5:00."

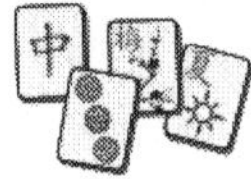

When Rhonda arrived, Myra led her to the sitting room. Rhonda paused and gripped the back of a chair to stop the trembling her anticipation was causing her. Rhonda took a measured breath and surveyed the room much the same way she did when she went to the estate sale. Judging, appraising the signs of wealth. Her grandmother represented so many things Rhonda had longed for her entire life, and now she was about to find out if she would receive the most prized treasure— acceptance and belonging. A family.

Rhonda had two scenarios playing in her head all week. Best case scenario—one where Myra apologized profusely for not embracing her wholeheartedly the minute she heard the news and laying out a plan for her to meet her aunts and cousins as soon as possible.

Worst case? Myra would leave a message at the salon cancelling all future appointments. That would be a clear message she didn't want to see her again. But Rhonda imagined that something in between those two scenarios would occur. Perhaps a small apology and hopefully a hug, with a statement like, "Now that we've found each other," *not that Myra had been looking*, "let's talk about how we can make up for lost years, all that time we could have been together. But first tell me about your mother."

Rhonda gazed longingly at Myra, trying to read her body language to determine which way it would go. With Myra's first words, Rhonda suspected Plan B.

"Rhonda, I'm sorry if I didn't appear as happy to hear your news as you might have expected. You can understand how it was such a shock to me after all these years. I think sometimes people shut out painful events of their life so much, they start to believe that they never happened. Some things are less painful that way, wouldn't you say?"

"I suppose. I guess I didn't think about how painful it must have been to give up your baby. I mean it probably was, wasn't it?"

"Of course it was. Extremely painful, also because I was deeply in love with the father. So not only was I losing the baby—our baby—but I was giving up a life I had hoped to spend with him."

"Why didn't you marry him?"

"I would have in a minute. But his family had grandiose plans for him. He had an appointment at the Air Force Academy. A great future ahead of him that didn't include a wife and baby at age eighteen. Remember, Rhonda, this was the sixties. Things have changed a lot since then, but those were different times."

Rhonda nodded slightly, but she didn't fully understand.

Myra looked away with a wry smile. "I'm not sure we would have ever married anyway. His family envisioned a daughter-in-law of better social standing. A college grad or a girl from a finishing school befitting an Air Force officer. Me, the high school sweetheart with no money for college from the wrong side of the tracks? I wouldn't have been their choice. I'm sure they were hoping our romance would fizzle out after high school even before they knew of the baby. But the baby gave them the chance to remove me from his life forever, and he could do nothing about it." Myra shook her head as if remembering how helpless she felt in that situation.

"I really didn't expect him to give up the rare opportunity to attend a military academy. Although the sixties is labeled *the rebellion generation*, most of us were still under our parents' thumbs." Myra gave a half smile and shrugged.

"His family wasn't wealthy but far richer than mine. The right side of the tracks. They lived in a neighborhood with manicured lawns, and mine was in a row of narrow houses. We had a postage stamp for a back yard. Mark's parents offered mine money in exchange for silence and an agreement that I would give up the baby for adoption. I imagine they didn't want me coming back into their lives years later for support. Those closet skeletons could be costly, I'm sure." Myra paused and took a deep breath.

"As much as I hated my parents when they sold out for cash, years later I realized they were thinking of my future. The bribe money would allow me to go to college. Otherwise, I couldn't have afforded it. A fresh start, a new life for me and a good home for the baby."

Rhonda said, "A good home for my mother."

"Yes. Tell me, Rhonda, was it a good home for her?"

Rhonda told her what little she knew of Momo and Popo. "From everything my mother told me, they were good parents. It was medical expenses that wiped them out later in life."

Rhonda pulled a book from the tote bag she had carried in. "Would you like to see some pictures? I brought my mother's scrapbook."

Myra hesitated. She closed her eyes for a moment, and when she opened them, she said, "I'd love to see them, Rhonda."

"It's not a big album, but there are photos of my mom, Dottie Feder, as a baby and a toddler."

Myra searched the face of the little girl in the photos but saw no resemblance. There were also a few of the teen years, but when she turned the page to Dottie as a young mother holding Rhonda, she gasped. It was almost as if she was seeing herself as a young mother. The resemblance was striking and eerie.

"Excuse me a moment." Myra walked into her bedroom and returned with a photo in a pearl frame. It was a younger version of Myra holding a baby. Strangely enough, her grandmother's stance was almost the same as Dottie's with Rhonda on her hip. There was no denying that Dottie was related to Myra.

"I guess we won't need a DNA test, will we?" Rhonda replied with a full and confident smile that implied, "See, you should have believed me the first time."

Rhonda didn't tell her that she had already done a DNA test with a strand of Myra's hair along with her own. She was going to use it as evidence if Myra denied their relationship. No use letting her know now how sneaky she was, and perhaps it was a crime without a police order. Whatever. She paid a high price for the quick results test. Three nights with that nerdy greasy-haired lab technician granting him all the sick favors he wanted.

Myra closed the album and cleared her throat. "Rhonda, what I need to tell you is, as much as I'd like to embrace you . . . you are my flesh and blood after all, I have to consider my other children too. I have three daughters, but mainly I'm thinking of Janet."

Rhonda blurted out, "I know about your daughters. I know all their names and ages and where they live." She only meant to show Myra how much interest she had taken in her life, but it came out wrong, somehow perverted.

Myra's hand went to her chest. She took a step backward and then abruptly changed the subject. "I've been so rude. May I offer you a glass of water? Lemonade, tea?"

Rhonda sensed Myra was nervous. Had she said the wrong thing? “Yes, I’d love something to drink.” *Obviously, we aren’t going to crack open a bottle of champagne to celebrate this momentous occasion, but a glass of wine might be nice.* She suspected that it wouldn’t be Two Buck Chuck. She was curious as to what it might be.

Rhonda asked, “Would it be okay if we had a glass of wine? I guess this is making me a little nervous too.”

“Excellent idea!” Myra said a little too enthusiastically and went to the china cabinet, taking out two crystal wine glasses. Then she turned to Rhonda. “Do you prefer red or white? I have both.”

“Whatever you’re having. I like both. I mean either.” She almost said, “I like anything with alcohol.”

“I opened a nice Viognier last night.” Myra poured each of them a glass, took a long sip out of hers and refilled it again.

“This is nice,” Rhonda said, sipping the wine. “Very nice.”

“Let’s start over,” Myra said. “I’d like to tell you some things about Janet you may not be aware of. Perhaps you know this. You seem to know quite a bit already. Janet is single. At age thirty-eight, when most people her age have a husband and a family, she doesn’t have anyone special in her life. She was jilted twelve years ago by her college sweetheart. They were engaged, planning the wedding and she had the dress, a lovely Vera Wang.”

Myra rolled her eyes and shook her head. “Oh, what does that matter now what kind of dress it was? When she found out he was cheating on her, with some little tramp no less, it devastated her. Since then, she’s thrown herself into her work and seems to have given up on love and sharing her life with someone. She became involved with politics on a small scale with her community. Trying to block a truck bypass coming through that would have eliminated many homes and a beautiful church. Not to mention having eighteen-wheelers barreling down the backyards of a sleepy community.”

Myra was rambling. She took another sip of her wine, a deep breath and continued. “What I’m trying to say is that Janet is excited about her life once again for the first time in a long time. The other day, we had lunch and she told me about a mud-slinging campaign against her opponent. She didn’t instigate it, but you know what politics are like. Someone in her party was determined the opposite party wouldn't prevail. Once that mud hits the wall, it's hard to remove. Her opponent is struggling to save face. I'll be honest, Rhonda. When you told me you were my granddaughter, as much as I wanted to shout it from the mountaintops, all I could think of was how it could possibly damage Janet."

Rhonda doubted that mountaintops were what Myra first thought of, based on her initial reaction.

"Not that my giving up a baby for adoption was a bad thing. It was probably the best thing for the baby. For your mother."

Why doesn't she say the words *my daughter*? Why won't she admit it?

"But you know how nasty politics can be. And especially when you told me your mother was in jail. It could destroy Janet's career. I can't do that to her. It doesn't mean I don't want us to become acquainted. I want to know you, Rhonda. I really do."

Myra took a deep breath and another sip of wine. She let out a big sigh and looked directly into Rhonda's blue eyes.

Rhonda focused on Myra's every word and by the time she finished, the slow burn of rejection was building and sparking like kindling on a fire. She felt it was about to burst into a flame. What should she do? What should she say?

"I understand," is what came out of Rhonda's mouth, almost too calmly with no emotion, in an effort to squelch her anger. Was that relief on Myra's face? But Rhonda didn't understand why she couldn't be acknowledged. What she really understood was that she would never have the place in Myra's life that the other girls did. Her mother, Dottie Feder, who died in a seedy apartment with few comforts in her life, would never have Janet's privileges. Her mother with her sordid background would never be welcome in this family. And if Dottie didn't matter, how could she, once removed, count for anything?

Now Rhonda felt like Myra did when she first received the news. She needed to be alone. She needed to think about this. Plan C? She didn't have one yet. She had to escape before she said something regrettable. Something stupid. Something hateful, because hate was what was filling her throat right now. Rising like bile.

She composed herself and said as calmly as she could, "Thank you for the wine. It was lovely. I'm tired all of a sudden. On my feet all day. I think the wine has gone to my head, and I do have to be at work early tomorrow. Can we talk about this again another time?"

"Of course, dear, of course," Myra said. "Should you be driving home alone? Let me call you a cab. I'll pay for it and for the cab to come back tomorrow to get your car. Please, Rhonda, let me do that."

"Thank you, but no thanks." Rhonda turned her back, strode to the door and had to refrain from slamming it.

So Grandmother doesn't want to claim me, but she can afford a cab. What a joke. I came here for a birthright and all I get is cab fare. Well, if that's the way she wants to play the game. I'll get as much money as I can out of the old bag. What difference will it make? Who needs a big loving family?

Mah Jongg tiles can be made of wood, bamboo, ivory, Bakelite, bone, ivory or jade. Bakelite tiles became fashionable in the seventies when Andy Warhol's affinity for it inspired collectors.

Chapter Forty

Present

Myra's daughter, Janet, walks into Angelina's home carrying a beautiful mahogany Mah Jongg case.

"My sisters and I were going through Mother's things to see what we would divide as keepsakes. We all agreed the Mah Jongg set should go to you—actually, to all three of you who played with Mother. We thought she would like you to have it."

Angelina is taken aback. "Janet, are you sure? Perhaps you girls will learn the game someday? In fact, Clara and June were hoping one of you might take your mother's place in our foursome. Like the daughter did in *The Joy Luck Club*."

"Mother always encouraged us, but it seemed we could never find the hours to devote to learning it. But you might ask Debbie."

"I'll do that, and you must promise me that if you have the interest, you'll let me know and I'll gladly teach you. Until then, I'll take good care of it, I promise."

"I have no doubt of that." Janet gives Angelina a hug.

"I also found this book which you gave her. I saw your note on the inside cover." Janet hands Angelina a small red book—*Mah Jongg from Shanghai to Miami Beach.*

"That is so thoughtful of you. I'd love to have it. There are some beautiful quotes as well as the history of the game and Chinese culture. For example, one of your mother's favorites. Now where is it?" Angelina turns pages. "Here it is. 'In China there is a belief that an invisible red thread connects those who are destined to be together in life.'"

"That is lovely," Janet agrees. "I don't believe Mother ever mentioned that to me."

When Janet leaves, Angelina thumbs through the book and lays it beside the Mah Jongg case on the coffee table. She glances at the clock. Only thirty minutes to get ready for Guy. She's already decided what to wear. A light blue cotton sundress with a short jacket and a sea-shell pendant. She bought it at Chico's with the gift certificate her son gave her last Christmas. She was saving it for a special occasion, and a Sunday morning at the Phoenix Botanical Gardens with Guy was indeed special.

She's looking forward to the morning walk through the gardens and the elegant brunch served at the outdoor café. There is usually a string quartet. Angelina feels young and light.

When Guy arrives on time as usual, she says, "I'll be ready in five minutes. Myra's daughter, Janet, stopped by to return a book I once gave Myra as a gift. It has some interesting Chinese history if you're interested." She motions to the book on the coffee table as she returns to her bedroom for jewelry.

Guy picks up the book and says hello to Henry who rubs against his pant leg as if he's going to befriend him, but then turns away snootily to follow Angelina.

Guy is thumbing through the book when she returns. He says, "Some interesting history here. I didn't realize the game was so ancient."

"That's one thing I love about it. To think how many years it has survived. And how it came to the States. Did you notice the part about why it became so popular in the Jewish communities?"

"No."

"Shanghai was one of the few places not requiring an entry visa during World War Two. Many Jews escaped the Nazis by fleeing there and adapted to the local Chinese culture, eventually bringing the game to America."

"Interesting," Guy says.

Angelina goes on, “The quotes of the Eastern philosophers give me a sense of serenity. And wisdom to ponder.”

“Let’s ponder over brunch,” Guy stands and leads Angelina to the door.

“Hungry?” she asks, although she knows the answer.

“Always,” he replies.

Chapter Forty-One
Prior

Rhonda was halfway home when she turned the car around and returned to Friendship Village. Her anger was building, and she needed to vent. And to share her idea with Myra.

Money was the perfect solution. Money, she convinced herself, was what she needed—more than a large family. It would be easy to demand it now that her warm feelings for Myra were turning to cold anger. Myra. The bitch. And she had Janet to thank. Ambitious Janet who wouldn't want to tarnish her political career with a mother who'd had an illegitimate child. Oh heavens no. More like heavens, yes, the heavens were going to pay. The planets would align to pay Rhonda for her silence as her great-grandfather paid Myra's parents years ago. Myra was going to experience what it was like being on the other side.

It could be the perfect way to realize her pipe dream of owning a classy salon. She would do the research as soon as possible. The cost of opening a salon—the finest—no mediocre cut-rate spa for her. After all, now she was the descendent of a first-class lady. Maybe she would flatter the old bitch and name it after her—Myra's Mystique. Let Myra think she was fond of her. Then she'd take that nice loose curl and weave it into the tightest, ugliest perm one could imagine.

Chapter Forty-Two

Present

As they stroll through the gardens, Angelina feels out of sorts.

"Is everything all right?" Guy asks. "You look serious for such a carefree morning."

"I can't pin down the nagging thought in my head. Like something I should be remembering that I'm not."

Guy wraps a reassuring arm around her shoulder. "I bet it will come to you in the middle of the night. Keep that speckled notebook handy. I practically sleep with my Steno." He rests his hand on her elbow as they turn into the outdoor café.

At brunch, they indulge in eggs Benedict, watermelon balls, and lemon scones, which they share. Myra likes the intimacy they're enjoying at meals, like a couple that has been together years.

Guy eyes the string quartet. "Vivaldi's "Spring" is my favorite of his *Seasons Overture*."

"I'm impressed. I didn't know they played classical music at Dunkin' Donuts."

He laughs. "Well, we Italians have to stick together. And speaking of impressed, I saw you wield that hammer the other day."

"Anyone can hang a picture," she says.

"It seemed more complicated to me. You were doing something with molly bolts. That's quite advanced, I'd say."

"I've learned to do a lot of things since Peter died. Did you cook before Monica passed or was it survival afterwards?"

"I knew how to grill burgers and steaks. Like most guys, that was about the extent of it. But after she died, I lost my appetite. I lived on cereal for weeks."

"Sounds like a well-balanced diet."

"I did vary it. Cheerios, Rice Krispies. Do you know how many kinds of cereal there are today?"

"No, but I think I'm about to find out." She rolls her eyes.

"Lots. And lots of people love to eat cereal, not just for breakfast. There's a store in Chicago on Michigan Avenue called Cereality. That's all they serve all day long. Rows of every kind of cereal in large plastic bins. Everyone serves themselves."

"Really? Another Food Channel find?"

"No, my daughter took me there. She knew I'd love it. It was fun to gorge on sugary kid food again. Like Captain Kangaroo Peanut Butter Crunch."

Angelina laughs at how he can make a kid's cereal sound so enticing. During a lull in their conversation while they listen to a Mozart piece, Angelina reflects on the man sitting across from her. She's getting to know Guy bit by bit. It reminds her of a favorite picture book for adults. Something about comparing friendship to artichokes. How they can't be rushed. You have to peel off one layer at a time to reach the core, the best part.

As the music stops, a chime sounds from her purse—a text message.

She reaches in and apologizes to Guy. "Excuse me. That must be my granddaughter. She's the only one who sends me texts."

"Whoa, I'm impressed again," Guy says. "You are in the 21st century."

She laughs it off but likes the compliment. "Grandkids rescue us from the dark ages. I want them to think I'm cool. And it seems to be the only way they respond. Phone messages take forever to answer, but if I send them a text—bing bing—they reply immediately. My son told me that 2007 was the first year people sent more texts than phone calls. Do you text?"

"Most of the guys I work with still pick up the phone. Cell phones and pagers."

"Do you mind if I read her message? In case it's important?"

"By all means." Guy also pulls out his cell phone and plays with his keyboard for a minute.

As soon as Angelina reads her granddaughter's text, she smiles. "She's letting me know they'll be coming to dinner as planned. I try to do a Sunday night family dinner."

Another text chime, but she ignores it.

"So your daughter and son both come? That's nice."

"Lately it's just been my son's family. My daughter's been so . . ." Angelina starts to say "busy" as she stuffs her phone in her purse. "To be honest, I'm ashamed to admit it but my daughter and I have become a little estranged. It's my fault and I'm trying to correct it, but I'm not making much progress."

Guy starts to say something when Angelina's phone chimes again.

"Do you mind if I check it again? This is so rude."

"No please. I insist."

She glances at the new text. *You look lovely in blue. It brings out your eyes. Signed Guy.*

She peers up at him, her eyes wide.

"You! You do so text."

"I didn't want to get left in the last century either. Blame my daughter."

Their eyes linger on each other across the table as the quartet resumes.

"That's a coincidence, "Angelina says.

"What?"

"They're playing one of Myra's favorite songs. 'Lara's theme—Somewhere My Love' from *Dr. Zhivago*.

"Great movie."

"Myra had a music box that played this song. When she moved to Friendship Acres, she left it in the estate sale by mistake. She'd meant to give it to her granddaughters, but it sold. She said she would give anything to have the box rather than the fifty dollars."

As they leave the gardens, they pass a brilliant red bougainvillea bush.

"Look at that color," Guy says. "Most of them are pinkish red, but that one is a true brilliant red."

"That's it," Angelina says and grabs Guy's arm. "That's it."

"What's *it?"*

"Red. The color red. It's what's been nagging me."

"Oh?"

"I went to the cemetery two days after the funeral. Safeway had a sale on beautiful potted begonias. Myra loved begonias, so I felt compelled to take one to her grave. That's when I saw the red ribbon at the base of the headstone. I don't know if it was there the day of the funeral. It could have been, but with all the flowers and people, perhaps I didn't see it. But when I returned, it was so obvious. And now the quote about a red ribbon in the book Janet brought me. Do you think there's a connection?"

"It's possible. Very possible. As I said, you're an observant woman. Perhaps one of the daughters left it there."

"I read the quote to Janet this morning. She said she'd never heard it. Didn't know it was a favorite of her mother's."

"Well, someone did."

"Who?" Angelina asked.

"That's a very good question."

"Shouldn't we go get the ribbon?" Angelina's eyes were bright at the prospect of finding a potential clue. "We could go together." *Nancy Drew joins forces with the Hardy Boys."*

"It's already done, Angelina. I have the red ribbon in my possession."

"You knew this already? I feel foolish," she says. "I . . ."

"Please don't." He stops, turns to face her and touches her lips with two fingers. Instead of objecting, she stares into his blue eyes. He takes both her hands in his. "I have the ribbon, but you provided the possible connection."

When they return to her home, Guy walks her to the door. "I had a wonderful time. Thank you so much," Angelina says.

"Me too."

Their eyes remain on each other, and Angelina feels a flutter in her stomach and a twinge in her chest. He gently pulls her toward him. A tender hug. She hugs him back, just as gentle at first and then firmer.

They separate and look at each other.

"Could we have lunch one day this week?" Guy asks.

"I'd like that."

Angelina retrieves her speckled notebook and writes the quote from memory. *In China there is a belief . . .*

She makes a list of questions. Who left the ribbon there? Why? What's the connection? Is there a connection? Who is destined to be with Myra?

She closes the notebook and smiles when she remembers Guy's hug. She likes that they are taking baby steps. Like an artichoke. One layer at a time.

Chapter Forty-Three

Present

When Guy returns home, he opens his desk drawer and carefully pulls out an envelope containing the red ribbon, which was still on the headstone when he decided to return. At that time, he didn't know if it was relevant but thought it could be. He'd handled it gingerly on each end, using gloves, and took it to the lab for fingerprinting. As he suspected, there were no fingerprints as they rarely stick to cloth. In the meantime, he kept it in his desk drawer waiting for it to make sense or reveal a significance. Perhaps the quote in the book is the key. Who in Myra's life was destined to be connected?

He opens his Steno and makes notes. *Who and what on the red ribbon? Was it there during the funeral service and Angelina hadn't noticed it? If it wasn't there during the funeral service but there when I returned for my missing phone, that meant someone put it there in the short time it took me to drive to the cemetery gate and back again. I thought all the guests had left. Perhaps one hung back. Why hadn't I noticed? How about the car that drove away? Had it stopped or was it passing through from another site? A '76 Dodge Dart. Not too many of those still around. Who drives one? Possibly a resident from Friendship Acres?*

Further notes. *Warrant for bank accounts and recent activity. Talk to Myra's financial advisor. License plate search on '76 Dodge Darts.*

He closes his Steno and smiles at the thought of Angelina frantically recording her "red" notes in her black and white composition book. She knows about his Stenos. Something only

Monica knew and now Angelina. It gives him a sense of pleasure—a sort of intimacy.

His thoughts are interrupted by a ping on his cell phone. He assumes it's his daughter, The only person who sends him texts.

To his delight, he reads, *Thanks for a perfect morning. A walk through the gardens, Vivaldi, decadent scones, eggs Benedict and your charming smile. Blagodara.*

He texts in return.

My pleasure, bella signora.

Chapter Forty-Four

Prior

As Myra changed into her nightgown, her phone rang.

"Myra, could I come back for a few minutes? I had an idea I wanted to run by you."

"Of course." Myra tried to sound cordial, but their previous talk disturbed her, and she anticipated the worst about Rhonda's idea.

When Myra, now in her blue robe, opened the door, Rhonda strode past her and skipped any formalities.

"I was thinking as I drove home that since you're ashamed of me, why don't we settle it, so I can stay in the background where I've always been. I'll do that if you at least give me what I'm entitled to." With hands on her hips, Rhonda regarded her grandmother with a look of cold defiance.

Myra shuddered. "Rhonda, I'm not ashamed of you. But what is it that you feel entitled to?"

"My mother died penniless and you didn't even know or care. I only told you about her past thinking you'd be sorry you weren't there for her and you'd want to make it up to me. You'd want to surround me with the family I never had. But you're too worried that your precious daughter might not be the first lady President. Whatever. Fine. I'll stay in the closet like a skeleton, but it will cost you." She spat out a final word, "*Grandmother.*"

"*So* how much is your precious secret worth? I'm not greedy. Only asking for enough to open my own salon. Who needs a big family anyway?"

Myra was horrified. Her eyes were wide, and her face drained of all color.

Then Rhonda's defiant composure seemed to crumble. She began sobbing. "I'm sorry. I didn't mean to upset you. I'm only asking for what's rightfully mine. Wouldn't you agree?"

The girl was psychotic. Myra began agreeing with her in an effort to pacify her. Stifling her own anger, she took measured breaths, not wanting to make it worse.

Then Myra said, "Please let's be rational. I know I may have hurt your feelings. I didn't mean to. You must understand. It's painful for me to bring up the past, a time when I was deeply hurt myself. So much of that has nothing to do with you. None of it was your fault, and I am so sorry your mother's life wasn't better. Let's be sensible. Let's not cause each other further sadness. I'm sure we can work something out."

"We can?" Rhonda peered at Myra as if she were given an executioner's reprieve.

"Of course," Myra said, although she had no idea what she was going to say or do next. "This is hard for both of us. Let's give ourselves a little time to get used to the idea. What do you say to that?"

Rhonda's shoulders sagged. "Perhaps you're right."

"Let's not talk any more tonight. We're both exhausted. This is emotionally draining. Let's get a good night's sleep and we'll talk in the next day or two. How would that be?"

Rhonda nodded as if she agreed, as if she calmed down, but then without a word, she stormed out the door and slammed it behind her.

Myra collapsed on the sofa. She drank another glass of wine. If only this was a bad dream. Myra knew she hadn't handled Rhonda well.

Rhonda said she needed time to think. That statement, combined with the wild look in Rhonda's eyes, brought fear to Myra's heart.

Should she have told Rhonda how often, almost daily, she'd thought about the baby she'd given up for adoption? Where was she? How was she? How she hoped the parents loved the adopted daughter as much as she loved her daughters. Didn't adoptive parents feel especially blessed and often love their children more because they chose them? That's what she told herself through the years. She should have expressed those thoughts to Rhonda.

She wished she had someone to talk to. There was no one. She missed Richard deeply. He would know what to do, but he wasn't here. She was alone. Alone and frightened.

Not one to have more than one glass of wine, she felt sedated by the second glass and fell into a dreamless sleep.

Chapter Forty-Five

Prior

Rhonda left Myra's feeling rejected and wounded. Like a helpless animal. As she drove, the hurt turned to anger, and the little animal grew into a ferocious beast inside her. She needed to do something to tame it. She thought of calling Todd with the raging hormones, but she didn't feel like making love. *Hmpff. What I have with him could hardly be called love. It's purely sexual release. What I need now is a different release. I need to hurt someone or something the way I've been hurt. If that's the way her grandmother wanted it, she could play the game, but it would cost her.*

She glanced at the time. The shooting range had evening hours. She went to her bedside table and took the twenty-two pistol. Another trade for sex. She drove to the range, donned the earphones and shot at the targets. She preferred those that had the outlines of people and she named them as she shot. Myra, Crack. Janet, Crack, Debbie, Crack. And don't forget the spoiled little granddaughters, Brittany and Ashley. Why should they be spared? She pictured them holding those little dolls as they came out of Myra's house the first time she saw them. She aimed at an imaginary silly smile on the doll's face. Crack. She was a good marksman.

Once her anger was spent, she could hardly keep her eyes open on the drive home. She fell into bed and a deep dreamless sleep.

If Mah Jongg is called in error and no one exposes their hand, the game continues with the remaining players.

Chapter Forty-Six
Prior

The next Monday, when the Mah Jongg Mavens met, Myra was thankful for June and Clara's endless prattle. It kept her from having to contribute to the conversation when she was still so preoccupied with Rhonda.

"You'd think, wouldn't you, that for all the times we've played, one of us would get that seventy-five point hand. I mean, have any of you even tried to go for it?" Clara asked.

"I almost had it once. Last year, remember?" Angelina said. "I only needed one tile. A four crack, and wouldn't you know it, the very next hand, the first tile I picked up was a four crack. Life is weird like that sometimes, isn't it?"

"Yes," Myra said. "Sometimes things turn up when you least expect them. And sometimes it's too late to enjoy them."

"There's a Yiddish saying, 'When you least expect it, expect it,'" June said as she searched through the Gummy Bears for her favorite flavor—green.

Clara said, "I've heard 'hope for the best, expect the worst.'"

"Sounds to me like you ladies are talking about a lot more than Mah Jongg tiles here," Angelina said. "Philosophical today, aren't we?"

No one responded. She went on, "I love the Chinese culture. The roots of Mah Jongg. The sayings of Confucius and Buddha."

"I love the fortune cookies," June said. "They always fit my situation perfectly."

"June, they're written to fit everyone's situation. Like, 'A pleasant surprise is in store for you soon,'" Clara said.

"Once I opened one that said, 'You will be hungry again soon. Order takeout now.'" Angelina discarded a five crack.

"So, did you?" June asked.

"Did I what?"

"Order takeout?"

"Of course. I thought it was a great marketing gimmick and should be rewarded."

Clara said, "My fortune cookie was empty one time. Now what kind of message is that conveying, I ask you?"

June said, "Don't count your eggs before you put them in the basket."

Clara remains stuck on Confucius. "And why would anyone ever take advice from someone with a name like Confucius? Sounds like he was bipolar or something."

"I don't think they had bipolar in ancient China," June said, discarding a two bam.

"Oh, they probably had it; they just didn't have a name for it. And that foot binding? Did you ever see pictures? How painful that must have been. Wish someone would invent something for butt binding." Clara laughed.

"Clara! "June said.

"Okay, hip binding. Think about it. What if someone had swaddled, bound us—whatever you want to call it—as infants and our hips didn't expand?"

Angelina laughed, "Clara, not that you should worry. In my next life, I'm wish to have long thin legs like you. You have a fine figure."

Clara shrugged off the compliment. "Well, how about some chin binding for turkey neck skin that hangs down. I could do without this." Clara pulled on the skin under her chin and made a horrid face.

"Did you read that book by Nora Ephron, *I Feel Bad About My Neck*"? Angelina asked.

"Didn't read it, but I could have written it," Clara said.

"Speaking of old men," June said.

"Were we speaking of old men?" Angelina asked.

"The foot-binding thing. You know it was a man's idea. And I personally think it must have been some old men passing the opium pipe when they invented this game. Some of the rules don't make sense." Clara shakes her head.

"I could use some opium after some sessions. My brain gets fried," June said. "Like the one bam-bird. Why does it look so different than the other bams?"

"It's about confusion. That's what it's about. See? That brings us back to Confucius. I'm sure he invented this game," Clara adds.

"The bird represents a sparrow or sometimes the lucky crane," Angelina said.

"How do you know that?" Clara asks.

"I don't know. I read it somewhere. Or maybe on that trip to China. The word Mah Jongg in Chinese means sparrow," Angelina said. "Something about the shuffling of the tiles. The sounds they make are like sparrows chirping."

Myra normally enjoyed the sound of the tiles clicking, but today the chirping sparrows were saying, "why, why, why?" She remembered the last fortune cookie and its message. Her daughter, Debbie, had teased her about it, saying perhaps a handsome gentleman at the retirement center had designs on her. *An unexpected relationship will become permanent.*

Myra shuddered.

Chapter Forty-Seven
Prior

Rhonda devoted every spare moment in the following days to researching the cost of opening a salon. There were franchises she could buy into, or she could do her own unique one-of-a-kind. The more she explored the possibilities, the more excited she became. Some apprehension surfaced, but each time the familiar anger that she would never be good enough for Myra's family fueled her ambitious drive.

She spoke to a small business banker, Brenda, who told her how much money she would need up front and other requirements. At first it was overwhelming. Not only the cost but all that went into a sound business plan. Projections. Short term, long term.

It would take some time to draw up a plan for the bank but not a plan for Myra. She didn't want to delay her request. The time was right to take advantage of Myra's guilty emotions. When she finally came up with a dollar figure that could get her started, she doubled it for good measure. Inflation. Who knew what could happen while she was in the planning stage? Better to ask for more than she needed. What seemed monumental to her was probably chump change to Myra.

Money was better than family, Rhonda told herself. You couldn't take hugs and kisses to the bank.

Chapter Forty-Eight
Present

Guy phones Angelina. "*Ciao, signora.*"

"*Dobre utro,*" she answers. "That's good morning in Bulgarian as you probably surmised."

"Yes, I'm a real quick study," he says. "I was thinking instead of lunch, how about if you come to my place one night and I'll make some pasta. Those wonderful stuffed peppers call for a return meal. Now I'm not saying the pasta will be wonderful, but …"

"Oh my, someone else cooking for me is wonderful enough. It doesn't even have to be good." Then she adds quickly, "But I'm sure it will be."

Guy laughs. "Good recovery. How about Wednesday? Say about six?"

"Wednesday is good."

"Okay. See you then. *Arrivederci.*"

"*Dovizdane.*"

Angelina hangs up and feels a warm glow flushing through her. He's charming, quite charming.

A thought occurs to her. She begins a text message to Guy. "One minor detail. I don't know where you live."

His response is quick. "Would you like me to pick you up?"

"Thanks. But I'd like to drive myself."

"1705 E. Hummingbird Lane."

"That's pretty."

"So are you."

She feels giddy and wants to keep texting but decides that's a good note to end on. She does a Mapquest from her house to his. Twelve miles.

Guy opens the door with an oversized white dish towel tucked into his belt as an apron. The fragrant aroma of spaghetti sauce and garlic and Andre Bocelli's familiar tenor fill the room.

"Oh my, a true Italian bistro," she says and starts to giggle in spite of herself.

"What? Is it too much?"

"No, no, it's wonderful. And I don't know why I'm laughing when you answer the door with a butcher knife," Angelina gestures toward his hand.

"No, signora, this is bread knife. Bigga difference."

He leads her to the kitchen where Angelina surveys much activity. The sauce is simmering in a large saucepan on the stove and oregano and basil scents mingle with the garlic. On another burner is a large kettle of water. A bottle of bubbly Lambrusco is open on the kitchen counter.

He hands her a glass. "Join the cook in a taste of wine? It wouldn't pass the wine snob test, but it goes well with pasta."

"I would never question an Italian on his choice of pasta wine."

"Yes, it's an offer you should never refuse," he says in a halfway decent Godfather imitation. "Would you like a mini-tour?"

"Absolutely."

He shows her the formal dining room. "But we'll eat in the kitchen. It's more intimate. Like family. The dining room table is way too big for the two of us."

In the living room, she notices the framed photograph on an end table.

"Your daughter? She's lovely."

"Thank you. She looks like her mother, thank goodness."

"Do you have some photos of Monica?"

Guy walks to the fireplace and takes one off the mantle. It's the two of them with shimmery blue water and sailboats in the distance. “Taken on our last trip to Rocky Point. She loved the beach. Pristine. Quiet. We drove there often before it became so popular. And crossing the Mexican border was safer than today.”

“Unless you want to play cops and robbers,” Angelina says. “I’m sure you have enough of that at your day job and don’t need it on vacation.”

“Yes. But there’s no thrill like finding the vital clue, the missing piece—the one that ties it all together.”

“I would agree,” Angelina says with a sparkle to her eye as if he’d suggested a romantic moonlight walk on the beach.

They circle back to the kitchen. Next to the Lambrusco is a loaf of Italian bread.

He places several cut pieces sets the basket on the table. From the refrigerator he pulls out two salad bowls full of crisp greens.

“Don’t look in my fridge,” he says.

“Why not? Do you have some science projects brewing there like most bachelors?”

“Evidently. Every time my daughter visits, she throws away all the expired salad dressings. I call her the Salad Nazi. Shall we have our salads while the pasta cooks?”

“You’ve been doing some serious chopping,” she says as she looks at the garnish of green onions and black olives on top of the salads.

Guy pulls out a chair for her at the small kitchen table, covered with a red-and-white checkered tablecloth. The music is now Mario Lanza’s, “When You Are in Love, It’s the Loveliest Night of the Year.”

“I love the ambiance. Feels like I’m in Italy.”

“Well, maybe that’s a stretch.”

All of a sudden, water splatters on the stove top. The pot is boiling over.

Guy jumps up, “*Mama Mia. Mi puo aiutare*!” He grabs two pot holders and moves the boiling pot to a cold burner.

Angelina laughs. “See, we weren’t watching it. Had we been, it would have never boiled.”

Guy sprinkles some olive oil and salt in the water and slides it back on the hot burner, now turned down a few notches. He takes a handful of spaghetti and throws it in. “Well, I’m going to watch it now," he says as he stands beside it. He sets the timer for nine minutes. "*Al dente*, right?"

"What did you say when the pot boiled over? Was that one of those words you said you couldn't use in front of a lady?"

"Oh, no, that was a desperate cry for help. *Mi puo aiutare.* Help me please."

"I'll have to remember that if I run into any of your Mafia relatives."

"Seriously, Angelina, do you have ICE on speed dial on your iPhone? In your contact list?"

Angelina looks at Guy who has become very serious. "No, I don't. I guess one reason is because I don't know what ICE is."

"You should. Everyone should. Let's do it now so you don't forget. ICE is a list of In Case of Emergency contacts. Most police, medical personnel and ETMs are trained to look for ICE on a person's cell phone these days. It lists numbers to call in case of an emergency. Your family, of course, and please add my number there too."

Angelina feels a warmth spreading through her that she knows is not the wine but his protective words and concern.

"And of course, you should have 911 on speed dial. You never know."

"Do it right now? In the middle of Lambrusco and pasta sauce?"

"Please do it for me?" He gazes at her with sincere pleading in his eyes, and she realizes again that he cares for her. It touches her in a way she hasn't experienced in years.

She pulls her iPhone from her purse and enters 911 under favorites and adds ICE as a new contact with her daughter's name, son's name and Guy's name. "Done."

"Thank you." He raises his wine glass to her and she follows suit. When they clink, he says, "*Alla vostra salute.* To your good health."

She responds with "*Nostrove.* To yours."

"Now back to our salads." They sit again. A few minutes later when the timer dings, he drains the pasta, then returns to the table.

"I told you how Monica and I met. Tell me about you and Peter."

Myra touches her napkin to her lips and blots. "As I said, he was quite a bit older than I was. The funny thing is my immigrant parents were still old-world. They wanted to arrange my wedding as theirs had been."

"I hope you were going to get more than the ten minutes in the room." Guy says as he butters a slice of bread.

"When I was a senior in high school, a wave of immigrants from Bulgaria came to our hometown. Most of the men were older than me, probably early twenties. I ran as fast as I could from the whole notion. They seemed not only ancient but like dirty old men, although they never did anything to warrant that. I wanted nothing to do with them. Ironically, five years after graduation, I married someone much older than any of them might have been."

"So how did you meet this older, or should I say, mature man?"

"I married my boss."

"Oh, that's one way to get a raise, or was it a promotion you wanted?" Guy teases.

"I was a legal secretary to three lawyers in a small firm. They were all married, but Peter's wife died in a car accident about four years before I met him. He was so kind and seemed so lonely. One night I worked late preparing a brief for court the next morning, and he took me to dinner afterwards as a thank you. I never suspected that he had any feelings for me, and I'm not sure he realized it either until that dinner. I don't think it was something he plotted. He was such a gentleman." Angelina sips her wine.

"When did you know you loved him?"

"Somehow sitting across from him at a nice candlelit table, I saw him as a man rather than an employer. The next day when he returned from the courtroom, I felt shy and embarrassed and he behaved differently too. I think we both knew our relationship had changed the night before. A year later we were married. Even though it was his second marriage, he humored my parents and agreed to the big wedding my mother always wanted for me."

"Did you want the big wedding?"

"Of course. Doesn't every girl? Did you see the movie, *My Big Fat Greek Wedding*?"

"I did. Don't tell me."

"Uh huh. Exactly. But you know, there's nothing like tradition."

"Say, I have the sound track for *Fiddler on the Roof.* Want to hear it?"

"I'm enjoying Italy right now, but thanks. Maybe next time."

Guy clears the salad plates but encourages her to stay seated. From the kitchen he brings in a large serving bowl of pasta covered with sauce and returns to the kitchen for a gravy boat of additional sauce.

"Please, help yourself," he encourages her, handing her a claw utensil. "Be sure to get some meatballs. Not bragging, but they are my specialty."

"Oh, you have a signature piece?"

"You tell me," he answers as he raises his wine glass. "*Bon appétit.*"

Angelina takes one bite of the meatball. "Yes, definitely. So moist and tender. How do you do that?"

"Add soft white bread crumbs that have been soaked in milk. Another teaspoon of milk in the mix, and don't handle the meat a lot."

"Ah, sharing your valuable secrets."

"It's fun to cook for someone again. Hardly worth it for one person,"

"Tell me about it," she adds. "I miss it too."

"What else do you miss the most about bring married?" Guy asks.

Angelina is taken aback for a minute. "I don't think anyone has ever asked me that. I guess one thing is the realization…and I heard this from Myra. It's the realization that you are no longer the most important person in another person's life."

"Wow, I never thought of it that way, but it's true. It's that person who cares about every little detail of your day, whether it's the traffic jam you were in or what you had for lunch."

Angelina nods in agreement. Then she smiles. "Before we get too maudlin in our memories, here's something about Peter I really miss. He was the one who cleaned the litter box."

Guy laughs and says, "And I've become an expert on laundry."

He raises his glass and proposes a toast, "To learning new skills."

They clink their glasses and smile at each other.

As they finish their meal, Angelina says, "Let me help you clean up." She rises to carry her dish to the sink.

"Oh, no, *la mia donna bella*. You are my guest."

"*Donna bella* means your guest?"

"No, it means beautiful lady. You are both beautiful and my guest."

"The wine is going to your head."

"Speaking of winos," Guy says as Dean Martin begins singing, "When the moon hits your eye like a big pizza pie, that's amore."

Guy throws the dishtowel over the back of the chair, takes Angelina in his arms and twirls her out of the kitchen into the living room. He holds her closely and they dance. He's light on his feet and Angelina feels younger than she has in years.

When the song ends, he brings her hand to his lips for a gentle kiss, then releases her while he walks to the kitchen. "Please sit. I have one final course."

He returns with a pink box. "I knew you'd never believe I could bake anything, so I won't try to pass this off as homemade. I'll get a couple of plates if you'll open this box from my favorite bakery."

When Angelina unties the white string, she sees two perfect cannoli side by side.

"Beautiful," she says. "I mean *bella*. No, I mean *krasiv*."

"Beautiful?" He asks.

"Handsome, actually," Angelina replies. "Beautiful is *Ubova*. So would a cannoli be masculine or feminine?"

Guy looks at the cannoli as if he can determine gender. "Hmm, a beautiful dessert. It works for me. *Ubova*."

Angelina takes a bite and the delicious crème filling melts in her mouth. A fit ending to a perfect meal.

Angelina glances at her watch. "Oh my, it's late. The time passed so quickly."

"You know what they say about when time flies."

"I'll admit it. I was having fun. Am still having fun. But I should go."

After they clear the table one more time and he refuses her help in the kitchen, he walks her to the door.

"I wish you had let me pick you up. I could still drive you home."

"I'm fine. I like driving, and now I know how to get here. When I'm a passenger, I don't pay attention to the way."

"Will you call or text me when you get home?"

"Of course."

He wraps his arms around her and holds her close to him. The scent of his aftershave is something woodsy. He nuzzles his head into her neck for a second. Is it her imagination or is this hug a bit longer than last time? They're getting closer to the center of the artichoke.

Chapter Forty-Nine

Prior

Myra went to the salon at five o'clock as usual. She sat in a waiting chair as Rhonda finished a cut for Kathy Sulser and swiveled her chair around.

"Do you like it?" she asked.

"I love it! You're so good. I want my friend to come here and see what you can do with her hair. Don't say I said it, but it looks awful most of the time."

She walked to her purse. "Can you work on people who don't live here?"

"I don't know. No one has ever asked. I'm sure if she's your guest, it would be fine. And what you said will be our little secret." Rhonda patted her shoulder.

"Well, I heard," Kathy whispered, "Since you've come here, most of the ladies want their hair done on Mondays. You're so much better than our regular beautician."

"Oh, come on now," Rhonda said. "That's not true." Although she suspected it was. She tried to create younger looking styles for the ladies rather than the ones they came in with. Happy people, big tips, happy Rhonda.

When Kathy left, Rhonda said, "Myra, let's get you started." She motioned for her to go to the shampoo chair.

Because it seemed that it would be business as usual, Myra complied.

"Looks like you're having a busy day," Myra said.

"Yes, and I like it that way. I hate to sit around. Time drags. I always bring something to do, like homework for my next class.

But the last couple of Mondays, I've hardly had a chance to crack a book."

"What are you studying?"

"My current class is New Color Techniques."

"Well, as your former client said, the word is out that you are good. You should have your own shop." Myra settled into the styling chair after her shampoo.

Rhonda couldn't believe it. Myra was making this so easy.

"I've thought about it quite a bit. In fact, I've spent this whole week researching exactly what it might cost."

Myra was about to comment when two little girls rushed in.

"Surprise!" they squealed.

With them was the daughter Rhonda had followed to the grocery store. Debbie. With the super white teeth. Of course, the dentist's wife.

The white teeth spoke. "Hope you don't mind us popping in like this. We were shopping at The Borgatta, and when I told the girls that you were around the corner, they insisted on seeing you."

"Well, that's so sweet of you," Myra said.

"So, this is the reason your hair looks so nice. My mother has bragged about you for weeks."

"Debbie, where are my manners? This is Rhonda, our new hairstylist. Rhonda, my daughter Debbie and granddaughters, Ashley and Brittany."

Rhonda smiled at them. "I guessed as much." To the two little girls, she said "Aren't you lucky to have such a nice grandma?" Her stomach was churning at the words. Acid reflux was streaming up through her throat.

They smiled and stood beside Myra's chair as if expecting to be invited up on her lap.

"Girls, we can't stay. Grandma is busy getting her hair all pretty. We'll come back another day. You can show Grandma your paintings and then we'll go."

Debbie pulled two sheets of paper from a large purse she was carrying and the girls each took one and held them up like chauffeurs do to greet arrivals at an airport.

"Those are lovely," Myra said.

"You can tape them on your refrigerator if you want to," the taller girl said.

"Well, of course I want to. They will brighten my whole kitchen."

The girls rushed toward Myra and placed their works of art across the blue cape spread on her lap.

Their mother laughed. "Girls, just set them down here on this table. Grandma will take them upstairs when she's done. Nice to meet you, Rhonda."

"Same here," Rhonda replied as she continued combing Myra's hair.

When they left, neither of them spoke for a few minutes. Then Rhonda said, "You have a lovely daughter." It had given Rhonda a start to make eye contact with Debbie. For a minute, she saw a glimmer of her own mother in Debbie's face. Something about the eyes. Yes, the shape of the eyes. More almond than round.

Myra answered, "Thank you. I'm sorry . . . sorry you had to . . ."

Rhonda cut her off. "Sorry? Oh, please. No need to apologize. Those are your grandchildren."

"But, but . . ." Myra stammered. "But you are too," she said.

Myra's words surprised her. Was Myra relenting? Reconsidering? Was she ready to claim her publicly as her granddaughter? No, probably a weak moment. *Best not to get my hopes up. Proceed with my financial plan. No emotion. Just business. Just money.*

"Myra, can we talk privately for a few minutes when we're done here? Perhaps upstairs again?"

"Of course."

They didn't speak as Rhonda finished the comb-out other than Myra saying, "Lovely," as usual when she was done. Then she handed Rhonda her payment and a tip. Rhonda didn't refuse it this time. She thanked her and slipped the money in her smock pocket.

"Why don't you go ahead and give me a minute to close the salon. You're my last appointment today."

When she reached Myra's apartment, Rhonda didn't waste a minute on small talk. She started in as soon as she entered. "I've been thinking. It's unfair of me to expect you to embrace me and welcome me into your life after all these years. I do understand that."

"You do?" Myra asked.

"Yes, with Janet and all. And from the little I know of you, it's probably causing you a lot of concern and conflict. You're torn with what's the right thing to do, and you don't seem like a person who would neglect or hurt her family in any way. And now here I am springing a new family on you out of the blue."

"I'm not one to hurt anyone, Rhonda, let alone my family. You are so perceptive. And mature. That's what has been troubling me so much."

Rhonda continued. "I know I left here angry last time we talked and said I was entitled to some things. Maybe that was a big assumption on my part, but I was thinking that if there were a way you could help me without hurting Janet, you might feel better."

Myra sighed. "Yes, I think I would. I'd love to help you."

"I've been doing the research on the cost of opening a salon. My own, as you suggested. It's been a dream of mine but seemed so far in the future, so unobtainable on my salary. You know it takes a long time to save that kind of money, although I'm a good saver. I've been saving since high school."

"Are you suggesting, or should I say, are you asking for some financial help from me?"

Rhonda acted embarrassed by the thought of it. "Well, I was wondering." Then she stopped as if it were too hard to go on, when in fact she knew exactly what she needed to say and had no qualms about asking.

"Yes, go on," Myra encouraged her.

"Well, I was thinking you could perhaps help me get started."

"I'd love to," Myra said. "What does it cost to start a salon?"

"It's quite a bit. I'm sure it's too much."

"Just tell me."

When Rhonda gave her the figure, Myra gasped. "Five hundred thousand?" It was more a question than a statement.

Rhonda brought her hands over her eyes with dramatic flair. "I'm sorry. I knew that was too much to ask."

"You're asking me for the total amount?" Myra's expression was one of disbelief.

"No, no, I was saying that's what a good start-up is. I've done all the research. I can show you the figures. I thought that since you want to protect Janet, you couldn't really claim me, even if you wanted to. I know in your heart you want to. I thought it would make you feel better if you could help me this way."

"The problem is that most of my wealth is tied up in investments—stocks and bonds. I don't have that kind of cash lying around. I mean, how would I even explain to my financial advisor that I need to liquidate such a large amount of cash? Not to mention that with this awful economy now, my portfolio has taken a serious dip."

Rhonda hadn't considered that hurdle. She assumed someone as comfortable as Myra could come up with cash whenever necessary. Just open that fancy Queen Anne desk and write a check. She felt a flash of anger at herself for not considering this and now being stymied for words.

"Well, I'm sure I wouldn't need all the money up front. Maybe just some to get started. And then as it progressed, perhaps a little more?"

"I see," said Myra. The stricken look on Myra's face caused Rhonda concern.

"Myra, are you all right?"

"Yes, yes, I'm fine. I'm thinking of how I could get some ready cash to get you started on your project."

Rhonda smiled in relief. "Oh, thank you. You know, I was thinking, for your kindness, I would name the salon after you. Myra's Mystique. What do you think of that?"

Myra wasn't a designer name that ladies would flock to, but she thought she could say that until it was time to open. By then she would have all the funds she needed. If she decided to change it, so what? What could Myra do at that point? The beauty of all this was that Myra couldn't complain to anyone without endangering her precious Janet.

Rhonda continued, "I'll start a bank account strictly for the business, so you can be assured I won't be using it for anything personal. We could be partners. Business partners. How does that sound?"

"That seems like a good idea ...," Myra started to say when Rhonda interrupted.

"I could set it up with the first deposit." Rhonda had hoped the first deposit would be the total amount, but she could open an account with whatever amount Myra gave her. "I've learned that it should be a limited partnership. That would be best for tax purposes. And as it builds, I could use that as collateral for bank funding if I need it. You'd be helping me so much by giving me a wonderful start."

Brenda, the small business banker Rhonda spoke to, told her she needed twenty percent down to be considered for a business loan, but she didn't mention that to Myra for fear that would be all she might spring for.

"Well, you certainly have done your homework, Rhonda."

Myra went to the Queen Anne desk as if she were walking to the gallows and removed her checkbook. She returned to the kitchen counter and started to write a check for fifty thousand dollars. She wrote the date on the check and the amount and then she stopped. She wrote VOID across the face of the check. "How about if I go to the bank tomorrow and get you the cash? I think that would be better. We could meet there about noon. Perhaps on your lunch hour?"

Before Rhonda could respond, Myra gave her the location and said, "I wish only the very best for you. I hope you know that."

"I do, I do. Thank you so much, grandmother."

"That would be fine," Myra said and closed the checkbook.

Rhonda almost ran out the door, giddy with excitement, not believing her good fortune. How easy it had been. Not the amount she expected, but she knew she could get more. Myra was fearful, and she planned to play on that fear. To the hilt. If she didn't want to claim her, it was going to cost her. It was Myra's decision, after all. Rhonda was playing by her rules. The bitch. Then she laughed to herself. Not just a bitch, but a rich bitch.

She thought of her mother, silently thanking her for keeping the adoption papers and wondered again why she herself hadn't searched for Myra. It didn't matter now. Perhaps this was the best way after all. If it wasn't possible to have both the big family and financial help from Myra, she'd settle for the money.

Chapter Fifty

Prior

When Rhonda left, Myra fell into a deep despair. She had become exactly like the man she despised for so many years—Mark's father. Rhonda's great-grandfather. She returned the checkbook to her desk and when she closed the drawer, she glanced at the row of books on the first shelf. Walter Scott's poetry spoke to her. "Oh, what a tangled web we weave when first we practice to deceive."

Myra pondered what Rhonda was really saying. That if she couldn't claim her, she could relieve her guilt by giving her money? *What if I don't give her the cash? Would she go public with my secret? Maybe I should do it myself. Stop this outrageous blackmail.*

For a moment Myra pictured herself in the dining room at Friendship Acres, hitting her water glass with a spoon the way people did when they wanted to make an important announcement. "Hello, everyone. Today is Susan's Miller's birthday. Let's all sing 'Happy Birthday' to Susan." She could see it. "Hello, everyone. I'd like you to meet my granddaughter, Rhonda. She's the daughter of the baby I gave up for adoption forty-three years ago. The baby born nine months after Mark and I made wild passionate love in the toolshed in my back yard. The daughter of the baby my parents promised never to speak of in exchange for money."

Myra's mind raced. If she refused, what would Rhonda do? One never knew. But half a million? Preposterous. Even crazier was she couldn't even remember Rhonda's last name when she began to write the check.

She wanted to help this young girl who seemed resilient yet fragile. Sincere yet frightening. In some ways she appeared to be a floozy with her feathery blond hairdo, her multiple pierced earrings, the skull tattoo on her wrist and who knew where else. But possibly, she had more substance, more depth than Myra gave her credit for, wanting her own salon.

Rhonda was a paradox, but Myra wasn't taking chances, though it was obvious from the information she had about the adoption and the photo album that she wasn't a fraud. She was her granddaughter.

If a player wins Mah Jongg because of a tile discarded by another player, the player who discarded the tile pays double the worth of the hand.

Chapter Fifty-One

Present

Wanting to please Angelina, Guy asks her to set up a meeting with June and Clara. "Perhaps they have information about Myra we've overlooked. I might as well be thorough."

"They'll be thrilled," Angelina says. "They want very much to add their two cents and…and I guess feel important."

"Don't we all?" he says.

The following day they gather around Angelina's kitchen table. After introductions, June says, "I thought of another name we need to add to the suspect list."

"And just who would that be?" Clara asks.

"Gayle," June says in a matter-of-fact tone.

"Gayle who?" Clara asks.

Guy simply observes the one-upmanship conversation taking place between Clara and June, while Angelina's eyes dart from one friend to the other, her speckled notebook open and pen poised.

"Gayle Crews, the widow, who has designs on George," June says as if everyone should know it.

Angelina speaks up. "She does?"

"It's common knowledge. And everyone knows George was quite taken with Myra," June says confidently.

"Really?" Clara asks. "And you know this because . . .?"

"Myra wanted some extra apartment keys made for her daughters, and when she spoke to George about it, he brought them to her the very next day."

"Was that unusual?" Angelina asks.

"Gayle thought so. She was at the lunch table when he gave them to Myra, and Gayle said something about it taking her almost a week to get a new key. She also spouted something about some people getting special attention," June said.

Clara rolls her eyes. "And that makes Gayle a suspect? She's going to kill someone over a key?"

"No, not over the key, Clara. Over George. If you could have seen Gayle's face when George came around, you wouldn't be questioning me," June folds her arms across her chest.

"Were you there?" Clara asks.

"Yes, I happened to be there that day. I was in the gift shop buying one of those lovely handmade aprons and I stopped by their lunch table. I saw it all with my own two eyes."

"Who were you buying the apron for?" Clara wants to know.

June scowls at Clara. "That has nothing to do with this story, but if you must know, it's for my neighbor. Doesn't cook a lick but loves aprons. Has some real old ones like our mothers wore. When I went to Savannah, I bought her a Paula Deen apron. It said, 'Put some south in your mouth.'"

Clara replies, "What she means is put some butter in your mouth."

At this, Guy bursts out laughing, and both ladies look at him as if they've forgotten he's there.

Angelina pacifies June. "I'll add her name to the list. We don't want to rule out anyone."

June says, "Yes, A bird in hand is worth a thousand words."

Angelina glances at Guy who is stifling a smile.

He says, "June, that is very helpful information. If your observation is correct, and I'm sure it is, I'll speak to George again. Now that some time has passed, perhaps he'll remember something he forgot to tell us about the night he found Myra. If he had feelings for Myra, his observations may have been affected. Thank you."

Clara, not to be outdone, says, "Detective, I feel strongly that the son-in-law, Randy, was in desperate need of funds. Doesn't he stand to inherit quite a bit due to Myra's death?"

"I'm sorry, I'm not at liberty to discuss that, but I'll make a note of your observation."

Guy pulls out his tattered notebook and says, “Is there anything else you can tell me about Myra that might be helpful?”

“She was a lovely lady,” June says. “I can’t imagine anyone wanting to hurt her. I say, ‘take sleeping dogs with a grain of salt.’”

“Lie, June. Let sleeping dogs lie,” Clara says as she rolls her eyes.

Guy closes his notebook. “Thank you, ladies. Your observations are very helpful. I’ll leave you to your evening.”

Angelina walks him to the door. They smile as they shake hands. Angelina whispers, “Thank you.”

“We might as well play a few games of Mah Jongg since we’re together. What do you say?” June asks.

“Let’s play with Myra’s set. The one Janet brought over. That would be a nice tribute to her,” Angelina suggests.

They set the racks on the card table, spill the tiles out and begin the “washing” of them, mixing them around and around. They each start building their double walls of nineteen tiles. Everyone is done but June, and they discover that she is short two tiles.

“That’s strange,” Angelina says. “Let’s count again.” They count their rows and verify that there are three racks with thirty-eight tiles and one rack with only thirty-six. Angelina checks the case again to see if any of them were left there. Nothing.

“I wonder which ones are missing,” Clara says.

“Let’s not take the time now. I’ll check it out later. Let me get my set.” Angelina walks to her wall unit shelf. “ I’ll ask Janet if any tiles fell out of the case in her car.”

June says, “No use crying over spilled tiles.”

Chapter Fifty-Two
Prior

The following day, Myra and Rhonda met at the bank. Myra withdrew fifty thousand dollars and gave Rhonda a cashier's check in that amount.

"I'm taking this right to my bank to start our business account. I'm so excited. I now have a personal banker, Brenda."

Myra took some comfort in the fact that if she could help Rhonda financially, it relieved her guilt for not claiming her publicly.

"Brenda told me," Rhonda said, "if I had at least twenty per cent, or one hundred thousand dollars, in my savings as collateral, that would qualify me to get a small business loan. That's assuming my credit is good. She wanted to know where I was getting the fifty thousand, and I said was it was from a relative. I wanted to keep it confidential."

Myra felt the knot in her stomach returning but tried to console herself that Rhonda wasn't going to betray her confidence.

Rhonda accompanied Myra to her car. "Grandmother, thank you so much for these funds that will allow me to open an account." Then in the meekest voice she could muster, she asked a brazen question. "Do you know when I might be able to get the other fifty thousand dollars? To get the business loan. I won't ask for any more. I promise."

Myra clenched the car door handle for support. "I'll see what I can do. Give me some time."

As Rhonda drove away, Myra sat behind her wheel, too shaken to drive. Instead, she went into the coffee shop next to the bank and ordered a coffee to settle her nerves and regain her composure.

That night the sweats and dreams returned to Myra. Her nightmare was not of her parents this time, but of her children. All three of her beautiful daughters were looking at a photo of Dottie, the photo Rhonda had shown her of her mother holding her as a baby. But the woman in her dream didn't resemble the person in the photo. She had two heads, both with hair done up in big pink rollers. Myra's three daughters were screaming, "This can't be our sister; she has two heads. Mother, how could you?"

The next day Myra, feeling like a robot programmed by someone sinister and unknown to her, called her financial planner, hoping the final payment would put an end to her night sweats.

Chapter Fifty-Three

Present

Guy looks at the notes in his Steno. Myra's body discovered by George, maintenance man at Friendship Acres. He recalls George appearing to be in shock over his discovery. Guy also knows that with the passage of time, details often are remembered that might have been overlooked due to the shock. He decides to talk to George one more time. Make sure he isn't missing anything. Did George have feelings for Myra? According to the Mah Jongg Mavens, he did, if their gossip could be believed. Guy returns to Friendship Acres.

"I'm sorry to bother you again," he says when George joins him at the front desk.

"No problem. Just doing your job, I'm sure. We all gotta do our job. Mine is to keep this place running. Sometimes I have to impose on the residents, so I understand. Let's go in my office, small as it is."

George is willing to talk and seems glad to do it. Maybe there's something to the romance rumor. People like to talk about loved ones—even if they're gone. Maybe because they're gone.

"Coffee?" George asks, pointing to the Mr. Coffee. Wanting to be polite, Guy agrees and then regrets it after his first bitter sip. He wonders how long that pot has been sitting on the burner.

They review the details of the fateful evening. On the chance that George did have feelings for Myra, Guy tries to be more sensitive, as if he were talking to a family member and not the maintenance man who had the misfortune of finding a dead body.

George's extreme sadness makes Guy think Angelina's friends may have been right about his feelings for Myra. It's obvious he was quite distraught over finding her lying unresponsive in the shower. A ghastly way to say goodbye to someone he wanted very much alive.

George's story doesn't vary or shed any new light. He accompanies Guy to the parking lot, as if he doesn't want to stop talking about Myra. George's pager beeps so Guy waits until he answers it to say a proper thank you and goodbye.

When George finishes his call, Guy says, "They keep you plenty busy here. This looks like a fairly new facility, but I guess even new places have glitches and kinks to work out."

"That's for sure. And for some reason, people think maintenance covers a lot more than the building. Half the time, I help with things that have nothing to do with the building. But you know, I don't mind. There are lots of nice people here." Then he adds in a sad tone. "But one less than there was a few weeks ago."

Guy is about to offer condolences again when George goes on, "Most people are so kind and appreciate any little thing you do. Maybe it's because they don't have money worries. Evidently they don't, or they wouldn't be living here. Not like some people who get crabby in their old age. I told my wife, God rest her soul, if I ever get that way, just shoot me."

Guy laughs at George's Will Rogers' homespun manner. "My dad always said if kids and old people like you, you know you're okay 'cause they don't pretend to if they don't. And they're pretty good judges of character, aren't they?"

"Your dad was right there," George says.

Guy asks, "Do most of the residents have their own cars here?"

"Many do but still take advantage of our courtesy van." He points to a late model Lincoln. "Many of these cars have very low mileage. When they're sold, the dealer can honestly say, 'Only driven by a little old lady on Sundays.'

They stop at Guy's car, a sensible, dark blue sedan as Guy pulls out his keys.

George asks, "Does the department furnish your car or is this yours?"

"This one looks like a company issue, but it's mine. I like driving my own car."

"It's in good shape. What year?"

"2008. A far cry from my first car, but I don't love this one as much as I did that beauty. A '76 Dodge Dart. I delivered a lot of pizzas that summer to pay for that one. Your first car is always special, isn't it?"

"That's funny. One of our employees drives a Dodge Dart," George says. "Or did work here. Someone said she left. I'm not sure."

Guy reacts quickly. "Someone here? A Dodge Dart?" On a hunch, he had checked on Friendship's parking lot several times after the funeral but never saw one. He thought that lead was a dead end. The search he ran for Dodge Darts registered in the Phoenix area earlier was also fruitless. That didn't surprise him as most cars over thirty years old were not plentiful. He wished he'd caught the license plate of the car exiting the cemetery gate.

George says, "Rhonda, the young girl who worked in the beauty shop. I helped her with a jump start one time. She said it was a faulty starter, but she had battery problems too. Carried her own jumper cables even. But a pretty girl like her would never have any trouble getting help."

Guy shook George's hand. "Thanks George, you've been very helpful. Very."

"If you need anything else, I'm here 24/7. Have my own apartment in Building A. They treat me well here."

"Good," Guy says. "Glad to hear it."

Guy opens his Steno and jots *Find Rhonda.* He sits there a minute and then walks back into Friendship Acres.

The receptionist leads him into Kathleen's office and offers him a seat. "She'll be back in a minute. She had to check out a complaint from one of our residents about our menu. Someone thinks we need to offer more gluten-free choices. Last week it was the vegans."

Guy is always amazed at how much information people offer without being asked.

When Kathleen returns, Guy introduces himself again since it's been a while since their first meeting. He asks about Rhonda's schedule and contact information.

"Well, that will be easy. I haven't even filed the folder away from the last request a few days ago, or was it yesterday? Anyway, it's right here." She thumbs through a stack of folders on the top corner of her desk and pulls one out.

"Oh dear, I'm forgetting about confidentiality. Is there a problem, Detective?"

"We're just trying to tie up loose ends on Myra Anderson's death. I'm told Rhonda did her hair each week and thought Myra might have confided in her."

Kathleen's brow furrowed.

"If you need me to get a warrant, I can."

Kathleen hesitates. "That won't be necessary. It's a simple enough request." She jots two phone numbers and the address of Fuchsia Spa and hands it to Guy

"Thank you. Also, if f you don't mind my asking, who else was looking for Rhonda?"

"One of Myra's Mah Jongg friends. Her name is Angelina. Angelina Popoff."

"Did she happen to say why?"

"No. I assumed she wanted to get her hair done. Rhonda is a great beautician. We miss her a lot. Is there anything else?"

"No, just want to make sure I've covered all the bases. Myra's schedule, things like that. What she did the day she passed."

"Well, I can tell you she didn't have her hair done. That was a standing appointment on Mondays with Rhonda. Now that you mention it, I think I received Rhonda's resignation letter around the time Myra passed."

"Did she give a reason for leaving?"

"Something about too much homework in one of her classes, and she couldn't keep up with it all."

Guy thanks her and makes notes of his conversation with Kathleen in the Steno before he pulls out of the parking lot. Dodge Dart-Rhonda. Why was she at the gravesite? Then one final note. Why is Angelina looking for Rhonda? Hopefully it's about a hairdo. As cute as she is with her speckled notebook, he doesn't want her meddling at this point.

Chapter Fifty-Four

Prior

Rhonda called. "Myra, I'm so excited about my plans for the salon I can't wait to tell you all about it. After all, you are making it possible. Can I come over? Like right now?"

"That would be fine. Would you like a bite to eat? I'm just fixing myself some lunch."

"That is so kind." Rhonda said. "Could we have a glass of wine too? Like our first night?"

"I suppose we could," Myra hung up the phone while muttering, "I hope the girl keeps her promise and doesn't ask for more money."

When Rhonda arrived, Myra handed her a glass of Riesling. "We're having tomato soup and grilled cheese. That's what my girls always loved. How about you?"

"That sounds good," Rhonda said. She relished the fact that someone was taking care of her. But she didn't want to get complacent. Her mission had to be accomplished today. It was important that she get weepy and sentimental, and the wine would help.

Rhonda sipped her wine and began the speech she had rehearsed countless times in her car on the way back and forth to work.

"Grandmother, I do understand why this isn't a good time to introduce me to the family. Even though I haven't met her, I feel like I know Janet, and I have so much sympathy. How awful. Left at the altar." Rhonda gave Myra a look that she hoped conveyed, 'I can't imagine anything worse.'"

Rhonda went on, "I have to let you know, however, that since I've found you, I feel so bad, not so much for myself, but for my mother who never had the things your other daughters had. Her life was hard once she lost her parents."

Rhonda took another sip of wine for liquid courage. "I know you had the best intentions, doing the right thing, to give her to a good family. It probably started out that way from what my mother told me. And you had no way of knowing things would turn bad."

Myra shook her head. "Actually, Rhonda, my daughters won't benefit that greatly from my financial situation. My trust is structured so that most of my inheritance will go to my grandchildren. In Janet's case, she will inherit if there are no grandchildren."

Rhonda couldn't believe what she was hearing. The trust was for her grandchildren? She was a grandchild. "So that would include me?" she asked eagerly without even thinking.

Myra blurted out, "Rhonda, please, you must stop these demands. We had an agreement. I'm not able to do anymore, and the stress of it all . . ." Her voice tapered to a pathetic whisper.

"I understand," Rhonda said. "Really, I do. I'm not asking for more money. I'm keeping my word to you. But maybe you could do one more thing for me, and I promise I won't ask for another thing. I didn't know about the granddaughters' trust, but now it makes even more sense."

"What makes more sense?"

"I was going to ask you . . ." Rhonda paused and looked as sheepish as she could. "Do you think you could include me in your will? I didn't know you had one for the other granddaughters, but I was thinking it would be a way for you to feel good that you were helping me, even if it doesn't make up for the past."

Rhonda was rambling now. "I know it won't help me right now, but it would make me feel so good to know that you acknowledge my existence and consider me part of your family. It would be such a comfort to me, and I promise I won't bother you again. In fact, I'm thinking of leaving the salon downstairs. I want to focus on the new business."

When Myra didn't reply immediately, Rhonda continued, "So basically, I will bow out of your life, unless you contact me. But if you could include me in your will, it would give me such a wonderful feeling of acceptance, and I think you would feel better too, wouldn't you? Knowing that you had provided for all your grandchildren?" Rhonda took a deep breath as if the words she spoke depleted her of air.

Myra looked stunned. "Rhonda, I think that's a possible solution." She turned and walked into the kitchen.

Rhonda had a sinking feeling that Myra was lying. She'd answered too quickly. She would wait and see what happened.

When Myra called her to the counter for her soup and sandwich, Rhonda devoured her food like an Ellis Island immigrant who'd crossed the Atlantic in steerage. When she looked at Myra's dish, she noticed she hadn't taken a bite.

Chapter Fifty-Five

Prior

After a nearly sleepless night with scattered thoughts racing through her mind, Myra finally dozed off for a few hours. When she woke at six the next morning, she had a plan.

She sat at her desk and pulled out a sheet of fine linen stationery. At eight o'clock, she called her financial planner, Spencer Parsons, who was also her husband's longtime friend. She was grateful for his friendship as well as his conservative philosophy. Although her portfolio had lost some value in the economy downtrend, it hadn't spiraled out of control like others she'd heard of.

After they chatted about their families, Myra said. "This may be an unusual request, but I've given it a lot of thought, and there's something I'd like to do with some of my funds."

"Let's hear it," he said.

"A dear friend of mine passed away recently and her cancer medical bills left her almost destitute. Her daughter has no other family members, and I'd like to provide for her in some way while I can. I'd like to give her some cash now to help her get a good start in life. Would it be possible to do this?"

"Myra, are you feeling all right? Is there a medical condition I'm not aware of?"

"No, I'm fine. I just feel the need to help this young lady now."

"You're sure about this? For a friend?"

"A dear friend, Spencer. Someone who was there for me many times when I needed a friend. I'll spare you the details. Girl talk, you know."

"With two daughters of my own, I understand girl talk. I've been outnumbered for years, as was your dear husband. We commiserated often. What amount would you like to give her?"

When Myra told him the amount, she thought she heard a slight gasp on his end of the line.

"$150,000? Are your daughters aware of this, Myra?"

"I'm not saying anything to them right now. No need to. It doesn't hamper anything I want to do for them and the grandchildren. Despite the dip in the economy the last few years, you said last month that my account is doing well. Isn't it?"

"Yes, it is. I would have, of course, let you know if there was a problem."

"This means a lot to me. To pay it forward, so to speak. I'm leaving the girls a letter explaining it all. I'll give it to them at a future date."

"That's a good idea. Do you want to leave the letter with me for safekeeping? I could give it to them in the event anything should happen to you."

"I suppose that would be the wise thing to do. I wrote it this morning and then I thought of a few more things I wanted to say. If it's the last word to my daughters, I want it to be right, and you know how those ideas often come late—usually in the middle of the night."

"Tell me about it. I'm up half the night once the creative juices are flowing. Then I fall asleep when the alarm is set to go off."

Myra sighed. "Glad I'm not the only one. Of course, I have the luxury of no alarms these days. That internal one, however, seems to go off in spite of chances to sleep in. You know, when the girls were little, I would have given anything for a few more hours sleep. Now that I can, I don't."

"Life is sort of backwards, isn't it?" Spencer said.

Myra replied with a sadness in her voice. "Yes, in many ways." Then her somber expression lightened. "I overheard two ladies in the lingerie department of Nordstrom's the other day looking at a flimsy peignoir. One said, 'Isn't this lovely?' The other said, 'Yes, when I was young and thin, I couldn't afford it. Now that I can, I'm too old and too fat.'"

Spencer laughed, but Myra knew that if she were sitting across from him, as old-fashioned as he was, he would have blushed.

"Sorry," she said. "TMI, as my daughters say. More girl talk."

They said their goodbyes, and she hung up the phone with mixed feelings. She was eager to tell Rhonda what she had arranged, hoping it would pacify her. That it would be an end to the requests. After all, she was her flesh and blood. It was the least she could do.

On the other hand, she had a sinking feeling in her gut that she might be making a terrible mistake. That she was setting a precedent and that Rhonda would be a constant threat in her life.

She thought of something she heard last month at the AARP luncheon. "If you knew your days were numbered, would you do things differently?"

"Of course," everyone agreed.

The speaker said, "Well, they are. We just don't know the number."

If she knew the number, would she do anything differently?

Chapter Fifty-Six

Present

Guy reviewed his notes on Myra's financials. Through Global Investigations, he was able to obtain her bank records easily. He examines Myra's transactions prior to her death. A large withdrawal of $50,000 from her checking account. Why did she withdraw that amount? And another $150,000. taken from her trust account according to her financial advisor, Spencer Parsons. No paper trail of what she did with nearly a quarter of a million dollars. Guy is thankful that the confidential agreements between financial advisors and their clients state they could reveal information if requested by the government or in a criminal investigation.

After his meeting with Parsons, he calls each daughter, asking if they received a letter from their mother about giving financial help to a friend's daughter. None of the daughters are aware of such a letter and can't imagine who that friend in need would be.

Guy checks databases for Sophie Mae Joforsky, the name of the baby on the adoption papers. He finds a birth record but no death record. If a donation is made in memory of someone, it usually implies they are deceased. Is Sophie dead or alive? If alive, where is she?

The pieces of the puzzle sit in front of him but they're not fitting. He records the scattered pieces in his Steno.

Chapter Fifty-Seven

Prior

Myra peeked into the salon to speak with Rhonda. A client was sitting in the shampoo chair, so Myra motioned for Rhonda to come to the door.

She spoke softly, "Rhonda, I have some news for you. I think you'll be pleased. I'll tell you about it after my Mah Jongg games. Let's skip my appointment and just come up to my place."

Rhonda returned to the sink with a big smile at her pending good fortune. Things were going better than she expected. Money. No, more like manna from heaven.

When she glanced through the glass window, she saw a family in the lobby hugging and kissing their grandmother goodbye. If money was the answer, why did family gatherings such as the one she witnessed leave her feeling empty and worthless? For a minute, her anger flared up again. She didn't know what Myra was going to show her, but it'd better be good.

When Rhonda entered Myra's, she noticed a manilla folder sitting on the kitchen counter.

"This is what I wanted to show you." Myra opened the folder and handed Rhonda a sheet of paper. "There's no need to read all of it. Boring legalize," Myra said. "You might want to take a glance at the line where the sticky note is."

Rhonda saw a figure of $150,000. "I think you'll have to explain it to me, Myra. I mean grandmother. I'm not exactly up on legal terms."

"When you asked me to include you in my will, I thought it was an excellent idea. But I thought about it. You could better use the money now to get a start in your life. I want to see you opening that salon and being successful, as I know you will be. So, I've decided to find a way to give you the funds you need now, not after I'm gone."

Rhonda couldn't believe her good fortune. "Oh, grandmother. That is so thoughtful and generous."

"You're quite welcome." She paused. "Actually, there are some conditions you'll need to agree to. For now, I would ask that you keep this between us. Everything, that is. Our relationship and the funds. I hope someday that will all change and you can meet your aunts and cousins, but now is not a good time. But I hope it will be possible in the future."

Myra pushed the paper toward Rhonda. "There is a paper you must sign. In exchange for these funds, I am asking that you not make any further demands. Are we clear on that?" Myra asked with eyebrows raised.

Rhonda observed the stern look in Myra's familiar blue eyes. She didn't want to do anything that would cause Myra to change her mind about this large payment. "That seems fair and reasonable to me. I give you my word, but I'll sign the paper too, of course."

"It's a simple form. I typed it myself. I don't think this is anyone's business but ours—yours and mine. My financial planner will be depositing the funds in my account in three days, and at that time, I'll give you a cashier's check for that amount. You can deposit it in your business account."

Myra apparently wanted no paper trail connecting her to Rhonda. "Yes, yes, of course. That all sounds wonderful. I mean good. You can count on me to follow the conditions." Rhonda said.

Myra's hand went to her side as if she had a cramp. "Excuse me for a minute. I have to use the restroom." She hurried down the hallway.

Rhonda looked at the paperwork in the folder. There was a red sticky arrow tag on the bottom of the page and she saw her name typed beneath the line. She walked to Myra's desk to get a pen.

A corner of an envelope stuck out from under the blotter on Myra's desk. Rhonda turned to see if Myra was returning. She slipped the envelope out. It was addressed, *A Letter to My Daughters.* It wasn't sealed. She had to see what was in that letter.

As she opened the one-page letter, she heard the toilet flush and quickly stuffed it back in the envelope and pushed it under the blotter. Before she folded it, however, she thought she saw her name on the sheet. Rhonda Feder. She was sure that was what she saw, but it was so quick. Was Myra telling her daughters about her? What was she saying? Somehow, she had to get back in the room and read this letter.

She quickly stepped away from the desk as Myra returned.

"Where do I sign?"

"Right here," Myra pointed to the red arrow. "I made two copies. Would you like to have one?"

"Oh sure," Rhonda said, not knowing what else to say. The hell with the copy, she thought. I just want the money, but whatever. All the paper said was that she was going to keep her mouth shut and not ask for more money. With two hundred grand in her pocket, she could do that. And if in a few years, she needed more? Well, she'd worry about that later. What she had to worry about now was what Myra was telling her daughters in that letter.

She had to find a way to get a key to Myra's apartment, and she knew the perfect time to visit undisturbed. During Monday Mah Jongg.

But Rhonda didn't want to wait a whole week to find the key to Myra's apartment. She couldn't wait. She had to see that letter as soon as possible. She couldn't risk it being given to the daughters before reading what it said. Why would Myra tell the daughters about me? Wasn't that what she wanted to avoid?

When Rhonda left Myra's apartment, she didn't wait for the elevator but ran down the stairs, hoping Kathleen's office wasn't locked. She was in luck. The light was on and the room was empty. Rhonda was afraid to snoop around, not knowing when Kathleen might return. She made one pass through the dining room, which was starting to fill for early dinner serving. She thought the term "early dinner" was stupid. All the old bags eat early. Why did they even bother to have a later seating? She spotted Kathleen with an older gentleman. She was introducing him to two men seated at a table.

She returned to Kathleen's office and scanned the room. Where would they keep the master keys? She knew they existed.

She'd overheard two of the ladies in the beauty shop talking about whether management should have a key to each unit.

"They have to," one said. "Remember what happened last year? Poor Teri Dye fell and couldn't open the door for anyone. She managed to crawl to the emergency button but couldn't get to the front door."

Rhonda opened drawers, keeping an eye on the lobby with each move. Thank goodness for the large glass windows in Kathleen's office.

Her frustration mounted. Drawer after drawer revealed nothing. Then she saw a small panel in the far corner wall. It had a round keyhole in the top center. That had to be it, but where was the key? Rhonda stepped out and saw that Kathleen was still engaged in a conversation with the men in the dining room.

She opened Kathleen's center desk drawer again. Intermingled with paper clips and staples was a single gold key. It didn't have an identifying tag on it. She took it to the wall panel. *Eureka.* It opened. There on dozens of little hooks were shiny gold keys hanging as orderly as little soldiers. Each one had a tag and they were in numerical order. She went to the 200s and found 223. There it was. She grabbed it and returned the master key to the desk.

She entered the beauty salon using the key Kathleen had given her for late appointments and arranged some of the items on the shelves. In case anyone saw her there late, she could say she was restocking shelves.

After a few minutes, Kathleen and Mr. Prospective Tenant passed by. Rhonda waved and smiled, and they stopped in to show him where he might get a perfect haircut each month.

After the introduction, Rhonda left and peeled out of the parking lot, not sure where to have a key made. A few blocks away, she saw a sign for an Ace Hardware in a strip mall. She ran in and hurried by the checkout clerk holding up her key. "Keys?"

He pointed to the back corner of the store as he continued with his customer.

She ripped through the store, almost knocking over a broom display. Her pulse was racing like the times she used to shoplift. No, even faster. When she reached the key counter, she said under her breath. "Damn!"

An older man was standing there holding up a large ring of keys. *Rotten timing.*

She offered her sweetest smile and said, "You must have a lot of houses. Are you related to Donald Trump or what?"

The old man seemed flattered that this young lady with the big blond hair would strike up a conversation with him. He smiled sheepishly and pointed to his name tag which said, Howard, Maintenance. "Big apartment building," he said.

"Do you have to make *all* those keys?" she asked, staring at the large ring of keys in his hand.

"No, just eight of them." He singled out one key and handed it to the clerk.

Rhonda turned on all the charm she could muster. "I only have one and I'm supposed to have it done right away. My boss is such a meanie. Do you mind if I have one itty bitty key made?"

"You go right ahead, young lady." He didn't add, "You pretty little thing," but he might as well have. It was written all over his face. The old man stepped aside to let her hand her key to the young Ace employee in the red vest.

The young man winked at Rhonda with a knowing smile. She smiled back with one that said, "See, it works every time." She learned early that men like smiles, especially if you looked right into their eyes. Smiles were an easy way to open a door. Or whatever else needed opening.

She knew it was too late to return to Friendship Acres, but she didn't want to keep the office key for a week. She'd think of an excuse to return tomorrow and replace the one she copied. If her luck held out like it did today, no one would be in the office. If she was really lucky, Myra would be in the dining room or somewhere out of her apartment and she wouldn't have to wait until Monday to read the letter. She had a feeling the letter was not a good thing and every day, every minute counted.

Chapter Fifty-Eight

Present

Angelina studies her notes in the speckled notebook. The red ribbon at the cemetery headstone. Someone obviously felt it meant something to Myra. Or to the person who left it there. Or to both. Did this person also know the quote Myra loved? *Those destined are connected with a red string*. If so, who was destined to be with Myra? Obviously, the daughters, but Guy said he spoke to them, and they knew nothing of the ribbon.

Did Myra have a friend Angelina didn't know about? They were good enough friends that Myra would have confided in her. Perhaps a male friend? A boyfriend?

Then she scoffed to herself. People our age don't have boyfriends. They have male friends or acquaintances.

But something about the word boyfriend reminds Angelina of the time Myra recently used that word—boyfriend. Not long ago. Something to do with high school. Yes, the one who gave her the music box. The music box that she accidentally sold in the estate sale. The one she had hoped to keep for her granddaughter. It had sentimental value.

Angelina remembers something else about the music box.

Chapter Fifty-Nine

Prior

Rhonda returned to Friendship Acres the next day on her lunch hour with hopes of replacing the master key before it was discovered missing. What were the chances they would need Myra's key in the coming week? But why take a chance? She saw Kathleen on the way in.

"Rhonda, what are you doing here on your day off?"

"I left my homework for my Coloring Techniques class. Of course, if I don't have it, I can't do it. I can always use the standard, 'the dog ate it,'"

Kathleen chuckled, "But you're too conscientious not to do it. I think I know you by now. See you later. I have a meeting off-site."

Rhonda nodded. *Great.* She waited in the salon until she saw the receptionist head toward the restroom. She hurried into the Kathleen's office, quickly found the panel key in the center drawer and replaced Myra's key. Mission accomplished. She breathed a sigh of relief.

She peered into the dining room on the chance Myra was there. *My lucky day.* Myra sat at a table with two other ladies. *I have some time.*

Rhonda raced up the stairway and ran to 223, hoping to avoid any neighbors. Her heart beat sped up as she inserted the key into the lock. *This is a bigger rush than shoplifting. Any day.*

One more hope was on her wish list. That the letter was still under the blotter. It was. She pulled it out. Still not sealed. Still tied with the red ribbon. She untied it, hands shaking. Took it into her bedroom in case Myra surprised her. The thought of possibly lying under a bed for eight hours was not appealing but better than being caught with the letter in hand.

She opened it and read.

Dearest Daughters,

If you are reading this, it means I have passed. I want you to know how much I love you all. And I want you to know the truth about my life.

When I was seventeen. I gave a baby girl up for adoption. I never made any attempt to find her (your half-sister). Her father, Mark Cook, and I were high school sweethearts, but his family didn't want him to sacrifice his career opportunity at the Air Force Academy. They gave my parents tuition money for my college if we wouldn't acknowledge him as the father. Sadly, my parents agreed to this.

Although this child made no attempt to find me that I was aware of, recently her daughter (that would be your niece) found her mother's adoption papers in her personal effects and tracked them to me. Her mother's adopted name was Dottie Feder. This young lady, Rhonda Feder, is the hairstylist at the retirement center. Debbie, you met her one day when you stopped by.

Rhonda wants very much for me to acknowledge her and be a part of our family, but because her mother served time in jail for drunk driving and died penniless, a welfare recipient on the south side of Phoenix, I didn't wish to bring the skeleton out of the closet. One reason was so I wouldn't ruin your political ambitions, Janet.

As difficult as this is to admit, Rhonda has been blackmailing me. And even more difficult to write is that I have succumbed to her demands to protect the three of you and your families from possible scandal or harassment. I have given her to date quite a bit of money to start her own hair salon. As weird as it might sound, it has helped relieve some of my guilt for not wanting to acknowledge her—the guilt of knowing that the last years of her mother, my daughter, were not pleasant. In fact, quite destitute. I told Rhonda I couldn't give her any more money or discuss any further demands. I was losing sleep and felt like I was losing my mind.

I don't blame her entirely. She has had nothing, and when she saw our comfortable lifestyles, she felt entitled. This entitled feeling frightened me. I saw signs of anger and possibly psychotic behavior. At times I felt she was a frightened child merely looking for love and acceptance, but at other times, I saw her capable of violence.

I am writing this only to let you know that should I die unexpectedly or in a strange manner, perhaps you should have her investigated. I know this sounds dramatic, and I hesitate to write it. I am probably not in danger, but once in a while, she says something that causes me to think she could be unbalanced and dangerous.

Rhonda gasped for a breath. The room began to spin, and her face became flushed. Tears sprang to her eyes but she read on.

I am tying this letter with a red ribbon. My dear friend, Angelina, brought me a book about Mah Jongg that said there is a belief that people who are destined to be together are connected by an invisible red thread. Let this red thread represent my deep love for you in a manner that I hope has been visible each day of your lives.

Rhonda's hands were trembling, and the anger welled up. The bitch. The lying bitch didn't trust her. Fine. She'd have good reason not to trust her when she got through with her. Calling me unstable, unbalanced. She'd show her what that looked like.

She strode back to the desk to return the envelope to its place under the blotter. An empty envelope. She was keeping that letter. Then she heard a click. Was that a key in the door? Where could she hide? She ran back to the bedroom. She lifted the bedspread but there wasn't enough room between the mattress and the floor to slide under. She ran to the closet and squeezed in behind a rack of clothes in the far corner.

Please, please, please, don't let her look in the closet. A minute passed. A dresser drawer opened. Myra was in the bedroom. Rhonda held her breath and stood as still as she could. With the soft plush carpet, she couldn't tell which direction Myra was going. The toilet flushed. *Do I dare try to slip out? Is her back to me? No, I can't chance it.* She waited. Then the sound of water running. When it stopped, to Rhonda's horror, she heard the glass door to the closet slide open. The clothes on the rack from the other end of the closet moved toward her. From the corner of her eye, she saw a sweater slip off a hanger. Rhonda's heart was beating so loud she was afraid Myra could hear it.

She looked down and saw the toes of Myra's shoes. She stifled a gasp and held her breath. Then the shoes turned and disappeared. She released her breath only when she heard the front door close. She waited a minute and then tiptoed out of the bedroom.

She returned to the desk drawer and found identical stationery. Crème-colored fine linen paper worthy of her grandmother. Her hands were trembling. She took a blank sheet of stationery and folded it into the envelope. She secured it again with the red ribbon. Hopefully, Myra wouldn't open the envelope again soon. Thinking it was in a safe place. She gave a smirk. It was Myra who was no longer in a safe place.

Perhaps it was time to give Myra a new hairdo. Gratis. No charge. Myra's curls were getting a little too loose and her mouth was definitely too loose. Or should she say, her pen flowed too loosely.

Rhonda returned to the salon with her empty backpack and filled it with hair products.

At home, she also wrote a letter. A letter to Kathleen resigning her position. Apologizing for the short notice, but her work and class schedule had intensified, and she couldn't keep up with it all. She told her how valuable her experience at Friendship Acres was. What she didn't say was that it was more valuable than she ever imagined.

Chapter Sixty

Prior

Rhonda worried each day that Myra would discover the blank letter.

When Myra phoned to say, "the funds are in," Rhonda said she'd come right over. She still had the backpack with hair products in the back of her car as well as her letter to Kathleen. She drove to Friendship Acres for the last time.

Myra opened the door to Rhonda. "Come in," she said so softly Rhonda could barely hear her.

"Myra, you look exhausted. Are you all right?"

"I'm tired. I'm tired of all this. I want it to be over. You do understand by signing the paper it is over. Don't you?" She handed Rhonda the cashier's check. "Any other funding is out of the question. Even asking for it will be a violation of our agreement. It would hold up in court, you know."

"I am so sorry, grandmother, that I've caused you such agony. I didn't mean it to end this way. Really, I didn't. I only wanted to find my family."

Myra let out a big sigh. "I understand. But for now, I think it best if we aren't in touch for a while. Let things cool down and get back to some sort of normalcy.

"You'll be glad to know then that my letter of resignation will be on Kathleen's desk. I'm going to devote myself to the new salon. Thanks to you. How can I ever thank you?"

"Honor my request, Rhonda. That's how."

"I did have one thing in mind. . ." Rhonda started to say.

Myra turned pale.

"No, no, this isn't for me but for you. A way to thank you. A small way, but it's something I'd like to do. Please let me."

"What is it?" Myra asked, a trembling hand touched her throat.

Rhonda picked up her backpack. "I noticed last time we talked that your hair was ready for a color treatment. And since I won't be in the salon anymore, please let me do that tonight. It's the least I can do. I know it in no way is enough, but. . ."

"I am so tired. I don't think so. That's nice of you, but not. . ."

"Myra, look at it this way. Tomorrow is a new start for you. I will be out of your life. Your stress and worries will be over. And what better way to start than with your hair looking nice? You'll feel so much better. You know you will."

Rhonda started taking product out of her backpack, talking as she continued, ignoring Myra's refusal. "Let's go in the kitchen and have a glass a wine, and it won't take long at all. Let's turn this into a celebration of sorts; not a sad farewell. What do you say?"

Myra knew how headstrong and determined Rhonda could be. The last few weeks had proven that. What harm was there in this last request? Heaven knows it was a lot easier than the rest of hers had been. She walked to the kitchen with Rhonda and opened a bottle of wine.

Myra's glass touched Rhonda's. "To your new salon, or I should say, to your future."

Rhonda responded, "To you, grandmother, for your kindness and generosity."

They raised their glasses and drank.

Before Rhonda left, she washed her own wineglass out, returned it to the shelf, and wiped the wine bottle for any fingerprints. She left Myra's half-full wine glass on the counter. To take every precaution, she wiped Myra's desk, the doorknob, other places she may have touched. As she was wiping the coffee table, she noticed the beautiful mahogany case that held the Mah Jongg tiles. Tempted to take it, she opened it and admired all the designs on the tiles facing up. Well, it wouldn't hurt to just take one or two of them. Who would know? Not like Myra was going to play with this set again. She studied the tiles another minute and chose one with a red dragon symbol and one with a green dragon. She dropped the dragon tiles in her tote bag and wiped the case clean.

Perfect. Myra did become somewhat of a dragon lady writing that letter.

On the way home, Rhonda deposited the cashier's check in the bank's after-hours deposit drawer.

There is an investigation due to an unattended death. There is one wineglass on the counter and a half-full wine bottle. Myra's wineglass has her fingerprints; the bottle has none. They find no fingerprints other than Myra's in the house. In fact, they find very few of hers. As if someone has wiped down counters. It was the lack of Myra's fingerprints where they would normally be that raised the first red flag for Detective Lucchino.

Chapter Sixty-One

Angelina has an inkling, a hunch. *Should I run it by Guy? I don't want to risk looking foolish like I did with the red thread. Thinking I was on to something when he knew about it all along. Maybe I can redeem myself with this little bit of information.* She picks up the phone.

"Guy, it's Angelina."

"Bella signora, *come stai*?" he asks.

"*Dobro*," she answers. "I recalled something. Something about Myra's music box. Remember I told you she sold it by mistake in the estate sale? The one with 'Lara's Theme'?" Angelina knows she sounds like an eager schoolgirl.

"Yes," he answers and waits.

"One day Myra mentioned that the young beautician at Friendship Acres had one just like it. And that's kind of funny since it was so old. Or so Myra said. Don't you think that's a coincidence?"

"It could be."

"I'd like to talk to Rhonda about it. Maybe she and Rhonda talked about the box. Maybe she told Rhonda who the boyfriend was who gave it to her, and maybe the boyfriend is a connection. You know how we're looking for connections. Even Confucius says, 'To divine the present study the past.' I read that in the Mah Jongg book Janet brought me." Angelina says all this like a good student who memorized what would be on the final exam.

Guy doesn't respond.

Myra goes on, "And as crazy as it might sound, I'm thinking maybe I could buy it back and give it to one of the granddaughters like Myra wanted. But more importantly, I thought you should know, in case it was important."

Angelina expects some praise from Guy for her astute observation. She is surprised when his reply seems unlike the man she has been talking to all these weeks.

"I'd rather you refrain from contacting Rhonda. In fact, I think it's best if you let me do the investigating."

Tears burn her eyelids and she can't speak. When she finds her voice, she says "Fine. That's fine. I won't be bothering you with my observations. Sorry to have taken your time."

As she hangs up the phone, Guy says, "Angelina, please..."

She sits there stunned by the turn of events. When her phone rings immediately, she sees on the caller ID that it's Guy. *Should I answer? No, he doesn't need my help. He can do his own investigation and I'll do my own. Who is he to tell me what I can or cannot do?* She tries to stifle her hurt and angry feelings. How foolish to think she would find romance at her age. To get a second chance.

She finds her car keys and her note from her conversation with Kathleen at Friendship Acres where she wrote Rhonda's salon address. She'll go there now. Her cell phone rings again. It's Guy. She ignores it and walks out the door.

As she starts the car, she hears the ring again. She is tempted to answer but refuses to look at it. At the stop light, she glances at it, and to her surprise, she has missed a call from April.

At the next intersection, she pulls into a Walgreens' parking lot and listens to her voice mail.

"Hi Mom. I know it's short notice, but there's a break in my schedule, and if you're not too busy, I think lunch would work today. Call me back."

She calls April immediately. Her daughter is far more important than proving a point to Guy.

Chapter Sixty-Two

As Angelina drove to The Perfect Pear near April's workplace, she remembers Clara's words the other day, *Hope for the best; expect the worst.* She is prepared for whatever. Just glad that April called her. This might be the first step to setting things right. A chance to redeem herself.

When Angelina sees April in the restaurant entryway, she's shocked at how thin she looks. How long has it been since she last saw her? April was always mindful of her weight, but now she looks almost anorexic. She also notices a new stylish cut from her normally long hair.

Angelina resists the urge to embrace her, waiting for April to establish how they will conduct themselves. "April, your haircut is very becoming. And that suit is a great color for you." *Am I gushing?*

"Thank you," she replies as they follow the hostess to their table.

They look at the menu she hands them. "What do you recommend? You probably eat here often, so close to your office."

"I like the salmon salad, but it's huge. I get the half-portion."

"Then I'll do the same. My doctor said I should eat salmon once a week. Omega 3's and all that."

"Is your health good?" April asks.

"It is. All good." Angelina wants to ask April if her health is good but doesn't want to comment on her weight loss. She's walking on eggshells.

They place their order and when the waitress leaves, Angelina says, "Thank you for meeting me. I'm going to skip the small talk. Although we can if you prefer, but I want to say what's on my heart." Angelina takes a deep breath. "I was so wrong to interfere. I wish I could have, as the kids say, a do-over."

April's smile surprises her and encourages her to go on.

"You know I like Gary. I did the very first time I met him. And all the times we were together I thought, 'what a nice young man.' That's why I wanted it to be a permanent relationship for you—someone for you to share your life with. But obviously, that wasn't my decision. It was his and yours. When I think of what I did, I am so ashamed. I accomplished nothing good, and the worst part of it all—I lost you. But I know you wanted to start a family. You're so good with your niece and nephew." Angelina takes a breath. "Am I rambling?"

"Mom, please. It's all right. I was angry at the time, but I'm not anymore."

"You're not?" Angelina feels the tears brim but doesn't want to cry. "Can I make it right with Gary? If I apologized to him, would it . . ."

"Mom, there's no need to apologize." April takes a sip of coffee.

Angelina continues. "But I would be willing to. Really. What I said and did was rude."

"There's no need because . . . because Gary and I aren't together anymore."

"What? Why? What happened? Did I cause that?"

Their salads arrive.

April takes a nibble of salmon and continues to eat as if they are discussing the weather rather than a serious relationship. She puts her fork down for a minute. "As long as you're being honest, I need to be also. I was feeling the same about Gary and me as you were, Mom, but I think I was too proud or embarrassed to admit that I had let it go on so long with no commitment from him. That I didn't respect myself enough to say to him what needed to be said." She takes another bite, waves her fork and says, "Mom, try the salmon. It's really good."

Angelina takes a bite as instructed but doesn't taste a thing. She's glad she ordered wine and takes another sip of that.

"So, when? How long?"

"It's been a few weeks now. And you know what? I feel better about myself than I have in a long time."

"Why didn't you call me? Oh, never mind. I don't blame you. You had no way of knowing how remorseful I felt."

"Kinda had to wrap my head around it myself first. The fact that I was willing to settle for less than I deserve. And then the breakup itself."

Angelina stares at her daughter and feels a sense of pride and then realizes she needs to voice this. "I am so proud of you, April. So proud."

"I'm sorry I put you off for lunch so often, but I knew what I had to do with Gary and wanted to do it before we met."

"Of course."

"Now, bring me up-to-date on my niece and nephew. Between the Gary thing and some deadlines at work, it's been too long since I've seen them. I miss those kids."

"I'm sure they miss you too. Their favorite aunt."

They both smile at the standing joke as she's their only aunt.

"Does this mean you'll come to Sunday night dinner?"

"I can't wait," April says.

Angelina feels the tears sting the back of her eyelids. She digs into her salmon, visualizes Omega 3's flowing through her veins, or is it the good feeling of having her daughter back?

"Headed home?' April asks as they leave.

"No, I have one important task to do first."

Chapter Sixty-Three

Rhonda glances up to see Angelina standing at the reception desk. For a minute she doesn't recognize her but knows she has seen her before. Yes, from Friendship Acres, and then it dawns on her that this is one of Myra's Mah Jongg friends, one of her regular four-some. Rhonda tenses but tries not to show it. Perhaps this has nothing to do with Myra. Perhaps it's a coincidence.

With all the grace she can muster, she flashes her professional smile and asks, "Can I help you?"

"Do you by chance remember me, Rhonda?"

"You look familiar. I bet you're from Friendship Acres, aren't you? I met so many nice people there."

"Yes, what an excellent memory. Especially since I never got my hair done. I wanted to. Everyone came out of your salon looking so good, especially Myra. I played Mah Jongg with her on Mondays.

"I'm sorry I couldn't spend more hours there. I really enjoyed the ladies."

"I don't know if you are aware . . ." Angelina hesitates. "I believe it happened after you left, but Myra passed away recently."

"What? She seemed so healthy." Rhonda feigns surprise.

"Yes, it was sudden and unexpected. And that's what I wanted to talk to you about. Do you have a few minutes? Can you take a break, so we can chat?"

At that moment, two clients came in and Rhonda shrugs her shoulders. "I'd be happy to talk, but as you can see, it's not a good time."

"I'm not in a hurry. In fact, I have a few errands in this neighborhood. What time do you get off? Would that work?"

Rhonda doesn't want to appear uncooperative, so she agrees. "I have a class tonight after work, but I could take a few minutes. There's a coffee shop a few doors down. I could meet you there at 5:30."

"Perfect," Angelina says and steps aside.

Angelina exits and glances at her watch. She doesn't really have any errands, so she heads to the coffee shop. As she passes her parked car, she remembers a book in the back seat and grabs it and her speckled notebook.

Before she reaches the coffee shop, something catches her eye in one of the parked cars. Dangling from the rearview mirror above the dashboard are what look like a few Mah Jongg tiles. She peers into the window and sees one red and one green dragon, each one tied to a red ribbon. *Hmm…Another Mah Jongg lover.*

At the coffee shop, she eyes the scones on the bakery shelf and buys a lemon one. "What a guilty pleasure," she thinks as its buttery taste satisfies her taste buds. She thinks of Guy, remembering the lemon scone they shared at the Botanical Gardens brunch. Her cheeks redden to think of how foolish she's been the last few weeks. Their relationship obviously doesn't mean the same to him. His words and abrupt manner cut her deep.

She opens her speckled notebook and makes a few notes about what she might ask Rhonda. And if she discovers anything interesting, she'll lord it over Guy. If she speaks to him again.

She chooses instead to think of April and how wonderful that they're speaking again. Still ashamed of her interference, April's forgiveness is a great comfort to her. *But would it be expecting too much to have both a loving daughter and Guy's friendship? Why am I experiencing teenager angst over a man at my age?*

Chapter Sixty-Four

When Rhonda sits across from her, Angelina offers to buy her a coffee.

"Thank you, but I don't have much time. How can I help you?" Rhonda manages a gracious smile.

Angelia says, "I know Myra thought so much of you, and you became quite close. I was a little curious. Did she seem different to you the last time you saw her?"

Rhonda looks at Angelina but doesn't speak.

In her delay to answer, Angelina asks again. "I mean any little thing."

"I'm sorry. I'm just trying to remember what we talked about." Rhonda stalls. "You know, I can't think of anything different. We did become friends, as much as you can once a week. I knew about her daughters and her grandchildren. She was so proud of all of them."

"Yes, she was," Angelina replies.

"No, I can't think of anything unusual. I'm sorry."

"That's perfectly all right. I guess it doesn't matter now. Myra's gone, and nothing is going to bring her back. I was wondering if there was something I missed that I could have helped her with. It all seemed so strange that she was fine one day and gone the next."

"Yes, that is strange," Rhonda agrees.

"Well, thank you for meeting with me."

"You're so welcome," Rhonda says as she starts to slide out of the booth.

"There is one thing. Myra mentioned something once about a music box. A snow globe. Said she accidentally sold it in the estate sale."

Rhonda doesn't respond but wonders where this conversation is going.

Angelina goes on. "I know this is going to sound strange, but Myra mentioned that you had a music box like the one she sold in the estate sale."

"Yes . . ." Rhonda answers hesitantly.

"I think it played the theme from *Dr. Zhivago*. 'Lara's Theme'?"

"Yes, it does," Rhonda answers.

"So, you do have a snow globe like Myra's? That's so unusual. With it being so old and all."

"It was a coincidence." Rhonda decides to go along with this. "Actually, the greater coincidence was that it was Myra's. I was playing it one day in the salon, and she told me about hers and how she sold it in the estate sale, and I told her that's where I bought it. At an estate sale. At the time, of course, I didn't know her at all. Or that it was her house." Rhonda is talking faster now and twisting an empty sugar wrapper. "But I don't have it any more. I gave it to a friend. Her name is Lara too. That's why I bought it. She always loved the movie, *Dr. Zhivago*. It was the perfect gift."

"I see," says Angelina "Then I guess it wouldn't do any good to offer to buy it back. When Myra told me about it, she said she didn't realize she'd left it in the estate sale. She had meant to give it to her granddaughter, and I was thinking that if I could track it down, it might be one last thing I could do for Myra. But it's not important."

"Myra never mentioned that to me or I would have given it back to her."

"Did she happen to tell you why the music box was sentimental? Or perhaps who gave it to her?" Angelina asks.

'No, no, she didn't. That's so sweet of you to think of Myra's wish. Perhaps my friend would understand. It should go to the granddaughter. Let me take your number and I'll call you."

"Are you sure?"

"It's worth a try, isn't it? I mean, what's a song compared to the treasure of a loved one? Especially under the recent circumstances. I'll do my best."

"Oh, by the way, do you remember the cost of the music box. I want to be sure you'll be reimbursed."

"Yes, I think it was $100. Way over my budget. Guess I got a little sentimental that day."

"Oh, I totally understand," Angelina replies.

Angelina writes her phone number on a napkin and slides it across the table to Rhonda. She leaves money on the table to cover her scone and a tip.

As she steps out of the coffee shop she notices Rhonda getting in the car with

the dragon Mah Jongg tiles. She walks to the driver's side and taps on the window.

Rhonda rolls it down cursing the handle that sticks again. *That woman again*? *Now what does she want?*

Angelina says, "I notice you have some Mah Jongg tiles hanging there. Do you also play?"

Rhonda covers her eyes with her hands and shakes her head. When she looks up she says,"They were my mother's. She passed away and …well, it makes me feel she is with me."

"I'm so sorry," Angelina says. "That's a lovely gesture."

Seeing the two Mah Jogg tiles reminds Angelina that she forgot to sort out Myra's set to see which tiles were missing. Driving home, she feels certain she is going to get a call in the next day or two. The girl seems money hungry, or to be politically correct, financially motivated. She remembers that Myra said the music box sold for $50.

Other than thinking the girl's a bit greedy, Angelina leaves Rhonda feeling her hunch was wrong. How could she know anything about Myra's past, especially from high school? The music box was just a coincidence. Maybe Guy is right. Maybe she's trying too hard to connect dots that don't fit.

Angelina feels foolish for many reasons. Foolish to think Rhonda was important to Guy's investigation, foolish to say anything to him about it, and most of all, foolish to think he cared about her.

Chapter Sixty-Five

Angelina won't answer his calls. He'll go to her house if need be. But first he needs to speak with Rhonda about her car at the cemetery. And about her bank deposits that match Myra's withdrawals.

Motive, motive. What could be a young girl's motive?

He flips back to the information Kathleen gave him about Rhonda. Her place of work and the number there.

At the time Angelina and Rhonda are meeting at the coffee shop, Guy enters the salon. "I'd like to speak to a Rhonda Feder please."

"Rhonda is gone for the day. Would you like to leave a message?"

"Will she be in tomorrow?"

The receptionist checks something on her desk and says, "She's scheduled for the afternoon shift. Starts at one o'clock."

He drives away without noticing the Dodge Dart in the parking lot.

Chapter Sixty-Six

As Rhonda drives to class, she thinks, "That old bag, Angelina, is nosing around. First the music box and then the Mah Jongg dragons. Who knows what else she might uncover? What business is it of hers who the music box belongs to? It belongs to me. But I couldn't care less now if I have it or not. I'd rather have the hundred dollars. A nice profit of fifty."

At the next stoplight, she pulls up alongside a car full of children. They're singing and the mother's laughing. Why are there happy families everywhere I go? When the car in front of her doesn't pull out the second the light changes to green, she lays on her horn.

She is way too snoopy. This Angelina Popoff. I think it might be time I popped her off.

Rhonda calls Angelina after her class. "Mrs. Popoff? It's Rhonda, the beautician."

"Hello, Rhonda. Call me Angelina, please."

"Angelina, I've been thinking of everything we talked about, and it seems selfish of me not to return the music box. I called my friend Lara and she said, by all means, return it. She's sentimental too."

"Really? How nice."

"Do you live at Friendship Acres?"

"No, I only went there to play Mah Jongg with Myra.

"I could bring it to your home. And I wanted to let you know that you inspired me today."

"Oh, how's that?"

"Because you were doing something kind by getting the music box for the granddaughter, I thought I could do something nice for you, her best friend. In memory of Myra. She was such a nice lady."

"Oh?" Angelina asks.

"You said you never had time to come in for a hairstyle. I'd be glad to give you a stylish trim and set at your home when I bring the music box."

"Oh my, that's not necessary,"

"But I want to. I really do. If you came to the salon, they would charge you exorbitant fees. At home, there would be no charge."

"But, Rhonda, I can afford the salon."

"Please, just let me do this. For you and for Myra. She was such a nice lady. We could do it in her memory."

"Well, since you put it that way, I guess there's no harm. Thank you. A new do might be just the thing I need now."

Rhonda smirks at how women's vanity gets them to agree to anything. "I only ask that you shampoo your hair just before I arrive. I like to cut it wet."

"That would be easy."

"I have some time tomorrow morning. I work the late shift. Would that work for you?"

"I think so. My two friends are coming to play Mah Jongg but not until lunchtime. If you come in the morning, how much time should I allow?"

"An hour should be sufficient. Say about ten?" Rhonda suggests.

"Perfect. I'll have the girls wait until noon, so we're not rushed."

"Oh, that would be great. No, I don't want to rush my time with you. Not at all. Oh, and Angelina," Rhonda adds, "Would you mind not saying anything to anyone about this? The salon doesn't like us doing private appointments. They'd think I was homing in on their profits."

"Of course not, but I don't want you doing anything that could get you in trouble. Are you sure it's all right?"

"Oh, I won't get into trouble. I really want to do this to you. I mean *for* you."

"Thank you, Rhonda."

She hangs up feeling confident Angelina will keep quiet about the new hairdo, but now she has to figure out a way to keep her quiet forever. That will teach her to poke her nose in other people's business.

After dinner Angelina decides to sort the tiles in Myra's case to see which two are missing. Just as she opens the case her phone chimes a text message. From Guy. *Angelina, I'm sorry I was so abrupt in our last conversation. Can I please make it up to you at dinner tomorrow night?*

Angelina smiles and thinks perhaps she did overreact. She replies. *It's been a busy day. Let's talk tomorrow. Good night.*

Immediately he chimes again. *Good night, mia bella donna.*

She returns to the case and closes it. *It has been a busy day. I'll do this later.*

The last thing Angelina thinks of before she drifts off to sleep is how wonderful it is to have April in her life again. And that it might be nice to have dinner with Guy . . . with her new hairdo and all.

Chapter Sixty-Seven

The next day Rhonda arrives at Angelina's promptly at ten o'clock carrying a small duffel bag containing the hair products she will need as well as the music box in a gift bag.

Angelina answers the door wearing a light blue duster and a towel around her hair.

"How's this?" she asks, walking Rhonda to the kitchen and pointing to a chair. "With my highboy table, I hope the seat isn't too high."

Rhonda approaches the back of the chair but is careful not to touch it or anything in the house until she puts on her sheer plastic gloves. "It's perfect. Just my height."

Rhonda hands Angelina the music box.

"Let me pay for this before we begin," she says as she pulls five twenty-dollar bills from her purse on the kitchen counter.

Rhonda slips the bills into the pocket of her smock and pulls out another one with daisies on it. "I brought a smock for you, but there will be hair clippings on the floor. Do you want to put down a sheet, or shall we sweep it up afterwards?"

"I think we can get it with a broom and dustpan. No problem."

Rhonda takes a clean white towel out of her bag and lays it on the table where she sets her comb, brush and two pairs of scissors in different sizes. She also pulls out a large hand mirror. Then she snaps the plastic gloves on, the kind most beauticians use only for hair coloring.

"Please don't be offended by the gloves. It's one of the first things they teach us at school. Not everyone does it, but I try to make it a part of my daily routine."

"I think it's an excellent idea. And I'm not offended at all.

You certainly are prepared."

Rhonda thinks, "I better be." What she says is, "Have scissors, will cut."

What she doesn't pull out of her duffel is her twenty-two revolver, a large spool of strong red cord and a roll of duct tape. Also red. She found the cord in the craft section at Michaels. It was perfect. The right color and durable. Thick, but not too thick to twist and tighten. She played with it for several hours last night as she watched television, twisting it around and around until she felt sure she could pull it tightly with her rubber gloves on. She wrapped it around the neck of a teddy bear she'd had for years and twisted it tighter and tighter. Teddy's silly smile never left his face, but Angelina's smile will soon fade.

The best thing about the cord, besides color, is its similarity to the material used to make lanyards at summer camp. It symbolizes everything Rhonda needs. In one act she'll wipe out both Angelina and her painful camp memories of her friend, Nancy. And the final and best reason for red? It's the color Myra wrapped around her pitiful letter to her daughters. Red, the tie that binds. Binds families and other body parts. How ironic is that? It's all coming together so beautifully.

She's not going to rush this. She has over an hour. No one is to arrive for two hours. It's too much fun to anticipate each step of such a perfect plan. Maybe she can get Angelina to turn on the music box at the right moment. She didn't plan on it, but like everything else, it's all falling into place so perfectly. And at that moment, when she reveals how and why she killed Myra, and why Angelina needs to join her dear friend, she'll pull the red cord tight. Very tight.

She'll wrap up her tools in her own towel, careful to leave no trace behind, and no one will be the wiser. Who will ever suspect that she's been there? No one will connect her to Angelina.

To be certain, she asks, "Won't your family and friends be surprised? You haven't told anyone, have you?"

"Oh no, it's our little secret. Remember that commercial? Maybe you're too young. It went something like, 'only your hairdresser knows for sure.'"

Rhonda laughs, thinking, "Perfect. Absolutely perfect."

"You know you could do a great business making house calls

like this," Angelina says.

"I never thought of it." Frankly she hadn't, but perhaps Angelina was onto something good here. "The only thing is—ladies love having their hair shampooed. I know I do."

"You're right. That is the best part. Other than the finished look of course."

"Since I didn't get to shampoo your hair, would you like a little scalp massage?"

"I would never say no to that luxury." As soon as Rhonda slides her fingers into Angelina's damp hair, her fingertips gently massaging her scalp, Angelina sinks into a wonderful state of relaxation. "I'll give you a week to stop that."

Rhonda laughs. She likes Angelina and feels bad she's going to have to hurt her. *Better her than me. She's too nosy. I can't take the chance.* Rhonda's fingers go deeper and deeper.

After trimming Angelina's hair, she plugs in the blow dryer using the extra long extension cord she brought with her.

"Oh, Rhonda, I have a hair dryer you could have used."

"The ones you buy retail are not as good as the ones from the professional beauty supply store. This dryer won't damage your hair. It has settings and heat cycles for all types of hair."

She uses a round styling brush on Angelina's hair, turning it under as she dries. *This woman has a beautiful head of hair. What a shame this is the only time I'll be able to work on it. But I'll save the beautician at the funeral home a lot of time. She'll be so lovely for her viewing. Maybe I should leave a business card in her casket.* Rhonda laughs to herself.

After the blow-dry, Rhonda uses the hot curling iron with a small rod and turns strands of Angelina's shiny dark hair into soft curls around her face. Angelina, of course, can't see what she is doing yet.

"It is going to be so lovely. Trust me." Rhonda says.

"Oh, I do. This is so nice of you. You must let me pay you, of course."

"Not necessary."

"I insist. The service has been extraordinary. Now don't refuse me. I know a young lady like you has lots of expenses. Going to school and all. Please."

"If you insist." *Might as well get some money out of the old broad.* Then she realizes she needs to have Angelina stay in the chair. *Well, I can ransack her purse afterwards. I'm certain there will be some large bills in her wallet. I can make it look like a robbery.* That wasn't the original plan but the more she thinks about it, why not? Take some money, a few pieces of jewelry. It might look like Angelina caught her in the act. Bad timing for Angelina. Perfect timing for Rhonda.

She begins to wrap up her scissors in the white towel but perhaps she'd better keep them handy. *What if the red cord doesn't work? Good to have a backup plan. And, of course, there's always the revolver. Too noisy without a silencer.* She still has her plastic gloves on. Angelina starts to get out of her chair, patting the back of her head as she does.

"Oh no, stay here a minute," Rhonda says.

She pulls out her large hand mirror and holds it in front of Angelina.

"Oh my, it's lovely." Angelina seems so pleased.

"I'm glad you like it. I think Myra would approve, don't you?" Rhonda unties Angelina's smock and removes it.

"No doubt. She would have loved it."

"Please stay put now. Can we put the music box on for a minute? We'll play it in Myra's memory. Then I'll clean up. You relax."

Rhonda pulls the snow globe out of the gift bag, shakes it and turns the key at the bottom. Snowflakes fill the globe and "Lara's Theme" fills the room.

Angelina smiles. "It is lovely. Always was one of my favorites. And such a love story. Oh my."

"Yes, "Somewhere my love." I played this for Myra one day in the salon at Friendship Acres."

"You did?"

"Yes, you were right when you said an old boyfriend gave it to her. But see, Angelina, he was more than a boyfriend."

"Really?" Angelina asks. She gives Rhonda with a puzzled look. "I don't recall telling you it was from a boyfriend."

"You might say much more than a boyfriend." Rhonda pauses. "He was the father of the child she gave birth to in high school."

Angelina's face registers shock and disbelief. "What?"

"I know you fashion yourself a detective. Here's a bit of information I bet you didn't uncover."

"You see, that boy was my grandfather. His name was Mark, and he and Myra had a baby girl who they gave up for adoption. That was my mother. My poor mother who had nothing while Myra's other three daughters had every privilege. I don't think that was very fair, do you, Angelina?"

"Well, I . . . I . . ." Angelina stammers.

"You don't need to answer. The problem is you've been snooping around Myra's death a bit too much. And it's only a matter of time until you uncovered the adoption and discovered my identity. And although she refused to claim me publicly, she gave me quite a bit of money. She asked me not to say a word. Not a word."

Rhonda's voice is stronger and louder. "But then she, the bitch, wrote a letter to her daughters saying I might harm her or her granddaughters. I found the letter. The daughters will never see it. I destroyed that bit of evidence. But now your snooping is a problem for me. I don't need any problems at this point. No one connected me to Myra until you started snooping around."

Angelina's face pales.

"I don't think Myra was very nice to me. I didn't get her love, and that made me really angry."

Angelina opens her mouth to speak, but words don't come out.

"She made me so angry I had to punish her. I thought about hurting her other grandchildren. I mean, if she didn't want to claim me as a granddaughter, why should she have them? You either want granddaughters or you don't. Wouldn't you agree, Angelina?"

Angelina doesn't respond, blinking back tears.

"Wouldn't you agree?" Rhonda repeats her words faster and louder. "But hurting the granddaughters wouldn't have given me any more money. I hate that I had to kill the golden goose, so to speak, but she was done laying any golden eggs for me."

Angelina gasps.

"You seem like a nice lady, and you have beautiful hair. I'd love to do your hair again sometime but that won't be possible.

You see, although your hair is lovely, it's your other features that got you into trouble."

Rhonda waves the still-hot curling iron so close to Angelina's face she jerks away from it. "Mainly your nose. Too big. Too nosy. Rhonda touches the tip of Angelina's nose with the hot curling iron. Angelina flinches at the burn.

"Why did you have to go snooping around? Guess that'll teach you a lesson, huh? Too bad you won't live long enough to learn it. No need for amateur sleuths where you're going. They already have everything figured out by the time they get there." Rhonda laughs.

Beads of perspiration form on Angelina's upper lip.

Rhonda keeps her eyes glued to Angelina's while she pulls the red lanyard cord out of her bag. Then in a swift movement, while Angelina's eyes widen in horror, Rhonda grabs her wrists and fastens the cord around them. She puts another cord around her ankles and ties it to the bottom chair rung. She tightens it, enjoying the terror on Angelina's face.

Chapter Sixty-Eight

Angelina fears she's no match for this strong young girl. *Think, think. Keep the girl talking while I think of what to do. Should I scream? Would anyone hear me? Guy, Guy, how can I reach Guy? I was so foolish not to listen to him. If I could only get to my phone. In my purse. On the counter.*

As if she reads Angelina's mind, Rhonda reaches into her bag again and pulls out a roll of duct tape. Also red.

Red, red. All Angelina can think of is the day she and Guy walked through the garden. This was all about something red. *Guy, why did I go behind your back? You must have suspected Rhonda. You were trying to protect me. I was such a fool.*

Despite the scissors lying on the table, Rhonda tears a piece of the tape with her teeth like an animal and covers Angelina's mouth. "In case you decide you want to let the neighbors know about our little party. Remember it's our secret."

Angelina's face burns with shame. She was so vain to want a new hairdo. How costly her vanity.

"Now, relax while I tell you the rest of the story. I can't really tell anyone else, and I'm so proud of it. So clever. I guess a little boasting wouldn't hurt. Aren't you curious as to how Myra died with no trace of violence? Of course, you're curious. Or are you plain nosy? That's how you got into this mess to begin with, isn't it? Well, let me satisfy your curiosity. It was quite brilliant, if I do say so." She primps Angelina's hair.

"See, Angelina, there's a test that we beauticians are required to do on our clients before we apply permanent hair color. It's a small patch test done on the skin. Usually on the back of the ear or inside the elbow to see if they're allergic to aniline derivative. It's a substance in most permanent hair coloring. It comes from coal tar, which is some downright nasty shit. Some people have sensitivity to it, so much so that it can cause anaphylactic shock. Severe anaphylactic shock can kill. The first time I colored Myra's hair I did the simple test and she showed an allergic reaction to the patch. I didn't mention it to her at the time. I had no ulterior motive and simply used a different product to color her hair that didn't contain the aniline."

Angelina turns her head to look at the clock on the wall.

Rhonda pulls her chin back to face her. "Look at me when I talk to you. Now, where was I? Yes, I couldn't have her going around accusing me of blackmail and saying I was dangerous, now could I? Well, I decided what an easy way to mask a murder. Who would ever suspect it? So, after I left the salon at Friendship, I asked Myra if I could do her hair one last time because she'd been so kind to me. It was, after all, quite a bit of money she gave me. It was the least I could do." Rhonda laughs sarcastically.

"So, in the privacy of her apartment. I applied the permanent hair color all over her scalp. Worked it in and massaged her head. Rubbed it in good and deep so the reaction, if fatal, would come quickly. She did enjoy it, and I thought, that's a nice way to go out.

"And here's where I think I was so clever. I said, 'Now Myra, you need to rinse so it doesn't get too dark. We can't have you looking like that lady in the *Adams Family* now, can we?' Myra actually started to laugh as she rose to go to the bathroom, but I could tell her breathing was shortening already.

"I suggested she step into the shower, so she could rinse it thoroughly. The steam would also provide the perfect petri dish for the fumes she would inhale.

"I helped her adjust the water temperature and then said, 'I'll leave you some privacy now, so you can take off your duster and step in. Give it a good rinse and then you can come back to the kitchen. We'll dry and curl it. You'll look lovely.'

"I left the room and waited just outside the bathroom door. I didn't have to wait long. Her gasps couldn't be heard over the sounds of the shower, but I did hear the thud when she fell. I ran in. She was struggling for breath while the water was running over her. She tried to say something, sounded like my name. I thought it fitting that my name should be her last words. It was as if she finally did claim me.

"But it was too late, Angelina. It was too late. She should have welcomed me with open arms when I first told her. If she had, she wouldn't be lying in a bathtub dying while the water sprayed over her.

"Of course, I didn't turn off the water. If she were truly alone she wouldn't have been able to do that. I let it run while I went to the kitchen and cleaned up all signs of my having been there. I wiped the counters of fingerprints, as well as any surfaces I might have touched on previous visits, like her desk. I was meticulous as I will be when I leave today. There will be no trace of my having been here—in your kitchen or in your life. Your life that is about to end. Oh, I forgot to mention, I did take a few mementos. The cute little dragons from her Mah Jongg set? Yes, one red and one green."

The missing tiles. They *were* Myra's. Angelina feels terror like she's never known. Thoughts flash through her mind. The things she'll never see. Her granddaughter's prom, high-school graduations, weddings. Sunday family dinners. The books she'll never read, the places she'll never visit. Thank goodness she made amends with April. And Guy. If she lives to see him, she'll tell him. Tell him what? How much she enjoys being with him. Why hasn't she told him? What was she waiting for?

"So," Rhonda goes on, "To finish the story, after that I returned to the bathroom and she lay there with her eyes closed. I saw no signs of life but took her pulse. Mission accomplished. Her permanent hair dye was indeed permanent. She wouldn't be requiring any further touch-ups." Rhonda laughs again. The laugh borders on the hysterical, and Angelina knows she is dealing with a very sick person.

"It was a risky method. I didn't know if she'd suffer minor breathing distress or die, but the good thing—if it didn't work, Myra would never even know what I attempted. I could always resort to what I'm doing right now. But rather messy and so ordinary. I do think my idea was genius, don't you?"

Angelina stares at Rhonda, still in a state of disbelief.

Rhonda's voice rises, "Don't you think it was genius, Angelina?"

She quickly nods her head up and down. And then, of all crazy things, she remembers an Agatha Christie story. Her most famous one, *And Then There Were None*. All ten people on the island were killed, and the man who orchestrated it all confessed, even though he might never been discovered. It was his pitiful need for recognition that caused him to confess. That's what Rhonda is doing now. She wants recognition for her creative, dastardly deed. Despite her fear, Angelina feels pity for this disturbed child. She is a forlorn child in many ways.

"Well, I guess that's all we have to talk about, so no use putting off the inevitable. Oh, look at the time. As they say, it does fly when you're having fun. I know your friends will be here soon. Won't they be surprised what you cooked up for lunch? Angelina, well done. Done for sure."

Rhonda laughs again and pulls the longer red lanyard cord out of her bag.

"Don't be afraid. You should thank me. Who knows what illness you might have contracted in your later years. You're no spring chicken, you know. Cancer, chemo, radiation, Alzheimer's. This is so much better. You look lovely and what a way to sign out."

Rhonda comes behind her and puts the cord around her neck. Angelina feels it getting tighter and tighter. She tries to resist, to escape. Perhaps she can tip the chair over. She isn't going to take this without a fight. She thinks of Peter. As much as she believes she'll meet him in the afterlife, she isn't ready to die. She has so much more to live for.

As the cord cuts into the tender skin on her throat, the doorbell rings.

Rhonda startles, causing her to loosen her grip on the red cord. Angelina gasps and takes a deep lifesaving breath.

Chapter Sixty-Nine

"She's going to be so surprised." Clara tries to keep the hot casserole she holds with potholders from touching her chest.

"We're an hour early. What if she's not home?" June looks perplexed.

"Well, we had to come early before she started cooking lunch for us, like she always does. It's time we did something nice for her."

"I guess we'll wait and surprise her on her front porch."

"How about the casserole? It won't taste as good if it's cold." June is still stewing.

"This warming cover is good for two hours, June. And it's not like she doesn't have a microwave and oven," Clara says impatiently.

June carries a shopping bag in one hand full of salad makings, a stalk of celery sticking out of one end. In the other hand she holds a bottle of wine. She sets the shopping bag down and rings the doorbell, pressing it a little longer. "Maybe she's in the shower."

Chapter Seventy

"Who's that?" Rhonda asks Angelina.

Angelina doesn't know how she's supposed to answer with duct tape across her mouth. She looks at Rhonda and makes a desperate plea with her eyes as if to say, "I don't know."

Rhonda whispers in her ear. "I'm going to peel this duct tape off, but one loud word out of you and the scissors go right in the jugular. Is that clear? I'll do it, Angelina. Don't doubt me."

Angelina fears she would and nods.

Rhonda peels back the tape and whispers, "Who do you *think* it is?"

Angelina whispers back hoarsely, "I'm not expecting anyone except June and Clara. But it's early. They shouldn't be here until noon." Angelina glances at the clock on the kitchen wall. "That's an hour from now."

The doorbell again. A persistent double ring.

Rhonda says, "I'm going to the peephole." She takes the long extension cord from the duffel bag and ties it around Angelina's waist and through the rungs of the chair back. "You'll stay put." She puts the duct tape back on her mouth.

Rhonda walks to the front door, looks out and sees June and Clara standing there. The doorbell startles her again.

Rhonda hurries back to Angelina. "It's the other two bitches you play Mah Jongg with. Will they go away if we ignore them?"

Angelina shakes her head no.

Rhonda pulls back a piece of the duct tape.

"Why not?" she asks. "Whisper, Angelina. Answer my question."

"They'll probably wait. They know we have lunch at noon."

Rhonda puts the duct tape back on and goes to the peephole again

June and Clara are both sitting on the small glider on the porch. Rhonda parked her car a half block away but didn't check out a back entrance. This is not how the plan was supposed to work.

She runs back to the kitchen with a new glint in her eyes, desperate, wild. "Okay, let them in. I can kill three as easily as one. One at a time. In fact, I think I'll let you watch. That's what you get for being so nosy. For asking about things that don't belong to you. Like the Mah Jongg dragons and the music box. You had to wonder about it, didn't you? Well, now you can wonder how your friends are going to die. All because of you. Too bad they won't have pretty curls like you do."

Rhonda steps in front of Angelina, an inch away and whispers, "Listen to me now. Listen good, old lady. I'm going to let you answer the door. Anything unusual and you will get the scissors. All three of you. If you want to be responsible for your friends' bloody scars, go ahead and mess up. No funny stuff, Miss Lady Detective."

Rhonda holds the scissors in her left hand as she unties the extension cord and the red cord binding Angelina's hands and feet. "Act natural. Like I came here to give you a cut and style. Let them think I'm leaving as soon as I pack up my stuff. Is that clear?"

Angelina opens the door, aware that Rhonda is watching her every move and expression. She can't risk giving June and Clara any sign of danger. She can't help her friends if she's bleeding

from scissor wounds. *Be careful,* she tells herself. This Oscar performance could save or end their lives.

"Surprise!" June and Clara both shout at once.

Chapter Seventy-one

Angelina has no trouble looking surprised as she sees her friends' arms laden with food and wine.

"We're treating you to lunch for a change," June says.

"Your hair. It's beautiful." Clara says and then they both see Rhonda.

Angelina tries to talk in her normal voice. "Ladies, I was going to surprise you with a new hairdo. Do you remember Rhonda from Friendship Acres? She agreed to come to my house and give me a cut and style."

"Really?" Clara says. "She makes house calls?"

"Yes, this was sort of a special occasion. I'll explain later," Angelina says, hoping there will be a later. "Do you want to set those things down? This lunch is so sweet of you."

Rhonda is watching her intently.

Acting poised on the surface, yet Angelina's mind is scrambling. Thinking, scheming. If she can get to her phone and hit 911 or Guy. One touch. Maybe two at the most.

June puts the wine in the refrigerator. "It's a chardonnay. I'll keep it chilled."

Angelina says, "Something smells delicious, June. Do you need me to turn on the oven?"

"That might be a good idea. On low. How soon till we eat?" June glances at Angelina.

Angelina looks at Rhonda with a questioning expression and a slight shrug of shoulders. She says, "I think we're done here, aren't we, Rhonda? Here, let me get my purse to pay you." Angelina thinks this is the way she can get to her cell phone, which is in the outside pocket of her purse.

The purse is on the kitchen counter, and as she pulls out her checkbook, she asks Rhonda, “Do you prefer a check or cash?”

Chapter Seventy-Two

Rhonda watches. She still has the scissors in one hand, which she has concealed behind her. Her eyes glance furtively around the kitchen and she spots the knife rack. She starts moving slowly toward it, her eyes never leaving Angelina. June and Clara are busy emptying the sack and removing the quilted casserole cover. They seem oblivious to the red lanyard which is now strewn across the chair and kitchen floor. Rhonda grabs the biggest knife out of the rack, her eyes on Angelina. Angelina pulls her cell phone out of her purse. As she does it rings,
startling Rhonda and Angelina both.

Chapter Seventy-Three

Angelina glances at the caller ID. It's Guy. She can't believe her luck. What can she say to him to let him know the danger they are in? Angelina looks at Rhonda as she tries to hit the accept call button.

Rhonda screams, "No! That's not a good idea."

Startled by the scream, June and Clara swivel to look at Rhonda.

Rhonda says, "I mean no check. It's not a good idea to write a check. I prefer cash."

June and Clara peer at Angelina as if to say, "What's going on?"

Angelina drops the phone but manages to hit the answer button, hoping no one will hear Guy's repeated hello but that he can hear them. "Oh, that's right, Rhonda. You said you were going on a little shopping spree from here, and I'm sure the cash would come in handy." She hopes Guy can hear the word Rhonda.

Then the house phone rings. It's on the desk in the kitchen, a few steps from Angelina.

"Now what?" says Rhonda. "Is this Grand Central Station?"

Angelina looks at the caller ID. It's Guy again. Angelina blurts out, "Oh, that's my housekeeper. She always calls me when she's on the way over to make sure it's a good time."

"Your housekeeper is coming while you play Mah Jongg?"

"Well, she wanted to come today, but that's why I had her call first. In case we didn't play for some reason." Angelina is surprised how easy the lies come.

The house phone rings again. Angelina knows the answering machine will kick in after four rings.

"I really should answer, or she'll show up. We don't want that, do we?" She looks at Rhonda.

"No, we don't. It's getting crowded in here. But let me talk to her. I can tell her not to come today".

"Oh, she doesn't speak English. I'll answer and say don't come today. In Spanish."

By now, June and Clara realize something weird is going on. They know Angelina's housekeeper who speaks perfect English and her regular day is Friday.

"Go ahead and pick up the phone. Don't say anything else."

"I won't." She picks up the receiver and says, "*Aiutare. Golemo aiutare.*"

"Hang up," Rhonda says.

Angelina does as she says. She prays Guy gets the Italian message. *Help me.* She threw in the Bulgarian word she'd taught him although it makes no sense. *Golemo. Big. Big help me. Please, Guy, get it, get it.*

Clara, hands on her hips, moves toward Rhonda. "What is going on here?"

Rhonda pulls out both hands, one holding the knife and the other the scissors.

"Stay right where you are. All three of you."

Clara steps back, her mouth wide open, unable to speak.

June screams. "I knew I should have worn my Depends today. Of all days. Please, I need to use the restroom."

"No one is going anywhere," Rhonda says. "This is even better than I thought. I was only going to dispose of your friend, Angelina. Snoopy Angelina. Did you know she was trying to find out what happened to Myra?"

June says, "Oh, she's good at clues. She solves mysteries before anyone on TV."

Clara says, "Hush, June."

"Well, I'll tell you both what happened to your friend, Myra. Your bitch of a friend. A better friend than family member. My dear grandmother who wouldn't claim me. She was afraid it would ruin her precious Janet's career."

Clara and June look stricken and confused.

June starts whimpering either over the knife or her uncontrollable bladder. She peers down at the spot appearing on the front of her pantsuit. "This is so embarrassing.".

"June, would you please stop worrying about your wet panties? We have bigger things to worry about." Clara glares at her.

"Yes, that casserole is going to be so dried out; we should take it out of the oven," June says as if she's totally lost her mind.

Despite her fears, Angelina shakes her head and gives June a half smile, trying to reassure her friend that everything will be all right, when in fact she knows it won't. She looks at Clara, tall, solid, and well built. *Maybe the three of us can take this young girl on, but we need a plan. How?*

Rhonda fires directions like a drill sergeant while waving the knife. "Angelina, get the red cord. Good thing I bought the whole friggin' spool. One false move and I put the knife in your back. I'll do it, so don't call my bluff."

Rhonda, with her hip, slides two of the high boy chairs side by side, their backs facing out.

You two," she waves the knife now at Clara and June. "Back up to the chairs. You," she barks to Angelina. "Start wrapping. Tight."

June and Clara inch backward to the chairs, afraid to turn their backs. Angelina takes the red lanyard cord and wraps it around them and the chairs. Her hands are trembling. Rhonda watches her, standing so close she can hardly make her turns.

"Tie it tight," Rhonda says. "Duct tape their mouths."

Before Angelina can tape Clara's mouth, Clara says, "Junie, I'm sorry for every mean thing I ever said to you."

"Shut up!" Rhonda shouts.

Tears roll down June's cheeks.

When Angelina gets to June, the loose end of the duct tape becomes stuck.

With shaking hands, she tries to get it started again.

Rhonda says, "Never mind. You, blondie, one peep out of you and you're history."

"Please don't say a word, Junie," Angelina whispers to her.

"What did you say?" Rhonda asks.

"Just saying I'm sorry."

"And that's another thing. Myra, the old bitch, didn't say she was sorry she couldn't accept me. Well, once, but it wasn't sincere. My mother died penniless. She never had enough money to get the prescriptions she needed while Myra's three other daughters are wearing designer jewelry. One piece would have paid my mother's rent for a month." Rhonda wipes her eyes with her sleeve.

"And how about me? I saw that room she decorated for her granddaughters' visits. The furnishings would have put me through the best beauty school in the country. But no, my mother and I had nothing. And did she ever look for us? No, not once. Did she care? No, she had her nice little family now. All intact. All perfect. Sure, forget the past and that child born out of teen lust. Like that child was nothing. Like she was imperfect and tarnished."

Keep her talking. Stall for time. Maybe Guy understood her message. She speaks to Rhonda. "I understand how hurt you must have been. Really I do."

Rhonda goes on. "This could have been so different. If she had once said, 'Rhonda, I have worried about you all these years and wondered where you were.' With DNA tests and adoption searches, she could have found us."

Rhonda sidesteps to the music box, watching them all the time, and starts playing it again. As she does, she bursts into tears and swipes them away with the back of her hand, never letting go of the knife in her left hand or the scissors in her right. "And then Miss Private Eye here," she waves the knife toward Angelina, "had to start snooping around, and I knew I had to get rid of her too. Now all of you."

Angelina peers at June. Tears are streaming down her face. Her lip is quivering. Clara doesn't cry, but her eyes hold a fierce determination Angelina has never seen. *If anyone is going to save us, it will be Clara.*

"Okay," Rhonda says, wiping her eyes again. "Enough of this drama. I'm ready to go. By the way, I might as well clean out your purses before I leave. Bet you golden girls have lots of cash. Angelina, get their purses and yours. Dump them out on the table. Stack up all the bills you can find. Take off their rings. A little robbery is a great motivation. And you all had to catch me in the act."

Chapter Seventy-Four

Angelina dumps all three purses on the kitchen table.

A package of Gummy Bears falls out of June's purse along with a few pieces of jewelry.

June exclaims, "There's that turquoise earring I've been looking for everywhere."

Angelina looks at June and puts a finger to her mouth.

Rhonda says, "I bet this is more exciting that your Mah Jongg game, isn't it? Too bad you won't be able to tell your friends how thrilling it was. No one will be expecting any of you for hours. I know you used to play till four at the retirement center. By then I'll be long gone. From your kitchen, your city, even your state. As far as my Dart can take me. I'm starting over. With two hundred thousand."

Rhonda looks at Angelina. "Sit here." She points to another chair. "I still have the extension cord for you." She wraps the cord around her waist and the chair.

"Now here's my dilemma, Blondie," she says to June. "I was going to strangle Angelina with the red cord, but it's got you all tied up. I'll have to try something else." Rhonda tilts her head to the side.

"Hmm. What should I use? Knives and scissors are so messy. The gun's too noisy. There must be something else in the kitchen. How about under the kitchen sink? Any poisons, Angelina? Surely, you have some. What a great way to go out. A party. Girls' night out. Really out, if you know what I mean." Rhonda's laugh is hysterical, and all three women shudder.

Rhonda checks their knots and looks under the sink. She finds a jar of Drano. Next to it is a yellow and green box of fertilizer that boasts, "help your flowers bloom."

"Oh, they'll bloom all right," she mutters. "One final bloom before they fizzle out completely." She holds up both the Drano and the fertilizer. She opens the refrigerator and spots a bottle of orange juice.

"I'll mix it with a little juice to sweeten it. See, I'm not completely heartless. Who wants to go first? Think of it as Kool-Aid. Happy face Kool-Aid. Sorry I don't have the big pitcher with the smiley face on it." She gives a laugh and then her voice turns harsh again. "And if any one of you refuse, I will use the knife on your friend while you watch."

Henry prowls into the kitchen with a pitiful, "Meow."

"Oh, aren't you a pretty kitty? Such a big boy. I'd hate to have to hurt you too. Maybe we'll find out if you really have nine lives." Rhonda chortles as she waves the knife, and Angelina shudders.

"Try anything funny, Angelina, and the fat cat gets it too. They'll be making tennis rackets out of this one when I'm through with him."

Angelina's heart sinks, thinking of innocent Henry walking into a terrible trap.

Rhonda glances at her watch. "Guess I'll have to hang out a while and make sure it works. I would hate to have any of you lingering on to tell this great story. There's no big rush. No one will be looking for any of you before four o'clock. Perfect. Now do you all want to do it at once? One for all and all for one. What are friends for?"

Rhonda opens a few cupboards and finds three glasses. She pours a small amount of juice into each. She pours Drano and Miracle Gro into each glass and stirs.

"I'm giving you a few minutes to decide who goes first." She looks at the clock on the stove. "Say, that casserole smells good. I might as well have some while you decide. I've got a lot of do when I leave here and will need every ounce of energy."

Rhonda, still wearing the plastic gloves, hangs onto the knife but sets the scissors down. She grabs the potholder Clara left on the countertop, opens the stove, and sets the casserole on the burner with one hand, watching the three of them the whole time.

"Mmm. This looks good. What is it?"

June takes a deep breath and says, "It's a Mexican dish. Chicken and cheese enchiladas. You use Campbell soups too." She gives the details as if her life depends on it. Perhaps it does.

Angelina wonders if June thinks she'll be spared if she shares her recipe.

Rhonda finds a fork in the drawer, never letting go of the butcher knife in her left hand. She takes a bite out of the corner of the casserole not bothering to find a plate. "This is delicious."

June keeps up her prattle. "The secret is to use good tortillas. I like the ones at Safeway, the raw ones you have to cook for a few minutes. They're a little thinner and not so doughy."

"Good to know," Rhonda says. "I'm not much of a cook."

"Oh, you could do this," June reassures her. "You simply layer the tortillas, the chicken and the cheese and then pour cream of chicken soup over it all and bake."

Angelina rolls her eyes and shakes her head. The absurdity. They are tied to the stake, so to speak, and a deranged girl with a knife is talking recipes with Junie, who for some reason, seems to have calmed down as if she's talking to a friend over the backyard fence.

June goes on, "You can add green chilies if you like it spicy."

At the word spicy, Angelina thinks again of Guy. *Guy, where are you?*

As if on cue, the doorbell rings. Everyone flinches, and Rhonda drops her fork from mid-air, gooey cheese sauce spilling onto the floor.

"Now who?" Rhonda says.

Angelina sees panic in Rhonda's eyes. Angelina has seen only one other pair of eyes that color. Myra's.

The doorbell rings again.

Chapter Seventy-Five

On the way over, Guy had a gut feeling and called for backup. Something was fishy about the phone call. He could hear Angelina talking but she didn't answer him. He couldn't make out what she was saying. When he tried her house phone, he recognized her cry for help in Italian. *Help Me. Big help me.* How he remembered that Bulgarian word for *big* surprised him. Maybe the grey cells were not as rusty as he imagined.

This ache in his gut is beyond police work. He just wants Angelina to be safe. *Please, let her be safe.*

His backup call was a better-safe-than-sorry approach. A few misjudgments through the years still haunted him. The two cops now standing behind him are out of peephole visibility when Rhonda looks out. Now at Guy's command, they push against the door. It doesn't budge.

Rhonda hears the push. Hurrying back to the kitchen, she sweeps the money and jewelry off the table into her duffel bag and runs through the laundry room and finds the back door. Rounding the side of the house, she runs the half-block to the Dart. She tries to start the engine. Nothing. "Damn, damn." She keeps turning the key. "Come on, come on."

The second it turns over, her car door opens with a violent jerk and she feels herself being yanked out by a tall police officer. One holds her while the other one cuffs her hands.

Chapter Seventy-Six

Angela hears the front door shatter and heavy footsteps. Guy and two other officers appear in the kitchen, one with his arm on Rhonda, whose hands are cuffed behind her back.

June shouts, "I knew we'd be saved at the last minute. That always happens on TV."

Clara rolls her eyes.

Guy unties all three of them. Once free, Guy enfolds Angela in a long warm embrace, not caring who sees. He whispers something in her ear.

Angelina, who hasn't shed a tear through the whole incident, sobs. Is it relief or is it gratitude she feels for this man who saved her life? All their lives. She clings to him like the savior he is at the moment.

Then she glances over his shoulder and sees the expressions on June's and Clara's faces as if to say, "Why are you getting hugs and we're only getting untied?"

Guy lets go of Angelina and says to the officers, "Take her in."

Rhonda looks stunned and confused. She mumbles something, "It was all so perfect. It was going to be so perfect."

At that moment, for no known reason, the music box starts tinkling, slowly. The tune is barely recognizable. "Somewhere my love."

With her hands in the cuffs, Rhonda can't wipe her tears as they stream down her face. Angelina thinks she looks like a child who has lost her favorite stuffed bear.

Through her sobs, Rhonda says, "I never meant to kill my grandmother. Just the opposite. All I wanted was some recognition.

Well, a little love would have been nice too. Was that asking too much? I didn't think so. Had she given me that, she might still be alive."

No one says anything.

Rhonda continues in a whiny pleading voice, "The music box. It's all I have of my grandmother. Please, please let me keep it."

Guy looks at Angelina.

Angelina thinks about Myra. Would she really want her granddaughters to have it now? So tainted. She doesn't think so.

"Can she take it with her?" Angelina asks Guy. "It's all she has. It might be a comfort where she's going."

Chapter Seventy-Seven

When the policemen leave with Rhonda, Angelina says to the rest of them. "Let's open that chardonnay you brought." She knows she is going to have to answer to Guy, and a sip of wine might make that easier.

Guy says, "I'll need to ask you all some questions. Do you want to do it now or take a breather?"

Angelina glances at the other two. "We might as well get it over with." Then she looks at June's soiled clothes.

"Come with me." In her closet, she goes to the section with the smallest clothes. In spite of her variety of sizes, she doubts she has something small enough for June. "Do you mind wearing a robe?" She asks as she hands her a soft yellow chenille. Angelina takes June's mauve pantsuit and says, "Let me take this to the dry cleaners for you."

"Oh, Angelina, don't bother. It's not like I'm ever going to wear that outfit again. Bad karma as they say."

"I'm so sorry I got you into this mess, Junie, but you're right. This duster is going in the trash too." Angelina goes into her bedroom and slips into a loose black summer shift. "Black seems appropriate for this day."

When they return to the kitchen, Guy is standing over the casserole on the stove.

"Hey, this looks good."

"Help yourself," Angelina says, relieved that she might have a few minutes to gather her thoughts. She goes to the cupboard to get him a plate.

"The girls were going to surprise me with lunch. Guess it was surprises all the way around."

June says, "I suppose that dish will be forever dubbed Surprise Casserole, and I'm not talking ingredients."

"No use letting it go to waste, is there?" Guy asks as he spoons two heaping servings on his plate. Anyone going to join me?"

"I think I lost my appetite," June says. "Too many crooks spoil…."

Clara eyes Guy's plate and says, "Oh, what the heck? I have to eat sometime. I can multi-task. Eat and talk."

Guy sets his pocket notebook aside and digs in. Clara eats alongside him while June sorts through the items dumped from her purse. She pops a stray gummy bear in her mouth. Angelina leans against the kitchen sink, sipping her wine.

He says to Clara, "Did you all ever hear of a place called Chino Bandito? Not very far from here. Great Mexican and Chinese."

Angelina rolls her eyes.

"Oh really?" June says.

"Yeah, saw it on the Food Channel."

"You watch the Food Channel?" Clara asks.

"All the time," Guy answers and winks at Angelina, who is shaking her head as if to say, "I can't believe this conversation."

Angelina smiles and says, "I think this is where I came in."

Chapter Seventy-Eight

While they sit around the table, Angelina relates to them what Rhonda told her, gruesome as it was. She is waiting for Guy's reprimand for sticking her nose where it didn't belong, but it doesn't come. He simply nods, shakes his head at times, and makes notes in his tattered Steno.

When Guy finally closes his book, he says, "I guess that's all the information I need for now." He looks at Clara and June. "I might call on you again, if that's all right with you."

Clara smiles, "Anytime, Detective, anytime."

Angelina hugs them and apologizes again for involving them.

"You didn't involve us. We showed up," June says.

"Yeah, at the wrong time," Clara says. "It's surreal."

"Wrong for you, but right for me. You saved my life."

Clara says, "I guess it wasn't the dentist with the drill after all. So much for my theory. I still think the son-in-law is a shady character."

Guy says, "Well, you might be right about that. He may not have committed a crime, but he might be in the penalty box at home."

As they leave, June says to Clara, "I think we should forget about Mah Jongg Mondays for a while. What do you think?"

"Junie, for once, I totally agree with you. I heard they play Canasta at the retirement center on Tuesdays. What do you say we try to get in on that?"

"Clara, I love your face," June says as they walk down the porch steps.

"What in the world are you talking about?"

"Don't you remember? The Jewish idiom. It means *I love all of you.*"

Clara smiles and puts her arm around June's shoulders.

Chapter Seventy-Nine

When Angelina returns to the kitchen, Guy sits patiently at the table with his notebook open. He looks at Angelina and shakes his head.

Angelina is worried and embarrassed, knowing she shouldn't have interfered with her own investigation.

She sits and is about to apologize when he says, "Lucy, you got some 'splainin' to do." He gives her one of his sweet smiles, and she realizes there's no reason to be wary of this kind man.

"Guy, I am so sorry. I shouldn't have meddled." Angelina puts her face in her hands and the tears well up. She can't stop them. She sobs. The events of the day have caught up with her.

Guy doesn't reprimand her. In fact, he says nothing. Instead he gently pulls her to her feet and envelops her in his arms. She melts into him.

He gently rubs the back of her head and keeps saying, "It's all right. Everything is all right."

"You tried to warn me. I wouldn't listen. I had to go and do my thing. It serves me right for being so hard-headed."

"Now, now," Guy says. "Actually, you were very helpful. I should have told you my fears about Rhonda before I said not to meddle."

"When did you suspect her? Did you know it was her?"

"Not at first. I began to suspect when every loose end had a connection with her, but I couldn't prove anything. She drove the Dodge Dart I saw leaving the grave site. Why didn't she come with everyone else? She opened a bank account and deposited the exact amounts Myra was withdrawing."

"So, Myra was giving her money?"

"Giving might not be the right word. Extortion or blackmail might be more accurate. But your finding the name Joforsky was helpful. It took a while, but I found a connection to Rhonda's mother. That was about the time you said you were going to talk to her. I had to stop you."

"Yes, stop me from sticking my nose where it didn't belong."

Guy lifts Angelina's chin. "By the way, speaking of noses, what's this?" He gently touches the burn mark.

"It's nothing," Angelina fibs, knowing she isn't fooling him one bit.

Guy's eyes are warm and something else. Loving. "You were very helpful to me, Angelina. But I'd rather you didn't attempt to solve any other crimes. Perhaps you learned your lesson, mia donna bella?"

"I know it's crazy, but I feel sorry for Rhonda. All she wanted was acceptance. A family. And to be loved."

"Isn't that what we all want?" Guy pulls her close to him again.

When she looks up at him, he says, "Do you believe in second chances?"

"In life or love?"

"Both," he says.

"I believe now I do."

"How about second helpings? That is a good casserole."

"*Dosta,* Angelina says. *Enough.*

Guy smiles. "*Mai Abbastanza.* Never enough of you, dear Angelina."

THE END